Missing You

D0417372

ALSO BY LOUISE DOUGLAS
FROM CLIPPER LARGE PRINT

The Love of My Life

Missing You

Louise Douglas

W F HOWES LTD

This large print edition published in 2010 by
W F Howes Ltd
Unit 4, Rearsby Business Park, Gaddesby Lane,
Rearsby, Leicester LE7 4YH

1 3 5 7 9 10 8 6 4 2

First published in the United Kingdom in 2010
by Pan Books

Copyright © Louise Douglas, 2010

The right of Louise Douglas to be identified as
the author of this work has been asserted by her
in accordance with the Copyright, Designs and
Patents Act, 1988.

All rights reserved

A CIP catalogue record for this book is available
from the British Library

ISBN 978 1 40740 993 1

Typeset by Palimpsest Book Production Limited,
Falkirk, Stirlingshire
Printed and bound in Great Britain
by MPG Books Ltd, Bodmin, Cornwall

FSC
Mixed Sources
Product group from well-managed
forests, controlled sources and
recycled wood or fiber
SA-COC-1565
www.fsc.org
© 1996 Forest Stewardship Council

ESSEX COUNTY COUNCIL
LIBRARIES

For my parents, Janet and
Michael Beer, with love

CHAPTER 1

Sean walks the short distance from his car to the front door, his keys in one hand, a wrap of flowers in the other. His steps are measured, but adrenaline is hurtling through his arteries. Belle, in her yellow sundress and slingbacks, is standing in the shade of the hall, sunglasses holding back her hair, her arms tanned, a silver bangle on her wrist. Her body makes a barrier between him and his home and he knows from the set of her shoulders what she's going to say. They have been careering towards this moment for weeks.

'Don't,' he says, 'not today, Belle, not on such a beautiful day.'

'I can't do this any more,' she says. 'I can't keep living like this.'

The engine of his car is ticking; the smells of hot metal and scorched rubber from the tyres drifting towards him. Sweat chills the hollow between the parallel swells of muscle on his back. He licks his lips to draw saliva.

'Please,' he says, 'please, Belle . . .'

'I'm sorry, Sean,' she says, 'but you have to go.'

Her eyes drift from his face and down to the left. He follows her gaze and sees the bulging suitcase by the radiator and, beside that, an assortment of bags, his guitar and his CDs stacked carelessly in a cardboard box marked *Virgin Wines*. The paperback that he left face-down beside the spare bed this morning has been jammed into the pocket of his sports bag. Everything that obviously belongs to him is piled in the hall.

'You can come back and collect the rest when you're ready,' she says.

The hand holding the flowers drops to his side. The cellophane crackles and two petals fall at his feet. Sean slips the keys into his pocket.

'Belle,' he says, raising his free hand, pleading. He touches her gently on her bare arm. Her skin is sun-warm. She takes a small step backwards and his hand falls away. She rubs the place between her elbow and her shoulder where his fingers touched her, and she frowns and shakes her head.

'I'm worn out,' she says. 'Please, Sean, no more talking. Just go.'

He passes her the flowers. She sets them down on the telephone shelf without looking at them. They are roses the colour of milk.

'I need to see Amy.'

'She's in bed.'

'I have to say goodbye.'

'It'll just make it harder for you, Sean. Don't.'

But Belle steps aside. Sean passes her. He runs

up the stairs, oblivious to the polished mahogany banisters, the cream carpet, Belle's beautiful, framed photographs of urban sunsets, and he goes into Amy's room. He leans against the wall with his head tipped back and presses his fists against his temples, trying to calm his heart.

The blue curtains patterned with stars and moons keep out most of the light and the room is warm, scented by talcum powder, wax crayons and sherbet. Sean bats the butterfly mobile that hangs from the ceiling. The paper insects bob and weave.

'Christ,' he says under his breath. 'Oh Jesus Christ!'

'Daddy?'

Amy is spread out like a starfish on top of her bedcovers. She's wearing a pale green nightie. Her hair is stuck to her forehead and Sean can just make out a red mark on the bridge of her nose where she has been rubbing it with her finger. He tries to make his face normal.

'I just came to say night night.'

Amy yawns, a little cat yawn. She smiles up at him sleepily.

'Can we have a puppy, Daddy?'

'Mmm,' he says, 'one day.'

'I'd prefer a girl puppy. I think we should call her Polly.'

Sean tries to reply but his mouth is dry as sand.

'I'll look after her,' says Amy. 'She can sleep in a basket under my bed.'

He closes his eyes. He feels the weight of himself against the wall.

'Then when I wake up in the night, I can put my hand down and she'll be there.'

Amy drops one arm over the side of the bed to demonstrate.

Sean rubs his mouth with the flat of his hand. Thoughts are chasing through his mind. There must be a way out of this. There has to be another way. He has to think straight.

'Ooh!' Amy laughs and pulls her hand back up. 'She licked my fingers!'

Belle is at the door.

'That's enough, Amy,' she says, smoothly, coolly. 'Settle down now. Daddy's busy. He has things to do.'

'Belle . . .'

'It's just prevarication, Sean. Go now. You can see Amy at the weekend. You can take her out on Saturday.'

'Belle . . .'

'It's for the best,' she says.

'Best for whom?' he whispers. 'A broken home is best for whom, exactly?'

'Don't let's fight any more,' she replies in a calm, reasonable voice, the voice of an executioner. 'Don't let's make it any worse than it already is.'

She follows him down the stairs. He is waiting for something to happen, something that will change the situation, put things back on track. He counts the stairs and at the bottom he sees that she has moved the suitcase and the bags from the hall out onto the drive. The roses are in the waste-paper basket, their stalks, bound by an elastic band, sticking up as uncompromisingly as the legs of a dead animal.

He turns; she shakes her head slightly.

'Belle!'

He takes her hands in his, her limp and cool, lifeless hands, and he holds them up to his chest. 'Belle, please!' he says. 'Please don't throw away everything we have, just think about—'

'There's no point,' she says, pulling away her hands. 'We've been through this a million times.'

'But you don't listen . . .'

'Because you say the same things every time.'

'That bastard has poisoned your mind, he—'

'This has nothing to do with Lewis . . .'

'Oh come on! We were fine until you started—'

'Shut up!' she cries. 'Stop it! I've had enough!'

'Mummy . . .'

They both look up. Amy is standing on the half-landing where the stairs bend. She is holding on to the banister with one hand. Her hair is messy and her eyes are large and worried.

'It's all right, darling,' says Belle, changing the texture of her voice and its cadence in a heartbeat. 'We're not fighting, we're just . . .'

Sean's heart is beating so violently that he is afraid he will not be able to conceal his emotion from Amy. He doesn't want to frighten his daughter,

5

so he turns and steps through the door. Belle immediately closes it, pushes it shut. He imagines her leaning against it on the other side, holding her breath. She will calm herself, he thinks, and then she'll take Amy back to bed and settle her. Then she'll fill a glass with wine and she'll take it out into the garden and sit on the swing-seat in the shade of the walnut tree, and she'll put her head back and close her eyes, breathing a sigh of relief into the blue sky. She will listen to the birdsong and clear her mind. Later, she'll telephone the Other to tell him the good news. Maybe she'll summon him over. Or maybe she'd prefer to spend her first night without Sean on her own. It would give her time to change the sheets.

Right now, Sean would like to hurt her. He'd like to hurt Belle like she's hurt him.

No, he doesn't want to hurt her; he wants to convince her of his love. He wants to love her.

He doesn't know what he wants.

He wants everything to be how it was four weeks ago, before she told him about the affair.

He wonders if this is really the end of their marriage. It can't be. That would be inconceivable.

He turns back to the door. He has to talk to Belle, he has to make her realize; she doesn't know how much he loves her, he hasn't convinced her, and he will do *anything* for this not to be the end. He's even proposed to let Belle see the Other if she wants to. Sean is prepared to wait for her; he is strong enough to put the thought of the two of them, together, from his mind for the sake of his family. She has been infected by her new lover, but sooner or later the venom will pass through her system and she'll be herself again and she will come back to him.

Sean raises his fists to beat on the door, and then he hears a polite cough to his left and turns and sees their neighbour, Mrs Lock. She is attending to her dahlias, and is poised, watching, secateurs in one gloved hand. She gives the slightest shake of her head.

She knows. She's heard the arguments. It is possible that, while Sean has been at work, Belle has gone into Mrs Lock's kitchen and confided her troubles to the older woman, asked her advice over a pot of tea and biscuits.

'I should give her a couple of days,' says Mrs Lock in a kindly voice. She smiles, all grey hair and gentle, sorrowful eyes.

Sean drops his arms. He nods.

He loads his things into the car. But they won't all fit so he leaves two bags at the end of the drive, beside the bins. Let the dustmen take them. What does it matter to him?

He wipes his face with his sleeve, gets into the car and starts the engine. He looks back at the house through the mirror, but the door doesn't open. Belle does not come out to call him back.

He drives to the end of the road and then he sits there, in his car, his shirt sleeves rolled up to the elbows, his forearm resting on the edge of the open window, vacillating between tipping the indicator switch up and tipping it down because he cannot decide whether to turn left or right.

Sean's face is wet with tears.

Left or right?

It doesn't matter.

Either way, everything he loves will still be behind him.

CHAPTER 2

Fen is up early, unloading the washing machine. She rests the basket of damp laundry on her hip while she looks out through the narrow window of the galley kitchen into the long, thin back garden, to the alleyway beyond, and on down the hill, just in case. Her heart is clenching. But nothing has changed. Nobody is out there; there are no unexplained shadows, no trampled plants and no cigarette smoke winding into the sky. Everything looks just as it did yesterday, except there's maybe the slightest hint of green-turning-to-gold in the leaves of the trees.

Tomas has not come back. Not yet.

She unlocks the door and climbs down the steps that drop into the garden. She puts the basket on the grass, removes the strut to drop the line that stretches from the house to the gate, and shakes out the first pillowcase. The long grass is cold and damp beneath her bare feet. It brushes her knees, the moisture soaking into the fabric of her jeans. In the sky, seagulls wheel and caw. The sun is already casting shadows through the leaves of the big copper beech tree at the corner of the overgrown alley that separates the gardens on this side of the road from the gardens of the mirroring terracc. Fen holds a peg in her mouth while she struggles to arrange a duvet cover on the line. Next door's little black dog is turning circles on her neighbour's closely shaven lawn, looking for the perfect place to pee. Fen catches sight of its owner, Mr Tucker, watching the dog through his kitchen window. He smiles at Fen, and waves. She smiles, waves back. She tucks her hair behind her ear and smoothes the linen on the line.

If the neighbours knew the truth about her, they would not be so kind.

The grass in her garden, unmown again this year, has turned from lawn to meadow. Feathery heads pepper her jeans with seeds. She likes the straggly buttercups and the poppies, but not the nettles that clump beside the wire fence, nor the ivy that creeps along the wall, fingering at the window frames. A long-limbed, woody shrub with shaggy, purple flowers has seeded everywhere; it attracts butterflies and birds but is untidy. Pink-flowering weeds are growing out of cracks in the paving stones and even the stonework of the house.

Fen's garden is not the worst. A little further down the hill an ancient Ford Escort is patiently rusting on a frame of bricks, its wheels long since gone; the Evans' garden is a shambles of masonry, broken kitchen units and an old settee; and right at the bottom is the frail old widower's garden, a jungle of sun-worn plastic ornaments, gnomes, signs and windmills.

One day, Fen thinks, she will make a real effort. She will get to grips with the garden, or at least clear a patch where she can lie out in the evenings, read a book and enjoy the views and the sun. Connor would enjoy the project and the neighbours would lend a hand. They are always offering to help, but Fen doesn't like to take anything from them, partly because she is used to managing on her own and partly because there is so little she can do to reciprocate.

Fen picks up the empty basket and goes back towards the house. She pauses at the top of the steps and glances out over her overgrown garden. The bed linen wafts lazily in the early September sunshine and a grey squirrel hangs upside down, gorging itself on the bird-feeder. There's still no sign of Tomas. That doesn't mean he is not out there, somewhere in the city, looking for her.

Fen goes back into the kitchen and she locks and bolts the door behind her. When Tomas *does* come back, she does not want to be surprised. She wants him to have to knock. She knows what Tomas is like, and she doesn't want him creeping up behind her, putting his hands over her eyes and holding her tightly.

He wouldn't mean to frighten her but these days she's less robust than she used to be; she scares easily and Tomas always used to go a little too far.

He never knew when to stop. He did not have the instinct for self-preservation that prevents most people from doing dangerous things. He thought he was invulnerable. He thought they all were and, because he believed it, it was as if it were true. When you were with Tom you felt as if you could do, or be, anything and that nothing could hurt you. It was one of the beautiful things about him.

Sometimes, when Fen thinks about what happened to Joe that night, the night that Tom went away, she tries to present the facts in a different way. She does everything she can to convince herself that Tom was the one who was responsible. But it's a lie. She, Fen, is to blame.

Her guilt is wrapped around her like a cloak she can't shake off. She's been wearing it for so long now that she cannot imagine herself without the weight of it, or the shame of it.

Every day of her life, Fen wishes Tomas would come back to her. He is the only person she could talk to, the only one who would understand how she feels, because he is the only one who knows the truth. Perhaps, together, they could find a way to live with their past and to reconcile themselves to what happened to Joe Rees. Perhaps things would be better for both of them.

Fen squeezes her eyes shut; she squeezes out her memories. Then she opens her eyes and looks about her, pulling herself back into the present. The kitchen is very small and the units are tired and old-fashioned, but it's clean and bright and cheerful, especially when the sun shines through the window. The splashy artwork Connor brings home from school is Sellotaped to every available vertical surface; a photograph of him laughing so hard that he is falling off his chair is stuck to the fridge by a magnet; his new school bag sits on the counter.

Fen opens the bag and extracts Connor's lunch box, takes out the previous day's yoghurt-smeared detritus and rinses the blue plastic under the cold tap. It smells of banana.

She feels safe in Bath, she likes living in Lilyvale. It's a small house, but it has a gentle, protective feel to it. She lived here for two months before Connor was born, and since then the two of them have been here for five winters and five summers, and in all that time their lives have been quiet. Nothing terrible has happened. Nobody has said an unkind word to Fen; people don't stare at her in the street or put their heads together to whisper about her and her family when she passes by. There is no speculation, no accusation, no finger-pointing and nobody she has to avoid. She has no history in the city beyond the first of the winters. Only Lina knew her before she came to Bath, and Lina doesn't know everything; and what she does know, she keeps to herself.

Fen dries her hands on the towel folded over the radiator, fills the kettle and switches it on. She checks the clock. It's still early.

★   ★   ★

On the kitchen table is a postcard she's going to put up in the window of the off-licence at the top of the hill. She has written in purple felt pen:

ROOM TO LET IN FAMILY HOME,

Crofters Road, Fairfield Park.
Would Suit Single Professional.

References required.

That sounds about right, thinks Fen, and she props the card up beside the cereal packet.

She checks the garden one last time, but it is still empty, and then she makes her tea and goes upstairs to wake her son.

CHAPTER 3

He wakes before six, not because he has had enough sleep but because his bloodstream is pumping liquid anxiety. Sean's breath is quick and shallow, and his nerves are on edge. He licks the inside of his mouth. His heart is a fierce hammer inside him; the sheet beneath his aching back is clammy with sweat. It takes him a few seconds to remember what is wrong, and when he remembers, he wishes he had not.

Everything is wrong.

Sean rolls onto his side and opens his eyes.

It is very dark in the room because of the blackout curtains. Sean is in a hotel bedroom, not a proper hotel, but a soulless, unstaffed place at the arse end of the motorway services.

He has been drifting. He has been staying in anonymous bedrooms in cheap hotels. Sometimes he sleeps in his car. He derives a masochistic pleasure from the loneliness of his existence. By punishing himself, he punishes Belle. It is perverse, of course, because she does not know that he finds himself in these miserable rooms, writing letters of increasing desperation that he

15

has the sense not to send, drinking to the bottom of the bottle just to stop himself thinking about the Other and what he is saying to her, how he is touching her, what he is learning about her, how he is knowing things that only Sean was supposed to know.

Sean yawns. He sighs and gets out of bed. Then he takes a shower to wash away these dirty thoughts.

When he comes out of the bathroom with a white towel fastened around his waist, he draws the curtains, and in the concrete-grey daylight the room is as grubby and shabby as he had known it would be. There is a crack in the mirror, the upholstery on the chair is frayed and stained, and the television screen is dusty and marked with fingerprints. His clothes are piled untidily on the chair. At least he didn't drop them on the carpet, which he knows from experience will smell of feet and commercial fabric freshener. There is an empty vodka bottle upturned in the waste-paper basket and several scrunched-up beer cans are scattered around.

Sean rubs his hair with the towel and then tosses it into the bathroom. He feels as if his entire self is one long, sore wound. His self-pity is humiliating but Sean has never been good at managing emotion. This was one of many personality traits that Belle cited as offensive. She said that any other man would have realized she was unhappy and would have done something about it, or at least discussed her feelings with her. He did not even notice that things weren't right.

She blames him for her affair. Perhaps she has a point.

On some rational level, Sean knows that Belle is not wholly to blame for their situation. He did not notice her unhappiness and so she fell in love with a different man. There is no crime in falling in love. Falling is not a deliberate action when you have been pushed to the precipice, as Belle apparently was, by the fact that she felt entirely unappreciated by Sean and was convinced of his ambivalence towards her. She has told Sean a thousand times that she never meant to hurt him, and he believes she is telling the truth.

Still he *is* hurt. He believes his love for Belle is so deep and intrinsic that he doesn't know how he can survive without her. She is everything to him. She is his reason for living. Whatever she thought, the truth is that he never took her for granted, not for one moment, ever.

Before, when he woke each morning, he would feel her presence beside him, her hand perhaps on the pillow beside his cheek, her hair, her sleep-soured breath, her precious little snores and sighs, and he would say a silent prayer of gratitude. When he went to sleep she was there, next to him; he could inhale the smell of her, see the way her hair tapered into silky down at the base of her neck; he could warm himself beside her lovely body, bask in the scent of the cream she used on her face. And he was amazed at his good fortune; he was astonished that a woman as wonderful as Belle could be married to a man like him. He imagined their future. He imagined more children, and although he loved the thought of these children, already, even before they were conceived, he looked forward to the time when they left home, and he could have Belle to himself. He thought they would travel. He imagined them, husband and wife, side by side on the deck of a ship, seeing a new continent take shape on the horizon in the sunrise, and he imagined how it would feel to share that experience with somebody to whom he felt so deeply connected. He imagined beaches, volcanoes, cities, seas, exotic hotels and savannah lodges, hired cars, tents, motels. The same life seen through two pairs of eyes, lovers, always, Belle and Sean, the perfect couple, the meant-to-be soulmates.

The trouble was that he didn't tell her how he felt.

He didn't think he needed to tell her.

He thought, because they were married, because every aspect of their life was so intimate, because they were forever united emotionally and genetically by the incredible child they had created together, that he didn't need to tell her that he loved her. He thought that fact was spelled out in every word he said to her, every action, every glance, every kiss and kindness. Everything he did was for Belle. Every mile he drove, every weekend he worked, every shitty, cold, thankless job he surveyed, every penny he earned, all of it was for his wife. She knew he was not good at articulating his feelings but wasn't it obvious that he loved her?

She said it was not.

She said she didn't tell him how unhappy she was because he didn't ask.

He didn't know it was something he was supposed to ask. He was happy and it never crossed his mind that Belle might not be. He didn't know what to do then and he doesn't know what to do now.

He knows one thing.

He cannot go on like this.

He needs to sort himself out.

One step at a time, he thinks, like an alcoholic. First things first.

He needs to escape these hotels. That's the first thing he needs to do.

CHAPTER 4

Lina tells Fen that she has given her telephone number to one of her colleagues. She says he's a decent man who has had some kind of 'major domestic'. Lina says she expects it will sort itself out in time, but, for now, Sean needs somewhere to stay.

Lina has known Sean for years. She says he's OK.

So when Sean calls to ask about the room, Fen invites him round.

'Hi,' he says, shaking raindrops from his hair. 'I'm Sean.'

He holds out his hand. Fen takes it. His fingers are red and cold but his handshake is firm. It is the first time she has touched a man deliberately in years and the feeling of his skin is strange. She lets go first and wipes her hand on the thigh of her jeans.

'Come in,' she says, moving aside. He wipes his feet on the doormat then steps through the porch.

'You're the one who . . .' she begins.

'Works with Lina, yes. She said you were looking for a lodger.'

'That's right.'

'I guess you would have preferred a woman but . . .'

'Well, it's OK,' says Fen. 'Lina knows you. This house actually belongs to her and Freddie. I'm their tenant. And she knows you're not . . .'

'What? A murderer? A drug dealer?'

He's smiling, although that's not funny. Fen can tell he's enervated. He's trying to act normally but he looks exhausted. She tries to rearrange her face into a polite smile, and tugs at the sleeves of her jumper.

'I didn't want a complete stranger.'

'Well, no,' says Sean, 'of course you didn't.'

'Would you like to see the room?'

'Please.'

She motions him to go upstairs. It feels odd to have a man in the house. He takes up space that is usually empty. Fen climbs the stairs behind him in a wake of cool, outside air and an unfamiliar, masculine smell; she is aware of an energy that is, in some small way or other, disturbing. His masculinity corrupts the balance of the house.

His jeans are loose about the waist and legs; his brown hair, which is slightly greasy and needs cutting, curls about the collar of a worn old jacket dotted with dark spots where the rain has stained the leather. He pauses on the landing. He is unsure of the etiquette of the situation, as is she, and this, she finds, is comforting.

'It's the door to your left,' she says.

21

He goes in.

It was a rather shabby room to start with, but now, with Lina's help, it is brighter. The window looks out over the back gardens and the alley, down the hill, over the city and beyond it to the opposite hills, so that in daytime the view is gloriously long-reaching and it's possible to track the progress of the sun, the cloud-shadows and the trains on the railway line way, way below. At night, the city of Bath twinkles and sparkles and shimmers like a girl dressed up for a ball. Fen has made new curtains, and she and Lina have painted over the woodchip on the walls. A fringed rug the colour of rubies, which Fen found in the Oxfam shop, hides the worst of the carpet; the old bed has been rejuvenated by new bedding; there are two lamps, both lit and casting egg-shaped pools of yellow light; a small, old-fashioned television is perched on a wall bracket.

'It's nice,' Sean says politely but Fen suspects, from the self-consciously emphasized affirmative, that it is less than he is used to.

'Have a look round,' she says. 'I'll put the kettle on.'

She trots back downstairs in her socks and goes into the kitchen, where she peers at her face in the mirror by the door. She pulls open a drawer and rummages for a comb, but there isn't one, just balled string, sticking plasters, odd screws and bolts, an ancient jar of Vick's Vapour Rub, broken pens and stray pieces of Lego and Playmobil. She fills the kettle, switches it on and looks in the mirror again. Her face is a small, pale knot of anxiety. Her hair is lank. It has not been professionally cut for several years. Fen combs it with her fingers.

She can't remember the last time she wore make-up.

She has run out of tea bags, so she makes instant coffee in her two best mugs. They don't match. Sean does not look like the kind of man who would be bothered by uncoordinated crockery, but still, she wishes she could do better. She hears his footsteps in the bathroom above; there is the unmistakable, loud splashing of a man peeing and then the toilet flushes. She blushes at the intimacy.

She searches the cupboards for something to serve with the coffee, but there are no biscuits, no anything.

She times it so that she is coming out of the kitchen with the tin tray as he reaches the bottom of the stairs. He follows her into the living room.

'The room's great. Just what I need,' he says, taking the mug from her and sitting down on the settee, leaning forward with his elbows on his knees. His face is tired, and the whites of his eyes are blood-shot. He blows across the surface of the coffee.

'I don't know how much Lina told you about me,' he says, 'only I have a daughter; she's six. I look after her most weekends. Would it . . .'

'No problem,' says Fen. 'I have a child too. Connor. He's coming up to five.'

She pauses. Oh, she might as well have it over with now. 'He has mild cerebral palsy,' she says, 'but you'd hardly know. He sleeps through the night. He's no bother.'

'Oh! Right. Fine, of course. And is he . . .'

'It was a difficult birth. It's not a big deal. He just has a little trouble with his right arm and leg.'

'Right.'

'And it can be hard to understand what he's saying. He backs up his words with signs, sometimes.'

'He sounds like a resourceful lad.'

'Yes.'

There is a silence. They sip their coffee.

'I could get a little bed, if you want,' says Fen, 'to go in the room. For your daughter.'

'No, no, I don't want to put you to any trouble.'

Fen tries to remember if it was always this hard to talk to somebody she didn't know, and she thinks that it wasn't. At one time she used to find other people easy. She had a nice way about her, that's what people said. Conversation was intuitive; she didn't even have to try. And now look at her. She shifts a little in her seat.

'How long do you think you'll want the room?' she asks.

'Not long, I hope,' he says, and then he coughs and adds, 'Sorry, that sounded rude. It's a great room, but things will soon be sorted out and I'll be back at home.'

She nods.

'Did you want me to commit to three months or something?'

Fen shakes her head. 'No, it's fine, you can decide week by week, if you like. That suits me too.'

She feels she should explain. 'It's my brother Tomas's room,' she says. 'Well, it's earmarked for him when he comes back. Only I don't know when that'll be.'

'Is he travelling?' Sean asks, curious, but reluctant to probe too far.

'Sort of. He's been gone a while.'

'Once you get the bug, it can be hard to shake it off,' says Sean.

'Yes.'

There is another silence.

Fen watches a daddy-long-legs quivering hopelessly against the wall. Sean follows her eye, stands up, cups the insect in his hand and slots it through the open fanlight.

'Thank you,' says Fen. 'I don't like those.'

'My wife is the same,' says Sean. 'She says they're purposeless. She worries they'll get tangled in her hair and their legs will come off.'

'Me too.'

'Well,' he says, 'I'm good with insects. Is there anything else you'd like to know about me?'

'What do you do?' she asks. 'At work?'

'I'm a surveyor.'

'What do you survey?'

'Old buildings, ancient monuments, bridges. Structures in need of restoration.'

'Do you restore them?'

'Not personally. But I work with the architects and the engineers and the craftsmen.'

'Have you ever surveyed a building you couldn't save?'

'There's always a way. Even if you have to take the whole thing down and start again.'

Fen nods.

She can think of nothing else to ask.

He lifts the mug to his lips, tips back his head and drinks, his Adam's apple moving up and down. She watches his jaw, the darker colour of his throat; he hasn't shaved for a day or two. He catches her glance and she looks away. He puts the mug back down on the tray. He is graceful in his movements, comfortable in his skin.

'Would you mind if I bring some of my stuff in now?' he asks.

'No, that's fine,' says Fen. 'Move in whenever you want.'

Later, as Fen walks around the corner store with Connor, picking items from the shelves, she imagines what it will be like to buy enough food for three. She looks at a pack of minced beef steak, too much meat for her and Connor, and thinks of what she could do with it: lasagne or cottage pie, Bolognese sauce, chilli, burgers, meatballs. She plans a week's worth of recipes in her head. She tells Connor about their new lodger, and Connor is pleased. He has reached an age when he wants to

26

learn more about men and their world. Now there will be somebody in the house who knows the names of cars and, better still, knows more than a little about the heavy machinery that Connor adores: bulldozers, piledrivers, cement mixers and cranes.

Connor sits in his buggy to go back down the hill. His legs are tired. Fen pauses at the crest because she catches sight of somebody moving in the front garden of Lilyvale and her heart pounds, but it's only the papergirl, a big yellow sack on her shoulder. The girl closes the gate behind her, picks up the bike that she had propped against the wall, and carries on down the hill.

CHAPTER 5

The Gildas Bookshop, in Quiet Street, is a poky little shop which mainly sells new and second-hand history and culture books, subsidized by a lucrative sideline in novels in a variety of Eastern European languages. Maps of the city are pinned to the spare places on the walls, greeting cards and postcards are stacked in racks. The shop's floors, ceilings, walls and windows slope, slant, dip and buckle. Everything is covered in a fine layer of white dust, the carpet is threadbare and faded, and countless spiders are enjoying life in undisturbed corners. Fen makes coffee in the tiny kitchenette, its window greened by climbing plants in the little courtyard behind, its creaky, lumpy old ceiling dusty with cobwebs. She stirs milk into Vincent's favourite mug, the one with the reproduction of the Penguin Classics *Pursuit of Love* cover. Vincent always says he doesn't care which mug his coffee comes in, but his eyes light up when she passes this one to him as he sits at his desk in its cubbyhole at the back of the shop, indulging in his favourite chore. He is rummaging through a box of old books which he has just bought from an apologetic, tired-eyed woman whose mother-in-law has moved into an old people's care home.

'You're an angel. Thank you,' says Vincent. He is old, whiskery, thin, too tall for the ceilings of his little shop, too elbowed, too jointed. What is left of his grey hair is combed over his head. He has a handsome nose and the confidence of the attractive young man he used to be. Photographs of the young Vincent leaning languidly and in a pseudo-aristocratic manner in the foreground of one exotic venue or another often turn up tucked into catalogues or at the bottom of drawers. Fen has seen him in front of the Taj Mahal, posing beside a lake at Band-e Amir, on the edge of Tiananmen Square and, in Arab clothing, sitting on a camel beside a palm-fringed water hole in the Egyptian desert. He used to write travel books at a time when travel beyond English-speaking countries was still the preserve of the wealthy, a small number of back-packers and sociologists. His books were very popular in their day, and first editions are highly collectible now. They are two of a kind, Vincent and Fen; their worlds have both closed in, although the passage of time and a wife he adores are what have tempered Vincent's ways, while Fen has been conditioned by life and by what it has done to her.

She returns to the counter by the window, and tidies the leaflets. Outside, crowds of people pass by. It's easy to pick out the workers on their coffee breaks: they skip on and off the pavement, check their watches, weave through the crowds. Little groups of tourists draw together like iron filings to a magnet, slowing down the locals, huddling over their books or listening to their leaders: Japanese, German and American guides identifiable by the coloured umbrellas they hold above their heads like flags.

'Is there anything interesting in that box?' Fen asks Vincent.

'Ever read *The Moon's a Balloon*? Very amusing, as I recall.'

'I remember my stepmother reading that,' says Fen. Vincent picks up a book in a green paper dust-sleeve with the title in white and the author's name below, in yellow. He turns the book over in his hands.

'Was she a book-lover?' he asks, peering over the top of his lenses.

'She used to read a lot. That was one of her favourites. I think she used to wish my father was more like David Niven,' says Fen.

'She wouldn't have been the only woman to feel like that. Not about your father, I mean . . .'

'No.' Fen smiles. A memory of her father, tall and imposing in his headmaster's robes, striding through the grounds of Merron College, flashes into her mind. She pushes it away. 'What have you got there?' she asks.

'Rachel Carson. *Silent Spring.*'

He opens the book to check the title plate.

'This one might be worth a bob or two.'

'Shall I have a look on the internet?'

'I'll do it,' says Vincent with uncharacteristic eagerness.

He doesn't like using the computer, as a rule.

'If this is worth what I think it's worth, I'll take you out for lunch,' he says.

'Sorry, Vincent, I have errands to run.'

'People to do, things to see . . .'

'Post office, bank, chemist, supermarket.'

'As your employer, shouldn't I take priority?'

'You just can't get the staff these days, Vincent.'

'Indeed,' he says, switching on the computer and wincing as it trills its welcoming five notes.

'So what did you do this weekend?' he asks, rubbing his hands, his face illuminated blue from the computer screen. The computer is elderly and inefficient. It takes a long time to boot up.

'Shopping, cleaning. The usual.'

'How long have you been in Bath now?'

'Five years or so.'

'Hmmm.'

'Vincent, I'm all right.'

'I know you're all right.'

'You don't have to worry about me. I'm perfectly happy.'

Vincent takes off his glasses and rubs the sides of his nose, where they have pinched.

'Five years of being on your own,' he says, 'it's such a waste.'

'I have Connor. I have Lina and you *and* my lodger has moved in now. I'm hardly lonely.'

31

'Are children and friends enough? Don't you want to be with someone? Properly?'

Fen looks up at him coyly. 'But Vincent, you're already spoken for.'

Vincent shakes his head and smiles.

'Whatever it is that's caused this drought, it's time to put it behind you,' he says. 'You're only young once, Fen. You only have one bite of the cherry. Five years is long enough.'

Fen nods as if she agrees, but she thinks: How would you know?

For the rest of the morning he is tied up with either the computer or the telephone. He is generating a buzz of interest in the Rachel Carson. Although he speaks quietly, for any talk of money embarrasses Vincent, there is excitement in his voice.

Meanwhile, a steady stream of customers comes through the door, tinging the bell which is linked to a sensory pad beneath the hessian doormat. Fen feels very calm in the shop, because of the clear view of the pavement outside. The level of the shop floor is lower than the level of the pavement, so people have to bend down to look beyond the window displays and past the posters; they put their hands above their eyes to shade them from the glare, and screw up their faces and peer in. People always look through the windows before they commit to entering the Gildas Bookshop. It would be impossible to be surprised, which is how Fen likes it to be.

If Tomas finds this place, if he looks through the window, she will see him before he sees her.

Fen can sometimes go for days without anything reminding her of what happened before Tomas left. She can go for days without thinking about Joe. But sometimes . . .

Sometimes she'll see a boy in the street, a young man with shaved hair and long legs in over-washed jeans, or she'll hear a certain snatch of music, James or Elvis Presley, and the memories will come back to her. On occasions, the past is more substantial to Fen – more real – than the present. She remembers the way Tomas used to sit with his bony knees apart, she'll think of the weight of his hand on her arm, his cheek on her shoulder, his eyelashes, the way he always offered her a bite of his hot dog, or a drink from his can, or a drag of his cigarette or whatever he had. The ways Tomas, impossibly, tried to look after her.

And always when Fen thinks of Tomas, she thinks of Joe standing just behind him, or beside him, watching.

Sometimes all it takes is a small change in temperature, stepping from shadow into sunlight, and Fen will look around her, certain that Tomas is close.

She waits and hopes . . .

She hopes her brother has been wrested from his addictions and is drifting through some other continent, picking fruit, perhaps, or working barefoot in a beach bar. She imagines him in baggy swimming

33

shorts, loose about his hips, and a shell necklace, maybe with long hair now, and a little beard, surfer piercings in his ear and eyebrow, tattoos on his arms. She hopes he has some good friends. Sometimes, if she's in a nostalgic, self-pitying, sentimental frame of mind, she sits on the top step, outside the kitchen door, staring at the sky and wondering which constellations he sees at night.

Mostly, Fen hopes only that Tomas is well and happy. She wishes he would come back. She wishes he would find her. Until he does, all she will have are her memories and her nightmares. She has had enough of those.

Sometimes she can hardly wait for the day when he returns. She can't wait to put things right.

And sometimes she has to fight to make herself believe that day will ever come.

CHAPTER 6

There is a man in the drive sweeping up the first fallen leaves of the autumn when Sean arrives to visit Amy, and for a moment he thinks it is the Other. Anger rises up in him and he has a fantasy of swinging the car round and hitting the man. He would catch him hard on the thigh, throw him into the air, break both legs maybe. He imagines the Other sliding cartoon-like down Sean's windscreen, the glass shattered, the frame dented, and the Other's hands leaving bloody trails as he slipped into a crumpled heap on the ground. But the man looks up, and it's not even a man, just an amiable boy, one of the three who live over the road – Chris, he's called, or Nick, or Mark – with his woolly hat pulled down over his ears and his jeans sitting low on his hips. The boy holds up a hand in greeting and Sean salutes back, trying to keep the humiliation from showing in his eyes.

Belle opens the door and a breath of warm, scented air drifts over Sean's face.

'Come in,' she says, like it's not his home, not his house, like his wages aren't paying the mortgage.

Her words are wounding, so is the cheerful tone of her voice; everything about her makes him feel crushed and also angry. Doesn't she realize how diminished he feels, being invited into his home like a stranger? Why hasn't Belle, blessed as she is with so much sensitivity and empathy, got a clue as to what's going on in his head?

He cannot bring himself to thank her. Already his heart is thumping and his mouth is dry. He steps over the threshold and follows the sound of CBeebies into the living room, where Amy is lying on the smaller of the two cream leather sofas, propped up with cushions and pillows and almost covered by her duvet. Her eyes are half closed and there is a bright red circle in the middle of each cheek.

'Hello, sweetpea. Are you in the wars?' he asks, and she nods solemnly.

'I have a chest infection,' she says, and she coughs with such polite theatricality that Sean has to turn his head to hide the smile. He catches Belle's eye and they share a moment of parental harmony, and he thinks: This is stupid, this is Belle and me, we are man and wife, we are a pair, we are as one.

'Cup of tea?' asks Belle, turning towards the kitchen.

'Please,' he says and goes over to his daughter.

Her eyes are runny and the lower part of her nose is sore and red, glistening with mucus.

'You poor little bugger,' says Sean, sitting down

36

by Amy's feet. He tweaks her toes. She sniffs and manages a brave little smile.

'Are you staying for tea, Daddy?'

'I don't think so. But I'll stay for a bit.'

'Have you got somewhere else to live now?'

'Yes. In Bath. You can come and stay.'

'Has it got a garden?'

'Yep. And there's an alley at the back where all the children play. And there's a boy who lives there, called Connor. He's a bit younger than you.'

'Oh.'

She looks disappointed.

'I would have actually preferred a girl,' she says. 'An older girl. Or a dog. But it doesn't matter.'

'Connor's nice,' says Sean with ersatz cheer. 'The house is all right too. You'll like it.'

'Does this mean,' whispers Amy, so that her mother can't hear, 'that you're the boy's daddy now?'

'No,' says Sean, silently cursing Belle for this situation, for riddling Amy with anxieties so frightening she has to put them forward in a quiet voice, 'I'll only ever be your dad, Amy.'

'And also,' she whispers, 'now you're living there, does it mean you're never coming back here to live?'

Sean shakes his head emphatically. 'No, it doesn't.'

'Doesn't what?'

Belle comes in with a tray of drinks and sets it down on one of the designer coffee tables. The whole room seems to have grown larger and plusher since Sean last saw it, but he supposes that is because of the contrast with the smaller floor-plan and cheaper, older furniture in Lilyvale. He feels a burst of shame at the thought of his lodgings, the old stains on the carpets, the throws which disguise the age of the rickety chairs and the over-soft sofa, the mismatched crockery. The shame is like a narcotic in his bloodstream and his prejudice, born of indulgence, disgusts him when he thinks of quiet Fen and how she works to look after her son, to keep the house clean, to make him comfortable.

'Did the doctor give Amy antibiotics?' asks Sean, to change the subject. Belle nods.

'She gave me a fright last night. She was so hot she was hallucinating.'

'Were you?'

Amy nods, and sits up to drink her Lucozade.

'She thought there were penguins in her bedroom.'

'They were evil penguins. They were standing on my shelf and they were singing a song,' says Amy.

'What sort of song?'

'"In a cottage in a wood". They knew all the actions.'

'You've been watching too much *Pingu*.'

'No,' says Amy patiently, 'these were real penguins, not cartoon ones. They were like soldiers. They were marching and holding up one wing.'

Sean shudders at the thought of the Nazi penguins.

Belle says: 'OK, Ames, enough of that,' and she passes a pile of envelopes to Sean. 'There's your wage-slip in there, and credit card statements, a postcard from your mum and dad, letters from the bank.'

'Thanks.'

Belle clears her throat and sits on the edge of the opposite sofa, her back straight, her hands resting on her knees. She is well manicured, as always. She has lost a little weight, thinks Sean, and she is wearing new clothes: plum-coloured trousers, a pale sweater made of the softest of wools, brown boots.

'Don't you think it's time you had your post transferred to your new address?' she asks in a voice so gentle it takes him a moment to realize the implications of her words. 'Don't you think you ought to let people know you've moved out? You have told your parents, haven't you?'

'There's no rush, is there?' he asks.

'There's no point not doing it,' says Belle. 'It'll be one job out of the way,' she adds. 'And what if there's an emergency? What if your family needs to get hold of you? What should I say if they call here?'

He gets the point. He takes a sip of tea.

'OK,' he says.

'It'll be better now you've got somewhere to take Amy,' says Belle. 'You can have her for the whole weekend, as soon as she's shaken off this cough. That'll be fun, won't it, Ames? Spending more time with Daddy?'

Amy glances from one parent to the other, unsure of the politic answer.

'You'll probably find that you grow closer, the two of you,' says Belle. 'I've heard lots of people say that the exclusive time parents and children have

39

together in these kinds of situations can be bonding. It can be a very positive experience.'

'Who are you trying to convince?' Sean asks. 'Why all the pill-sugaring?'

'Oh, Sean, don't . . .' She trails off. She looks at the backs of her hands. She is still wearing her wedding ring and she twists it round and round the base of her third finger. 'I'm just trying to be civilized,' she says. 'It's not as if I don't still care about you.'

'You've got a great way of showing it, Belle.'

'Sean . . .'

He takes a deep breath, holds it in his lungs, tries to exhale his anger. Amy's eyes switch from one parent's face to the other's. She is pressing herself deep into the settee.

'Sorry, Amy,' says Sean. 'Sorry, honey, I didn't mean to shout.'

He takes her hot little foot in his hand, but she winces and withdraws it.

Belle is giving him a 'see what you've done now' look.

'Is there anything you need?' she asks in a cooler voice. 'From the house? Do you need extra bedding? Towels? Pots and pans?'

'No.'

He will not thank her. He won't give her the balm to soothe her conscience. No. Her words sound attentive, concerned, but this generosity is all part of the eviction process. She just wants shot of him.

This is all wrong. It's like some kind of nightmare,

like one of those films in which the hero goes to work in the morning and comes home to find everything looks the same but everything has changed.

'Daddy?'

Amy has not changed. She stares up into his eyes and her own are wide and worried. She sniffs loudly and wipes her nose with the edge of her duvet.

'Amy, don't be disgusting. I've told you a hundred times to use a tissue,' says Belle.

'For Christ's sake, Belle, she's not well. Give her a break!' Sean hisses.

'Don't talk to me like that,' Belle replies in a voice that's quiet and brutal.

'Oh! Right! So you can fuck your bastard tutor any time you want but I'm not allowed to *talk* to you?'

'If you're going to use language like that I think you should get out of my house,' says Belle.

'*Your* house?'

'I'm sorry!' says Amy urgently. 'I'm sorry I didn't use the tissue!'

Sean closes his eyes and wishes he could rewind. He doesn't like himself at all. He used to think he was a decent bloke but now he's someone else, someone riddled with resentment and bitterness and spite, someone who goes off like a firework at the slightest provocation.

'Darling Amy,' he says, 'it's not your fault. Nothing is your fault.'

'Mummy and Daddy are just a bit cross with each other at the moment,' says Belle.

41

'We're not behaving very well,' says Sean. 'We should both go and sit on the naughty step.'

Amy tries to smile but it is not convincing.

'Listen,' says Sean, leaning down and picking Amy up and swinging her onto his lap. She is tangled in the duvet. Her head is hot and sweaty. She is a bundle of duvet and elbows and damp hair in his arms. She's grown taller lately. Her limbs are long and thin. She doesn't sit comfortably on his knees as she used to. He puts his lips against her head, to taste her. 'I'm going to go now. I need you to get better and then you can come and see my new –' he pauses: *room* seems too pathetic – 'my new house.'

Amy nods.

'We'll do something nice, OK?'

'Mmm.'

He wipes his daughter's face with his sleeve, kisses her forehead, and holds her close for a moment.

Belle is staring into her teacup. Her knees are clamped together and her elbows are tight to her side. She is sitting very straight.

'Belle, I'm sorry,' Sean says quietly. 'I shouldn't have come. It's too . . . difficult.'

She nods. Still she does not raise her head.

He is surprised to see a tear drop from her chin. It spatters on the thigh of her trousers, making a tiny dark stain on the fabric.

None of us is happy, he thinks.

★　　★　　★

Sean plays his music as he drives along the darkening road back to Bath. He plays Faithless: 'Mass Destruction', 'Don't Leave', 'Insomnia'. He has the volume turned up very loud so that he cannot think or feel; all he can do is drive the car and hear the music. Sean lets the music and the road take over. He drives too fast. The old car roars as he forces it down the fast lane, overtaking newer, shinier, more powerful vehicles. Every now and then his eyes flick to the mobile phone lying on the passenger seat beside him, but its screen remains inert. Belle does not call.

He braces the palms of his hands against the steering wheel and listens to his music. He watches the road roll out shakily before him like a film he has seen many times before: the M4 with its bridges, its banks, its hills and vistas, its promise of going somewhere and leaving something behind. What he used to like best about the M4 was its geography. In the mornings he started in the east and travelled west, like the sun; in the evenings the skies reddened behind him as he made his way home.

It doesn't work like that any more, because now there is no home.

Sean pushes the accelerator pedal down as far as it will go and drives close to the rear of a banana-yellow Mercedes, until the Mercedes' driver concedes and drops into the middle lane. Sean's car rattles, the temperature gauge creeps towards red. One day, Sean will push the old engine too far and it will explode. It will shatter all over the M4, bits of metal flying into the air, hurtling into windscreens, hot oil arcing across the carriageway, and the car will spin and the tyres will burn as the car bounces and rolls and smashes into the other vehicles. It will be a spectacular crash of biblical proportions, a testosterone-fuelled destruct-fest. Sean turns up the volume as high as it will go and he keeps his foot down hard on the pedal. The car trembles and groans, the road disappears beneath its wheels, the music screams through his head like wind in the desert, and he tries not to think about anything that has gone before.

CHAPTER 7

Fen walks the short distance to the city centre, weaving through the shoppers clotting around the stalls and looking at hand-made jewellery, scarves and pictures of Bath. She goes through the arcade, crosses the road and walks by the river to Pulteney Bridge. Its beauty, as always, catches her off guard. The three perfect vertical arches and, beneath them, the water rushing towards the longer, distorted, horizontal arcs of the weir – the stone, the architecture, the reflections of the trees, their leaves progressing from green to red and gold, and the berries in the bushes – it's all so perfect. People lean over the stone balustrades, gazing across the water, taking photographs. Seagulls stand reflected in the shallowest part of the river, where the water goes smooth and glassy, just before it foams down the weir.

Sometimes it worries Fen that Tomas might, somehow or other, find himself in Bath and spend days walking among the crowds looking for her, and then give up and move on somewhere else. Or else he might fall in with the wrong crowd. Bath has its problems; it's the same as any other city underneath all its beauty and its World Heritage Site umbrella. Fen has seen the dealers. She knows how to spot them. She has spent enough time with Tomas to recognize how they stand, how they keep their hands in their pockets, how they pretend to stare at the ground but how their educated eyes scan the crowds. They are on the lookout for people like Tomas. They know what to look for.

Tomas might be here, in the city, right now, walking a parallel journey, destined to turn left when Fen turns left, so that their paths never cross. It would be possible, in theory, to walk the streets forever and never bump into one another. But, in truth, it's unlikely. It is surprising how often Fen has met somebody from her old life, an old school friend from Merron, or the wife of one of her father's colleagues, and they have always just been down for a weekend, or for a day or two. It's not a big city.

Bath is less crowded now that autumn has set in and there is space on the benches outside the Abbey. Most of the street entertainers, like most of the birds, have gone to warmer cities and the pigeons have room to strut and peck without the constant harassment by children. Lina and Fen sit close together, for warmth, and they open their packs of sandwiches and balance cardboard mugs of hot coffee on the slats of their bench. The October sunlight slants across the pale Abbey stone, staining it yellow. People stride across the square:

shoppers clicking in their heels, business professionals with their dark coats and tourists, more relaxed, looking at their maps or eating food from paper wrappers. Fen crumbles bread between her fingers and throws it to the pigeons and they scuffle and peck in a huddle of pale grey, mauve and white feathers that reflect the sky like petrol spilled in a puddle.

They talk about this and that, but Lina is quieter than usual.

'Is something on your mind?' asks Fen, and Lina lets out a deep breath. It makes a small cloud in the cold air. 'What is it?'

Lina extracts a sliver of onion from her sandwich and drops it into the bin. Fen puts her sandwich back in the box. The dread unfurls inside her. She feels its tentacles in her stomach, her throat, her bowels.

'I spoke to my parents last night and they said there'd been a story about Tomas and Joe in the *Gazette*.'

Fen sighs. She peels the lid from her coffee carton and inhales the steam.

Lina glances at her friend sideways, unsure of whether to carry on.

'It's the tenth anniversary of the accident.'

'Yes, I know.'

'There were picture of Tomas, pictures of your whole family.'

Fen puts her coffee down.

'They ought to ask permission,' she says. 'They

shouldn't use those pictures without asking. They should give them back. It's not fair.'

'No.'

'They don't know what they're writing about,' Fen says, protective as ever about her brother. 'I bet they got it all wrong. Everything they said about Tomas before was wrong, it was all twisted. And the terrible things they wrote after Joe's inquest . . .'

Lina shakes her head. 'No, no, I don't think it was anything like that. Mum said it was a very sympathetic article.'

Fen exhales through her lips and gazes up towards the sky. She follows the trail of an aeroplane as it lazily skews white across the blue. She misses her brother so dreadfully.

'The reason I'm telling you about it, Fen,' Lina continues carefully, 'is because there was also an interview with Joe's mother, Mrs Rees.'

'Oh?'

'Mmm. Did you know she's still working in the kitchens at Merron College? Still supervising?'

Fen shakes her head. It's not that she doesn't care; it's just so difficult to think about Emma Rees.

'She still wants to get to the bottom of what happened the night Joe died,' says Lina. 'She wants to know who it was who dialled 999 from Joe's phone after the accident.'

'It doesn't change anything.'

'No . . . But it is a mystery, it is odd. It was definitely a girl. It can't have been Tomas.'

Fen lowers her head. Her eyelashes mask her eyes.

Lina speaks softly. 'They're speculating that another car was involved, or at least that somebody in a second car may have seen what happened, but didn't want to stay at the scene for whatever reason. They're appealing for whoever it was who made the call to come forward. Mrs Rees told the journalist she wouldn't rest until she knew the truth.'

Fen sighs. 'Oh God,' she says. 'It's awful for her, I know it's awful, but what's the point? Nothing can bring Joe back.'

'Honey, the point is that Joe Rees was killed when a car driven by your brother crashed, and his mother wants to know exactly what happened. That's all. She wants to know who called the ambulance and she can't understand why Tomas left Joe on his own, dying out there in the rain, in the woods. She knows how close those two boys were and it doesn't make sense. She says she needs to know and she can't let go of her grief until she does.'

Fen is overwhelmed with waves of hopelessness, helplessness and sadness.

'I just thought you ought to know about the newspaper article,' says Lina. 'I thought it would be better if I told you, rather than you hearing about it from someone else.'

Lina puts her hand over Fen's.

'Fen, I'm not saying you should, but maybe it would help you to go back to Merron and talk to Mrs Rees. You're in the same boat, you and her.

You're both anchored to what your brother did that night. Maybe if you talked to one another you could make sense of it all. You'll both understand how the other is feeling. You might be good for each other.'

Fen stares down into her coffee. Steam evaporates gently in wispy curls from its surface.

'I can't,' she whispers. 'Not yet. Not until Tomas comes back.'

'Fen, Tomas isn't ever—'

Fen shakes her head. 'Please don't say that, Lina. You don't know for sure.'

They are both quiet for a moment. A brightly coloured sightseeing bus trundles past at the periphery of Fen's vision. She catches the tune of the cheerful commentary, the up-and-down male voice, and hears the laughter of the sprinkling of passengers. Bath is full of historical anecdotes.

She sighs and stares at her knees. A tear runs down her cheek.

Lina puts her arm around Fen's shoulder and squeezes.

'It's OK,' she says. She licks her finger and gently wipes the tear from Fen's chin. 'I understand why you don't want to go back. It was a horrible time for you, Fen. Joe dying like that and Tomas . . . disappearing and your father being so ill and all.'

'Lina, you don't know how much of it is my fault. I could have—'

'Shhh. Stop it. Nothing you did or didn't do would have made any difference. Tomas would

50

still have had a drugs problem, Joe would still have followed him everywhere, your father would still have had cancer.'

Lina brushes the crumbs from her lap in a practical manner. She screws up her sandwich box and drops it into the waste bin at her side.

'Come on,' she says, 'don't start dwelling on it. Maybe I shouldn't have said anything.'

Fen picks up her bag. 'No, you were right. You're such a good friend to me, Lina.'

'I do my best,' says Lina.

In the evening, when Connor is in bed, Fen calls her sister, back in Merron.

'Lucy? Hi, it's me. How are you feeling?'

'Hello, you. I'm OK. Still a little nauseous in the mornings.'

'Have you tried eating a ginger biscuit before you get up?'

'I have. It doesn't help. How are things with you? How's my favourite nephew?'

'He's good, fine.'

'You sound tired, Fen. Is everything all right?'

'Yes. Oh . . . It's just . . . I had lunch with Lina and she said there was a feature about the anniversary of the accident in the *Gazette* and I was worried . . . I was worried the press might have been bothering you.'

'No, we're fine,' says Lucy, in her calm, big-sisterly voice. 'We're absolutely fine. A reporter did come round but she was very nice and she let

51

us see what she had written before it went in the paper, which she wasn't supposed to. It was all very civilized.'

'Good,' says Fen, quietly.

'They've set up a drugs-awareness campaign in Joe's name, did Lina tell you? The *Gazette*'s put some money in – a lot of money. They're asking people to join in and organize events and sponsored runs and things to raise funds. They want to get enough to employ a specialist youth worker to go around the schools looking out for vulnerable young people. It's all good stuff.'

'But it means they'll keep going over what happened the night Joe died. Every time they mention the campaign they'll write about the accident again as if it's the only thing that mattered . . . as if it was all . . .'

Lucy exhales. 'All Tom ever did in his whole life?' she asks.

'He did so many good things,' says Fen. 'So many people loved him. He was, *is*, such an amazing person. And they don't know what happened that night. They don't *know* that it was Tom's fault.'

'Fen, you have to accept the facts. We think this campaign is a good thing, Alan and I. It's something positive to come out of Joe's death . . .'

'I'm not sure,' Fen says.

'Well, I'll save the article,' says Lucy. 'Maybe you'll come and see us and we can look at it together.'

Fen gazes out of the window. She will never go back to Merron.

'Maybe,' she says.

The line goes silent. Then both sisters start to speak at the same time and they laugh, awkwardly.

'Lucy, I'm sorry but I've got to go,' says Fen. 'Connor's calling me.'

'All right. But let's speak again soon. Let's arrange for you both to come and stay for a weekend or something. How about bonfire night? It's always great at the school.'

'I'll see,' says Fen. 'I'll give you a call a bit nearer the time.'

'OK,' says Lucy, but both sisters know that she won't.

Fen switches off her phone. Then she opens the back door and sits on the top step in the cool air, staring out across the darkening valley. She wishes she had a cigarette or a drink or something. All this talk of the past, it's made her uncomfortable. She feels itchy, irritable, upset. She wants to cry, she wants to hide, she wants to run away and disappear into the background of life like she did before, in the years between her father's death and Connor being conceived. She wraps her arms around herself and shivers, and looks out across the valley. She wishes things were different, she wishes there were something she could do to change things, to put things right, but in her heart she believes there's nothing she can do, nothing at all.

CHAPTER 8

It's Friday evening. Sean lies down on his bed, just for a moment, with his hands behind his head and his ankles crossed. The last of the sunlight dies on the ceiling. A dead moth is caught inside the paper globe of the light shade. Water glugs in the radiator, warming the room, and the November chill, the smell of fallen leaves, hangs damply in the air beyond the cold window glass.

Sean wishes he could close his eyes and sleep. The bed is comfortable; he's used to it now and it's pleasant to sleep in the same bed every night. He likes the calmness of this room, this house. He likes to be on his own up here, but it's comforting to hear Fen downstairs, playing with Connor, doing his physiotherapy exercises before she puts him to bed.

Fen does not have to leave the house again. He does. And the effort he needs to make now, to do what he has to do, appals him, and his head is aching and his heart is sore. But he must leave soon if he is to pick up his daughter on time, so, after a few minutes, he gets up, goes to the bathroom and splashes cold water on his face. The darkness that's mustering beyond the window dismays him. Sean pats his face dry with his towel, goes into his room and picks up his jacket, his wallet, his car keys.

He meets Fen on the stairs. Connor is on her hip, in his pyjamas, his head on her shoulder and his fingers wrapped in his mother's hair. One of his delicate feet, one slender ankle, hangs by her knee. His pyjamas are a little too small. They have been washed too many times and the pattern has faded.

'Hi,' says Sean, stepping back up to the landing to give her space.

'Hi.'

He jingles the keys. 'I'm just off to fetch Amy.'

'Did you want me to leave some supper out for her? There's some pasta . . .'

'No, thanks, it's OK. If she hasn't eaten, I'll buy something at the services.'

Connor holds his hand out to Sean.

'High five,' says Sean, and the little boy laughs and throws his hand up, almost unbalancing Fen. Sean catches her elbow to steady her.

'Thanks,' says Fen, coming up onto the landing and setting Connor down. She looks up at him. There's a slight colour to her cheeks.

'I'll see you later, then,' says Sean.

'OK.'

'Fen?'

'Mmm?'

'That chain around your neck, it's pretty.'

'Oh, this,' she says, touching the gold chain. 'It belonged to my mother.'

'Belonged?'

'It was a sort of souvenir. She left us when I was very young.'

'I'm sorry,' says Sean.

'Don't be. We had a stepmother. She was very . . . competent.'

'What does the "M" stand for?'

Fen covers the letter with the palm of her hand. 'Mari.'

'It's a pretty name. Is it Gaelic?'

'Irish. My mother is Irish. My father's Scottish and my sister and brother and I were all born in England but we grew up in Wales.'

'Must have made things tricky in the Six Nations.'

Fen laughs politely and he laughs with her.

They both stop laughing at the same time, and there's an awkwardness.

Fen gives an apologetic shrug. 'I need to get Connor to bed,' she says.

'Yeah, sorry, of course,' says Sean. 'I'll see you later.'

It's not far from Bath to Swindon, but an accident has closed the eastbound carriageway of the motorway. Sean is listening to Nirvana, singing along, tapping out the rhythm on the steering wheel to put himself in a good mood, and when he turns on the radio to find out why the traffic up ahead has stopped, it is too late. He is trapped. Lorries dwarf his car on either side, their giant tyres and vertical walls of metal shimmering in the heat from their engines. Sean idles the motor and calls Belle's mobile to explain why he will be late. She is already at Membury services. She is unsympathetic.

'Why didn't you leave earlier?' she asks. 'Why didn't you come straight from work?'

Sean feels a tingle between his shoulder blades. He wonders whether it is feasible that the source of his pain is Belle. Could he actually feel the loss of her as a physical pain? The car in front of him moves forward a few feet, and then stops again. No, he thinks, shifting in his seat. It's just that I spend too long sitting in this bastard car.

'I had to sort out the room, to make it nice for Amy,' he explains. 'That's why I couldn't leave earlier.'

Belle sighs a long-suffering sigh. 'Sean, you've had all week to do that. You didn't have to leave it to the last minute.'

Sean sighs back. He can do patronizing too; she doesn't have a monopoly on that.

'I can't help the traffic jam,' he says. 'There's nothing I can do about it.'

'It's just,' she says, and he can hear the frustration in her voice, 'it's just you *always* do this. You're always messing me around.'

Sean holds his breath. He can't deny this. There *is* always some kind of problem when it comes to him honouring the rendezvous arranged by Belle. He doesn't do it deliberately, but some devil in him connives with the world to ensure something goes wrong every time he is on his way to collect Amy, or on his way to take her back to her mother. Belle, for whom life seems to run more smoothly, finds this intensely frustrating. These late changes in the arrangements set her weekends off to a bad start, but he invariably has a valid excuse so she can't accuse him of direct sabotage. For Sean, it's a Pyrrhic victory, for Belle's anxiety infects Amy and this minor discord seeps into his weekend. It's a victory, nonetheless.

He plans a little speech in his head which goes along the lines of saying he may be late, but if he were still living in the family home, that wouldn't be an issue, would it? And Belle, presumably, did not take into consideration the potential inconvenience to him, Sean, when she took up with the Other. He, actually, believe it or not, would rather be driving home, *home*, right now . . . home to his house, the house he and Belle chose together, the one they were going to stay in until Amy and their future children had flown the nest, the *family* home.

But if he says any of this, the conversation will deteriorate into accusations and the reliving of past hurts and slights. And it would be petty and mean and pathetic. It would confirm that Belle had made the right decision in choosing the rational, reasonable Other over Neadnderthal Sean. It would demean Sean in her eyes, and his.

'Belle, I *am* sorry,' he says, making an effort to

sound sincere. 'I can see the traffic moving up ahead. Why don't you get something to eat? I'll pay.'

'It's not that, it's . . .'

'What?'

'Nothing.'

'Are you doing something special this weekend?' Sean asks. 'Is that why you're upset?' Now he's trying to sound empathetic. It works. He hears her gentle, relieved exhalation. The texture of their dialogue is smoothed. If only he'd worked out how to do this before . . . If only he'd known that was what he had to do . . . He makes a fist and salutes his new-found, new-man self. He will win Belle back. He is learning.

'We're going to St Ives,' says Belle in a more subdued voice.

'Cornwall? That's a long way to go for a weekend.'

'It's our anniversary.'

'Your anniversary?'

'Yes,' she says quietly.

'Oh.'

And Sean thinks back; he thinks back to this time last year and how he took a week off work so Belle could join her tutor group for a study week in Cornwall, and how, when she came back, she seemed to have grown in confidence and energy, and how she changed her hairstyle and laughed a lot and kept going off for walks, on her own, with her mobile phone in her pocket, and how her eyes were bright and her cheeks pink, and how she said she was as happy as she'd ever been . . . and how he'd thought she meant that, now she was being intellectually stimulated by her degree course in creative writing, she was happy with him.

'Oh Christ,' he says.

'I promised you no more lies,' she says.

'I know, but . . . I wasn't expecting . . . a year, Belle? It's been going on for a whole year?'

'Sorry,' she whispers.

A year. That's twelve months' worth of lies, fifty-two weeks of unfaithfulness, three hundred and sixty-five days of deception, who knows how many hours and minutes and seconds of pretending.

'Christ,' says Sean. 'Shit!'

His brain is trying to assimilate this seismic new information. It is fighting back a tidal wave of memories, small inconsistencies in Belle's accounts of how she spent her days, sudden changes in her plans, how she would shower when she came back from her tutorials, the new clothes, the new perfume, the brittle laughter, the energetic, let's-get-it-over-with-quickly sex.

'Sean?'

'Sorry . . . The signal's going,' says Sean, and he puts the phone down so that she will not hear the effort he is making to stop himself fragmenting into a million little pieces of humiliation and hurt.

CHAPTER 9

'*Gëzuar Krishtlindjet e Vitin e Ri*,' says Vincent.
'Oh yes?'
'Merry Christmas and a Happy New Year. In . . . Albanian, I think.'
Fen smiles and shakes her head.

It's been a mad busy morning. The Christmas rush always starts early in Bath, and this year is no exception. Literary aficionados come into the shop in search of special gifts for like-minded friends, others are looking for something a little out of the ordinary, and some, Fen thinks, are just looking to escape the crowds. The Gildas Bookshop is an oasis of quiet and calm. The city is already filled with piped carols; shop windows are overflowing with energy-saving fairy lights, their political correctness tempered by the red and gold of tasteful, Victoriana point-of-sale displays; tens of thousands of shoppers are trip-trapping through the streets, bumping each other's legs with their smart carrier bags filled with delightful, shiny, well-packaged items; they are queuing to buy wraps of genuine roasted chestnuts and cardboard cups of mulled wine from entrepreneurial street vendors. At this time of year, Bath is a cathedral to Mammon, but the bookshop is devoid of glitter, twinkle and marked-up prices. The only concessions to the season are the foreign-language Christmas cards and a tiny, old, three-bar electric fire. The top bar doesn't work, but still the fire warms the air in the shop until it is heavy and thick and anyone standing within about a metre of the appliance will scorch their legs. The heater makes the shop smell of burned dust. It's not a pleasant smell and after a while Fen can taste the dust in her mouth and feel it in the moisture that coats the surface of her eyes.

Fen has been making a display of the greeting cards. They are beautiful things, photographs of winter landscapes of the countries they represent, each captioned in the appropriate language.

'Hah,' says Vincent. 'You'd have to go a long way to find another shop that stocks Christmas cards in, er –' he turns over the card he is holding – 'Lithuanian!' Normally a man given to self-deprecation, today he is exceptionally pleased with himself.

'What if the words are inappropriate?' asks Fen. 'What if they're wrongly spelled? What if that doesn't say, "Happy Christmas", what if it actually says . . .'

'That's what the internet's for,' says Vincent happily. 'When the shop's quiet, Fen Weller, you can make yourself useful by Googling the phrases and seeing what comes up.'

He wags an affectionate finger at Fen. 'You never stop learning, dear girl, that's the beauty of life.'

The migraine that has been hovering just outside Fen's field of vision all morning finally swoops in for the kill just before lunch. She sees a shimmering mirage before her, a pool of mercury that darts whichever way her eyes turn, and the familiar, spiteful vice has begun to tighten around her skull. She battles on, but Vincent, who is always attentive, notices that she is not right.

'Sit down a while; you've gone very pale,' he says, offering his chair, but Fen knows that if she gives in, the headache will win. 'Your skin looks bleached. Would paracetamol help? Ibuprofen?'

'No,' she says, 'thank you, but they won't touch it. If I ignore it, it may go away.'

Lina comes into the shop. 'Hello, gorgeous,' she says to Vincent, going over to him for a hug and a kiss. 'Hello, Fen. What have you done to your eyes?'

'Nothing, I . . .'

'She's not feeling well,' says Vincent. 'Migraine, I suspect, although she hasn't said as much.'

'Oh, Fen, nobody likes a trooper,' says Lina. 'It shows the rest of us up.'

'I'm fine,' says Fen.

'You blatantly aren't.'

'Is your car nearby, Lina?' Vincent asks.

'It's in the Waitrose car park.'

'Be a dear and fetch it,' says Vincent. 'Give Fen a lift home.'

'I'll be all right,' says Fen.

'You look like death warmed up; you'll frighten off the customers,' says Lina.

Vincent, who would never be so discourteous as to comment on a woman's appearance, unless it was to pay a compliment, does not contradict Lina. He pushes back the hair that has fallen from the top of his head over his eyes.

'Have the afternoon off,' he says. 'Go and lie in a darkened room until Connor comes home. And if you're no better in the morning, don't come in.'

'Thank you,' says Fen. 'You are a lovely boss.'

'I know, dear girl,' says Vincent. 'I know.'

Lina drives like a man, fast and tight, with one hand on the steering wheel and the other flat on the gear stick. Fen braces herself as Lina braves the car round the bends and through the lights at the London Road junction, squeezing through impossibly small gaps as she races up Snow Hill.

They reach Fairfield Park in record time and Lina drives down Crofters Road, skimming past the narrow, terraced houses trickling down the hill, but there are no spaces. She loops back up again along Claremont Road, and stops the Mazda in the middle of the road outside Lilyvale. A Range Rover pulls up behind.

'You'll be OK?' she asks Fen.

'I'll be fine.'

'Call me this evening,' says Lina. 'Let me know how you are.'

Fen leans over and kisses Lina's cheek. In the wing mirror, she sees the Range Rover driver make a frustrated gesture, both palms upturned.

'I'll see you soon,' she calls to Lina, 'and thank you!'

The fifteen minutes out of the shop, away from the heater, have made Fen feel a little better. Still, she thinks, she'll do exactly as Vincent suggested. She'll fill the kettle and put it on to boil while she changes into something less constricting than the demure navy-blue dress which Vincent says makes her look vaguely Jane Austen-y, a look which he believes appeals to the punters. Then she'll fill a hot-water bottle, make a mug of ginger tea and get into bed; she'll close her eyes and lie there until Connor is dropped off by the school transport. She'll have at least three hours to herself, and by then the flashing lights will have gone from her eyes and the worst of the pain will have passed.

The sky is hazy, silvery. There's a strange light over the city and the buildings are highlighted; they stand out like two-dimensional cut-outs, as if they were a film set. Fen recognizes the light. It usually precedes thunder, and she thinks this is one of the reasons why she has a migraine. As soon as the storm comes, her head will clear.

She goes tentatively down the steep, front garden steps, because she is still a little dizzy and the mirage has begun to zigzag giddily in front of her.

She holds up her key to unlock the outer door, but as soon as her hand touches it, it swings open.

Fen swallows. She remembers locking the door before she walked to work. It was only a few hours ago. She remembers rattling the handle to double-check. Or is it yesterday she's remembering? Were the blood vessels in her brain already constricting this morning? Migraines do weird things to her mind. They make her forget. Maybe she forgot to lock the door. Or maybe Sean has come back early. Maybe he's come to collect something.

Still her heart begins to race.

She pushes the outer door wide open, sweeps aside a flyer on the doormat with the toe of her shoe and opens the inner door with her Yale key.

'Hello?' she calls quietly. 'Sean?'

There is no answer. The doors to all three downstairs rooms open off the hall. They are all ajar. Fen can see into the kitchen, ahead of her. It is empty but there's a Starbucks carton on the counter that wasn't there before. Fen steps into the hall, and checks the living room and dining room. Both are empty. Both are as they were when she last saw them.

Her heart is beating so strongly that Fen can clearly feel the muscle contracting and pulsing in her chest. Breathing is difficult; she has to remember to inhale but the air only seems to reach the top third of her lungs and she exhales shakily. She stands still, listening, and she hears movement upstairs, she hears water.

At first she thinks that this is the sign she's been waiting for – the sign that Tomas is back. The water is the clue, the running water. But much as she wants this to be the truth, there's a more plausible explanation; she knows there is.

The cold tap that feeds the bath is broken. Sometimes she twists the handle tight into its thread until she is certain the tap is turned off but minutes, or sometimes hours, later water splashes from the spout. Sean said there's something wrong with the plumbing; air in the system, he said, and it needs bleeding. Sometimes, when one or the other of them flushes the lavatory, the whole house groans and rattles. When Fen suggested calling a plumber, Sean told her to save her money. He said he'd look at it. He is, she has noticed, inclined to volunteer for mending and maintenance jobs around the house, although he never seems to find time to actually carry them out.

Fen holds her breath to slow her heart rate.

Her head is throbbing.

'Which is more likely?' she asks herself firmly. 'That the cold tap has turned itself on again, or that Tomas is upstairs running himself a bath?'

Still she is careful. She pulls off her boots, takes hold of the banister and puts her bare left foot on the first stair.

Fen creeps up the stairs, moving one foot after the other, cautiously unpeeling her sole from the carpet at every step to make herself as light and quiet as possible. She treads carefully, breathing in little shallow gasps, trying not to imagine how she will feel if she taps on the bathroom door and Tomas is there, in the bath. What will she say to him? What will she do?

'Stop it!' she says, out loud, but very quietly. 'Stop.'

At the top of the stairs, she pauses, rests a moment.

The bathroom door is open.

It's not the cold tap making the noise. It's not the bath either.

It's the shower.

Fen takes two more steps forward, and looks through the narrow gap between the door and the door frame. The earthy, damp warmth of the bathroom, mingled with the metallic smell of hot water and the hot-plastic smell of the shower curtain, seeps through the crack.

There is no ghost in the bathroom.

It is Sean, and he's alive. He is very alive.

He is standing beneath the shower.

The shower curtain is drawn and water streams down it, steam billowing softly so his silhouette and his colours are blurred, like the Countryside seen through a rain-soaked window.

He is leaning forward. One arm is braced against the wall, slightly below the chrysanthemum-shaped shower head. The fingers of this hand are extended, spanned for balance, the palm supporting his weight. His head is inclined downward, so his face is hidden by the arm, and the water from the shower is firing onto the crown of his head, pelting down his back, which is slightly arched.

Although his body is hazy through the curtain and the water, Fen can tell that he has a beautiful shape from the way his back slopes into his buttocks, the length of his thighs and the tapering of his lower legs to his ankles.

One leg is bent gracefully at the knee, like a statue of an Athenian athlete about to run a marathon. The braced arm and the bent knee give Sean's body a heroic pose. But it's the movement of his other forearm that holds Fen's eyes: the V shape of the elbow, smudged behind the curtain, and the rhythm of the wrist working that private, universal, unmistakable sexual rhythm.

Fen is spellbound.

Everything drains from her mind.

She is aware of nothing but the man in the shower just a few feet away from her, the beauty of him, the movement beneath the raining water.

She holds her breath and she watches.

She watches as the steam plumes, as the water splashes into the bath and trickles down the curtain. She watches as the water streams out of the shower head and down Sean's wet hair, down the incline of his neck to the shadow of his shoulder blade, down the dark hairs of his leg to the bend of the knee. She watches the tension of his back, the movement of his elbow, his arm, his far shoulder arching even further, so muscular, so intent and intense. She breathes in his beauty as she watches and after a moment, after forever, he groans loud enough for her to hear. Then his head relaxes, and the working arm falls to his side and she sees the tension leave him.

He stands still, quite motionless for a moment or two beneath the shower water, and then he pushes himself upright with the braced hand. He stands up straight and tall, and pushes the hair and water out of his face with his two hands.

Fen holds her breath.

Then he turns, he turns towards the door, and she knows he cannot see her – there is a streaming, steamy shower curtain between them and she is just a shadow in the gap between the door and its frame; and he does not know she is there, she should be at work – yet she feels he looks right into her.

She sees the shape of his chest and the slightness of his hips and the dark, dark hair that trickles from his navel to his groin and the paler shape between his thighs, and she wants to groan like he has groaned, but she suppresses it.

He leans down, picks up a bottle of shampoo, *her* shampoo Fen notices with pleasure, and it is only then that she remembers she should not be here. She turns away and puts her back to the door frame, then slides down it until she is resting on her heels. She leans her head back and exhales, and it is as if she has been holding her breath forever. In a way, she supposes, she has.

'God,' she whispers. 'My God.'

CHAPTER 10

Amy falls asleep in her car seat on the way back to Bath after Sean stops at the off-licence and buys beer and whisky. Back at Lilyvale, he sees Fen has left the downstairs lights on for him and her bedroom light is on. Sean carries Amy upstairs and puts her to sleep in his bed. Then he takes his guitar and goes down into the living room. He shuts the door, turns on a small lamp and opens a can of beer. He fingers the strings of the guitar and makes up a song, which he knows he will have forgotten by the morning. The song is called 'Membury Blues.'

When he goes back upstairs, some hours, some beer and some whisky later, he finds Amy awake in the bed, watching *Poltergeist* on the television. The duvet is pulled up to her eyes, which are wide and round, terrified. Sean can't remember the exact plot of the film but he knows it has something to do with a child of about Amy's age being sucked into the mouth of hell, or something equally disturbing.

'There are ghosts in the television, Daddy,' she whispers, too scared almost to breathe. He switches off the set and scoops his daughter up in his arms.

She is shivering and doesn't seem to realize, thankfully, that she has wet herself and the bed. She would be mortified if she knew. Soon, the lap of Sean's jeans is also damp. He holds Amy very close, wraps her into his big body and kisses her head. He strokes her hair over and over, smoothing it against her warm little skull with the flat of his hand, feeling the delicate shell-shape of her ear, and he tells her that there are no ghosts, that it was just a scary story.

'I *saw* the ghosts,' she insists, whispering, trembling in his arms.

'Those were just pretend ghosts.'

'How do you know?'

'Because I know the man who made the film and he told me.'

Amy shifts her position; and looks up at her father, wanting to believe him, but still suspicious. Her eyelashes are sticky with tears that catch the light from the landing and reflect in her dark pupils.

'It's true,' he says. 'Shall I phone him up now and you can ask him yourself?'

'Your words don't smell very nice,' says Amy, pulling her face away from his. 'I think you should brush your teeth, Daddy.'

The next day, they sleep in late, and Sean wakes to find his little daughter clinging to him like ivy to a tree. He unwinds her and wakes her, and she is hot and strange, an alien Amy. She behaves nothing like the quiet, eager-to-please daughter he knows and loves. She won't let him comb her hair and refuses to brush her teeth or eat any breakfast. She says she does not want to go to Royal Victoria Park, she hates the park, she hates Bath, she wants her mummy, she wants to be at home. She works herself up into a desperate crying fit, sobbing as if her heart is breaking. Sean cannot touch her. She can't hear what he says so he sits on the bed and waits for her to work the excess emotion out of her system. He has never seen Amy like this. It's as if she has been broken.

He thinks: Is this how it's going to be from now on? Is this my life?

Over his daughter's wails, he hears Fen tactfully clatter Connor's pushchair up the steps in the front garden. He hears her collecting the boy, hurrying him along, pretending she has somewhere to be so that Sean and Amy have the house to themselves. He is grateful.

When Amy's crying has subsided into huge, swallowing, gulping sobs, he takes her downstairs and gives her little sips of sugared tea from a spoon, like a baby. He turns on the television out of habit, and Amy screams that the ghosts will come. She kicks the guitar that he left propped beside the settee. Amy knows that kicking his guitar is about the worst crime she can commit in her father's presence. She is never naughty. She is, by nature, the least controversial child. Once she has kicked the guitar, her hand flies to her mouth and she looks up at her father with wide, startled eyes, as if she cannot believe what she has just done. Sean doesn't care. He is tired and hung-over. He rubs his stubbly chin, rubs his eyes. He hitches up his jeans; he needs to buy a belt.

'Come on,' he says to his daughter. 'We're going into Bath.'

'I don't want to go into Bath.'

'There's a fairy shop,' says Sean, 'and it's full of nice things. Really, Ames, I think you'll like it.'

He noticed the shop some weeks back and has been saving it for an emergency.

They catch the bus down into the city centre and make their way through the Saturday crowds to the fairy shop, which is down one of the narrow little side streets that remind Sean of film sets; they are too authentic, too quaint to be real, he thinks. Amy holds his hand very tightly. She has gone quiet now. Occasionally she sniffs. The shop is tiny, a shrine to pink and glitter, fairy dust, wands, sequins, tinsel and fairy lights, all sparkly corners and mirrors and pink plastic.

Amy's mouth falls open.

'Oh!' she says, a little bubble-gasp of pleasure between her lips, and she is off.

Sean looks at his watch. He leans up against a shelf of tiaras and wishes he had brought something to read. He plugs his iPod into his ears, crosses his arms, closes his eyes and fills his head with the Pixies, only moving when Amy shakes his sleeve to show him some new wonder. After an inordinately long time, bored almost to tears, he persuades her out of the shop by buying her a fairy outfit, wings, wand, glitter dust, the whole shooting match. It's the sort of stuff he and Belle have always tried to steer Amy away from, hoping to nurture less stereotypical interests. Today he doesn't care. He'll do whatever it takes to make Amy happy.

They eat lunch in a cafe upstairs at the Podium. Amy, her hair messy beneath the tiara, picks at a bowl of chips, delicately dipping each one in mayonnaise and nibbling off its end, before discarding it at the side of her plate. From time to time she spoons marshmallow balls from a mug of hot chocolate, making a sticky mess on the table which she makes worse by painting patterns with her finger. She is talking to herself, her lips moving constantly, maintaining a private running commentary. She does not realize she is making a mess. Sean can't be bothered to stop her. He wolfs down a bacon burger and drinks a pint of Stella as the hair of the dog. The waitress, a pretty girl with a nice wide mouth and an Alice band, makes a fuss of Amy and flirts with Sean. He has no inclination to join in. He wipes the froth from his upper lip with the back of his hand and tries to keep his mind on his daughter. There is still a whole afternoon to fill in. There are five hundred or more weekends to be endured before Amy will be old enough to go to concerts with Sean, by which time she'll be too old for him to impose his musical tastes on her. He prays that the child will grow to like rugby because otherwise God knows

75

how they'll manage. What interests Sean bores Amy and vice versa. One or other of them will die of boredom. They'll grow to dislike and resent one another. The future looks grim.

After lunch, he shows Amy how the steam from the hot springs, which feed the famous Roman baths, comes up through the drain covers in the old roads around the historic building. She is captivated, putting her hand in the steam which, her father tells her, has come all the way up from the centre of the earth. She is almost back to her old self. She asks lots of questions about hot springs and the Romans who built the baths and what they wore when they were bathing. They walk through streets almost unchanged since Georgian times and lined with grand, tall, sash-windowed houses all in the palest, most elegant stone, houses with straight, high walls that catch the sunlight in geometric slabs and cast beautiful shadows. They go to the balcony that overlooks the Recreation Ground and Sean manages to watch a bit of rugby. Amy, in her fairy tiara, soon attracts several other little girls who want to play with her. Amy is flattered by the attention, but does not know how to take advantage of it. She hangs on to her father's hand and lets the other girls play with her wand.

This amenable state of affairs does not last long. Soon Amy is quietly unhappy again. Sean buys a paper and takes his daughter to the Royal Victoria Park. Amy runs off towards the sand pit. The grass is cold and damp, spattered darkly with fallen leaves, so Sean finds a discarded orange Sainsbury's carrier bag to sit on, and reads the *Guardian* from cover to cover, and all its supplements, even the Money section. He feels more at home, because he and Amy have already been to the park so many times, and because a lot of men on their own come here with their kids at weekends. Sean has even spoken to a few of them. He's thrown footballs and cricket balls back to boys. He's ridden the rope slide with Amy. He has not exactly made friends, but here he feels less of a social pariah.

With one arm tucked behind his head, Sean is half-sitting, half-lying against a grassy slope, chewing a piece of grass and watching Amy, who is being bossed about by an older girl. Amy is listening intently to instructions. She is slightly knock-kneed and her fairy wings are already bent out of shape. She looks up at the other child, nods and then crawls off through the sand, in search of something or other.

Sean smiles. He checks his watch and as he does so he is aware of somebody beside him. He looks up and it is his landlady, Fen.

'Hi,' she says.

'Hi,' he says, squinting into a metallic, wintery sun. He makes a visor with his hand. 'Do you come here often?'

She smiles, looks down. 'It was such a nice afternoon. I thought I'd come for a walk.'

The boy is in his buggy, wrapped up in a coat, boots and gloves, and a felt hat with ear-flaps is tucked around his head. He grins widely when he sees Sean and climbs out of the buggy.

'Hey, Connor,' says Sean.

Connor salutes Sean as he has been taught and says: 'How's it hanging?'

Fen laughs. 'Go and play, Con,' she says, pushing his shoulder gently. 'Where's Amy?'

Sean nods towards the sandpit. 'I'm sorry about the noise this morning.'

Fen shrugs.

'I was going to get a cup of tea,' she says, looking towards the ice-cream van in the corner. 'Would you like one?'

'I'll go,' says Sean. He jumps to his feet and indicates the carrier bag. 'Have a seat,' he says, 'I'll be back in a moment.'

She doesn't talk much. She sits quietly beside him, looking out over the park and watching the children, one hand shading her eyes. It's OK; he doesn't feel as if he has to make conversation. They have shared the same house long enough now to be comfortable with one another's silences. And she always seems half lost in thought.

'It's as if all the children in Bath come here on Saturdays,' she says.

'We always do. I tried to persuade Amy that rugby was more fun, but she wasn't having it.'

Fen laughs. 'Bath's nice in the summer,' she says. 'She'll like it better then. There are more things to do. Loads of things for children.'

They are silent again for a moment. Sean is thinking that he won't be here in the summer. He'll be back home by then.

'You know,' she says, 'you don't *have* to be out of the house all weekend. I don't mind if you want to take over the living room or the kitchen. It's your home too.'

Sean winces. He didn't mean to and he hopes she didn't notice, but she's wrong. Lilyvale is *not* his home.

'OK,' he says, 'thanks.'

A little later he says: 'You're not local, are you?'

'No.'

'You told me you grew up in Taffy-land.'

She laughs. 'That's right.'

'What brought you to Bath, then?'

She gazes over towards the giant gas tanks across the road. They are catching the falling sunlight, magnificent in their enormous ugliness.

'I was sort of passing through and I bumped into Lina. I needed somewhere to live and she had a house to rent.'

Sean glances at her. Her eyes are pale brown, almost yellow, glassy in the sun's rays.

'That's not much of an answer,' he says.

She smiles, but not at him; she smiles at Connor, who is methodically piling sand around the base of the climbing frame.

'Is that where Connor's father is?' Sean persists. 'In Wales?'

Fen picks at the dying grass and narrows her

eyes as if she's trying to remember and then she says: 'I don't know where Connor's father is.'

There's a pause.

'Doesn't he help you out at all?' asks Sean.

She shakes her head. 'It's not his fault,' she says. 'He doesn't know about Connor. I'm sure he'd help if he could.'

'Why can't you contact him?'

She looks into the distance. 'We were only together for one night. He was very nice, but I don't know anything about him. I didn't expect to fall pregnant.'

Sean can think of nothing to say to this.

She looks at him sideways.

'Do you think that's awful?' she asks.

He shakes his head and smiles. 'It's kind of romantic.'

She looks away again. 'I was a bit fucked-up,' she says, 'at the time.'

Amy comes over to the adults. She looks anxious, shy.

'Fen,' she says, 'has Connor hurt his leg?'

'Not exactly. He has a problem with his muscles, that's why he looks a bit strange when he walks.'

'What happened?'

'It's just the way he was born.'

Amy thinks about this for a moment.

'Does it hurt him?'

'No, not at all.'

'Can I ask him if he wants to play with me?'
'Of course you can.'

Sean is touched by the way Amy plays with Connor. The two get on very well. If Amy can't understand something Connor says, they work it out between them with signs. She enjoys mothering him; he is grateful for the attention and does everything he's told to do.

They are enjoying one another's company so much that the normally impeccably placid Connor refuses to get back into his pushchair even though the sun is so low that it has disappeared behind the gas tanks and the air is turning cold and the grass is already wet.

'Why does he have to go in the buggy?' asks Amy.

'Because his legs are tired and it's a long walk home.'

Amy hangs on Sean's hand to pull his head down towards hers. She stands on tiptoe and whispers: 'Can Connor come with us for a pizza?' Her breath is hot and moist in her father's ear. She smells of damp grass and sand, discarded lollipop sticks and fallen leaves.

Sean glances at Fen.

'Well, why not?' he says. 'Why don't you come and eat with us?'

'Thanks,' says Fen, 'but I don't want to intrude on your time with Amy.'

'You won't be intruding.'

'No, really.'

'Please come,' says Sean, 'you don't know how lonely it gets.'

It's only as the words leave his lips that he realizes they are true.

'My treat.'

She shakes her head.

'Go on. I'll put it on my expenses. I'll pretend you were clients, you and Connor. I'll pretend you had a restoration project you wanted me to look at.'

Fen looks down at Connor, who is looking up at her, pleading with his eyes.

'If you're sure . . .'

'I'm sure.'

'OK,' says Fen, 'thank you.'

They eat in Amy's favourite restaurant, pricey but classy with its high, ornate ceilings and rococo walls, big mirrors and tea-lights on the tables. Amy sits next to Fen and tells her about her life. Fen picks slivers of artichoke and olive from the surface of her pizza. Connor listens, but is too hungry to join in. Sean, temporarily relieved from having to worry about whether or not Amy is having a good time, slips back into his thoughts. He drinks his wine and watches Fen and how she smiles at Amy with her pale brown eyes.

'And Lewis, who is Mummy's partner, well, I'm supposed to call him Uncle Lewis, but he's not my real uncle, but Lewis is his real name, which is not as funny as Daddy's name, which is Sean,' says Amy.

'I know,' says Fen.

'Like Sean the Sheep!'

'That *is* funny.'

Amy leans forward conspiratorially. 'Daddy and me call Lewis "Pooey Lewey".'

Fen raises her eyebrows.

'But only when nobody else can hear. Anyway he's moving into our house today. He's going to share Mummy's bedroom. Mummy says Daddy will get used to it but he shouted at her yesterday when he came to pick me up.'

Amy stares at Fen with round, serious eyes. Sean holds his wine in his mouth.

'I expect he did,' says Fen in a matter-of-fact voice. Sean relaxes, swallows, tugs at his ear lobes.

'But he shouldn't shout at Mummy,' says Amy quietly, shaking her head to emphasize the point. 'I really don't like it.'

'No, I'm sure you don't. But I don't suppose he shouts very often and I'm sure he says he's sorry afterwards.'

'Mmm,' Amy agrees grudgingly.

She looks over at her father to see if he's paying attention, and he pretends that he is not. He is glad that Amy is talking about what's going on in her life. He supposes that she can't talk about Lewis and her mother to him, because she knows it would hurt him, and out of loyalty to Belle. He is grateful to Fen for acting as confidante, and for her calm impartiality. He hears Amy whisper to Fen: 'Mummy told me there's going to be a special present for me when I get back, to celebrate.'

'Oh,' says Fen. 'What do you hope it will be?'

Amy shrugs. 'I don't care. It won't be as good as the fairy things Daddy got me today.'

Amy is bathed and asleep by nine, lying on the dry side of the bed, her infant-red lips slightly ajar, her silky hair drifting across her cheeks, and her eyes moving charmingly backwards and forwards beneath her closed, delicately veined lids. Sean had forgotten how little she was. He could cup the top of her skull in the palm of his hand. He had forgotten details about his daughter. Now he sits on the bed and watches her sleep, while the sky darkens to black beyond the window and, far below, the lights of Bath twinkle as the air grows colder. And he thinks of Belle, and how tonight she will be lying in the Other's arms, between sheets that she and Sean used to share. He remembers the pattern of the curtain fabric in their bedroom: lemon flowers and leaves. He remembers the shape of the yellow spill of light on the pale carpet from the landing lamp, left on for Amy's sake. He remembers the silky texture of the padded headboard and the apricot colour of Belle's dressing gown hanging on the hook on the back of the door. And his loneliness cracks and forms a chasm inside him. He slides down into the space between the bed and the wall, and tries to lose himself in music but it doesn't work any more. All he can think of is what he has lost.

CHAPTER 11

On Monday, Fen's day off, she goes into his room. She stands for a moment, looking around her. Sean's collection of CDs is stacked along the wall beneath the window, and there are more in boxes beside the facing wall. His guitar leans against the wardrobe door. There's a small pile of coins on the chest of drawers, a can of deodorant, a comb, a handful of receipts and a hard hat. A high-visibility vest is hooked over the back of the chair. Fen sits on the bed and picks up the framed photograph which was lying, face down, on the carpet below the window.

It's a picture of Sean with his arm around the shoulders of a woman. The woman is beautiful. She has dark hair, almond-shaped eyes, a long nose, and the confidence in front of the camera that only ever comes with real beauty. In the picture, Sean's hair is a little shorter than it is now, his face less tired, and his forehead touches the woman's forehead, so she must be quite tall. The woman is wearing a chic, short-sleeved black dress. An expensive-looking, cream-coloured handbag is tucked under her elbow. Propped into the bottom corner of the frame is a smaller picture. It's a photograph of Amy as a chubby toddler on a Mediterranean beach, smiling, her hair in bunches, holding up her hands to whoever is taking the picture, asking to be picked up.

Fen puts the photograph back on the carpet, nudging it under the bed so that she can vacuum the room without Sean realizing she has been spying. She strips the bed and piles the linen, the duvet and the pillows on the floor. The mattress is stained and smells of ammonia, the familiar farmyard stink of stale child-pee. Fen pushes back her hair and then she grabs one side of the mattress and, heaving, hurting her fingernails and straining the muscles in her arms, she tries to turn it. She has pulled it half off the bed, when she sees the little blue notebook that had been hidden between the mattress and the bed frame.

Fen knows she shouldn't intrude on Sean's privacy, but having done so already, albeit accidentally, she has no qualms about what she does next. She opens the notebook, its cover circled with coffee-mug stains, and reads the words inside. It is filled with lines of poetry, scribbled out, amended – no, not poetry, she realizes, but lyrics. The songs are all love songs. On some pages are little sketches of a woman illustrating the sentiment of the lyrics. Some of the drawings are beautiful, some are ugly. On the second to last page, Sean has drawn a naked man with his head in his hands and then scribbled obscenities over the drawing.

★   ★   ★

Tomas used to write illustrated poems about love. He used to hide them too. More often he destroyed them so that nobody else could read them and misinterpret them. He set fire to them or else he tore them up and dropped the pieces over the side of the bridge that took the road over the river in Merron. The pieces of paper fluttered like leaves to the water, where they met their reflections, and were carried, spinning, downstream. And there was a beauty to the destruction of the words, there was a poetry.

He was fascinated by the conflict between water and fire. Sometimes he would make paper boats and float them at night, setting fire to their paper sails with the yellow flame of a disposable lighter.

'Water always beats fire,' he said, sucking the side of his thumb because the lighter wheel was rusty and had made it sore.

He and Joe wanted to go to Japan to watch the peace ceremony at Hiroshima. Tomas told Fen there was an eternal flame burning beside the peace pond and it would only be extinguished when the last nuclear weapon was destroyed. He said the beauty of this symbolism was designed to mask the horrors it hid. He said men would never get rid of nuclear weapons so the flame really was eternal. It would burn until the sun began to swell and sucked the planets and moons of the solar system back into it, like a multiple birth in reverse.

★   ★   ★

Now Fen sits on the unturned mattress and she reads what Sean has written. She strokes her lower lip with her middle finger. The lyrics could be turned into an opera, an elegy to Sean's marriage. She enjoys the gentle, funny, erotic and pleading words but does not care for the angry verses. She supposes the emotions they describe are part of what's happening to him, they have to be expressed, and at least Sean's expressions are creative, not destructive. She flicks back to the beginning of the notebook and reads her favourite lyrics again. She touches the pages. She whispers: 'Oh, Sean.'

He could have been describing her loss. His missing Belle, finding out things he did not know about her, and could not have imagined of her, wanting her back, is the same as her missing Tomas. It's the same terrible not-knowing. And the guilt. The thinking: If only I had done this, or that, or said this, or that, anything to stop what happened from happening.

Sean is as lost as she is. He doesn't know where he is, or what's going to happen next. The tentative stepping into each new day, feeling the way forward, blind because all certainty has been taken away, as if the projected backdrop to a life has been lifted and replaced by another and completely unfamiliar scenario, is the same for Sean as it is for Fen. And she wishes he would turn away from Belle because it is obvious there is no happiness for Sean with her; she wishes he would look forward, instead, towards a happier future.

And she realizes that this is precisely what the people who still care about Fen have been saying to her for years.

When she has read the notebook several times, she hefts the mattress back onto the bed. She cannot turn it now, or he would know she has seen the book. She switches on Sean's CD player, to listen to whatever it was he was listening to last night. A man's gentle voice comes from the speakers. He sings an appeal to a woman who is no longer his. Fen gathers up Sean's bedding and lies down on the mattress, her head on his pillows, and she holds to her face the used sheet he has slept on for the last week. She wraps her arm around the linen, nests her cheek in the sheet and inhales the musky, musty man-smell of his skin: the smell of Sean, sleeping.

She stays there, immersed in Sean's sheet, and his music, half-dozing on Sean's bed until she hears the hoot of Connor's bus outside and runs downstairs to greet him back from school.

Fen spends the first part of the evening in the dining room, sewing at the table by the window. The room is warm and cosy, the curtains are drawn, Connor is sleeping and Fen should feel content. She enjoys her work; she's making cushion covers for Lina and Lucy, Christmas presents, using scraps of fabric she has collected over the year and stored in carrier bags. The covers are turning out beautifully, and Fen knows her friend and her sister will be surprised and pleased, but all she can think about is Sean.

He is in the living room, watching television, and she is acutely conscious of him being there, and of the wall between them. All she has to do is cross from one room to the other, it's not far, only two or three metres, but she feels illiterate in the language of man-and-woman, and it is so long since she has practised. One clumsy move could ruin their quiet relationship, she knows that, and also she is terrified of humiliation. She would rather cut open her wrists than embarrass him and reveal herself as needy. Yet the connection she sensed when she watched him in the shower is deeper now, because she knows they have both lost somebody they loved. They are both refugees. They ought to be able to help one another. Only there is no way to broach a subject so intimate without sounding mad, or desperate, or like one of those people who enjoy probing into the unhappiness of others, peeling back the protective veneer that hides their misery and sticking their dirty fingers in the infected wounds that lie beneath.

When she finishes putting the zip on the last cushion cover, she turns off the machine, goes into the kitchen, tidies up and sets a load of laundry to wash. It's not even ten o'clock, and there are no other domestic chores to fill the time. Fen checks the fridge, to make sure there's a bottle in the chiller, then taps on the living-room door with her fingertips and goes in. The television is still on, friendly blue-grey faces in the corner are taking part in a current affairs quiz, but the volume has been turned low. Sean is sitting on the chair, very quietly picking out chords on his guitar. He raises his eyes and his hand in greeting when he sees her.

'Hi,' she says, nervously, and her voice sounds highpitched and stupid.

'Hey,' he says. 'Am I making too much noise?'

'No, no, not at all. It's nice . . . Sean,' she says, and she enjoys the sound of his name on her lips, 'this morning, I went into your room to change the bed and there was a CD on the player, and I turned it on. I hope you don't mind.'

'Beck,' says Sean. 'The album's called *Sea Change*. I was listening to it the other night.'

'It's beautiful,' says Fen. 'It's sad.'

'I'll make a copy for you, if you like.'

'Thank you.'

Sean's eyes drop down to the guitar again. It is cradled in his arms. Fen feels a pang of jealousy for the instrument. Sean's hair hides his eyes. She can see the top of his head, the pattern of the crown. She sees the way his arm is curled around the lower half of the guitar, his sleeve rolled up to the elbow, the dark hairs on his arm and the boniness of his wrist, and the way the fingers are splayed . . . She has to swallow the thrilling memory that floods into her mind and bloodstream. She steadies herself against the door.

'My brother used to like Beck,' she says.

Sean continues to play, but he looks up.

'I'm sure Tom saw him play live. He had all his CDs.'

'He's into music, then, your brother?'

Fen nods. 'Yes.'

Sean smiles politely, but he doesn't seem to want to talk. He looks as if he'd rather be left alone to play his guitar.

'I was just wondering –' Fen persists, and again she sounds gauche, far too awkward – 'I was going to have a glass of wine. Would you like some?'

He shakes his head. 'No, I'm all right,' he says, 'but thanks anyway.'

'OK,' says Fen. She stands there for a moment longer, but he is engrossed with his guitar and she can think of nothing else to say. 'Well, goodnight,' she says.

'Goodnight.'

And she goes up to bed with her book.

CHAPTER 12

S ean spends Christmas week with his parents. His old bedroom has been commandeered as the headquarters of his mother's new internet retro-fashion business. The room is full of faintly smelly, old afghan coats; brown, orange and purple mini-, midi- and maxi-dresses on wire hangers looped over the curtain rail and door; platform shoes, flared trousers and flowery shirts with matching ties. There's an ironing board and various paraphernalia for wrapping the ordered goods. On the desk by the window, where Sean was supposed to do his homework when he was at school, there now sits a flash little laptop with wireless broadband access. The computer is never turned off, and pings irritatingly through the night as orders come in from countries in different time zones. Sean has to move armfuls of newly washed charity-shop finds off the old single bed in order to lie on it. The overriding smell in the room is of Bold 2 in 1.

'It's my busiest time of year,' says Rosie unapologetically, as she climbs over Sean's rucksack to access the computer on Christmas Eve. Her cheeks are flushed like the cheeks of a Russian doll. She calls it her 'sherry blush' even though she's not drinking sherry but Southern Comfort and lemonade. She's pretending it's sherry because her mother-in-law, Vera, is over for Christmas and Vera is a stickler for tradition. Sean is pretty sure Vera is on to Rosie; he can sense disapproval emanating from her pores.

His parents are being unnaturally jolly and are trying to keep Sean busy so that he won't have time to dwell on his situation, but he knows what they're up to and nothing, not even alcohol, helps ease the ache. He misses his home, he misses Amy, but most of all, and angry as he is with her, he misses Belle.

His father says it's Christmas that's making Sean feel so bad. He says it's a bloody time of year at the best of times and that there's nothing more guaranteed to depress a man than being told he should be enjoying himself. But that can't be entirely accurate, because Belle was never one for making a big deal of Christmas. She refused to be drawn into the consumer frenzy. At home, their decorations were minimal: candles and some tasteful greenery, nothing that glittered or sparkled or played a tinkly tune, ever. They gave money to charities that supplied drugs to HIV-infected people in Africa, or to Amnesty International, and their house was a religion-free zone. No carols, no cards, no symbols. When Amy was two, Belle relaxed the rules a little, because she wanted to share

Amy's excitement over presents, and she concurred with Sean that Amy be told the Father Christmas myth so that she wouldn't feel out of things at play-group. Still, for Christmas dinner they usually ate a light curry or a risotto and then they would sit up late, the three of them, watching classic videos, the adults drinking wine and Amy snuggled between them in her nightclothes.

Last year, Sean realizes, Belle was already seeing the Other at Christmas. She must have wanted to be with him. He remembers how she went out on Christmas Eve and stayed out late. She said her tutor group was meeting for drinks. Sean thought it a little strange at the time, given that term had ended a fortnight previously. He watched her spray perfume on her wrists as she studied her reflection in the big mirror in the hall before she left. Her hair was glossy, straight, her eyebrows arched; her fingernails were perfect, polished, pale pink. She looked beautiful, so beautiful she took his breath away. He was flooded with that familiar sense of his own good fortune that he was married to such a wonderful woman. She must have felt his gaze on her back because she turned to smile at him over her shoulder and the earring in the curl of her lobe refracted a flash of lamp-light.

She said: 'For goodness' sake, Sean, have a shave. You look like a cowboy.'

'I thought you liked cowboys?' he whispered, slipping his arms around her waist. She pulled away.

'Don't,' she said. 'You'll crease my dress.'

Sean didn't remember seeing the dress before. It was ivory-coloured, simple, silky. It did not look like the sort of dress anyone would wear if they were going to be spending the evening sitting in a crowded pub with their fellow students. Of course *now* it's obvious that Belle was lying about the group social. She and the Other would have been enjoying some intimate evening somewhere private. His house? His car? A restaurant? A hotel? They would have been making up for the forthcoming enforced abstinence. They would have been regretting the time spent apart even before it happened, looking forward to the end of the holiday when they would be able to resume their relationship unencumbered by Sean being at home for ten days. Was Belle hoping, then, that it would be the last Christmas she ever spent with Sean? Or had she not made up her mind at that point? Sean's heart beats a little more slowly. He wishes he could stop remembering things like this.

They always threw a party on New Year's Eve. Belle approved of celebrating the New Year; she thought it would bring good luck, or karma, or whatever it was she believed. Sean wonders if the New Year party tradition will continue now Belle is living with the Other. Would their old friends still turn up if invited, or would they make their excuses out of loyalty to him?

Sean misses his friends too.

★　★　★

96

His parents' house, a 1960s semi on an estate on the outskirts of Reading, looks the exact opposite of what his and Belle's house used to look like at Christmas. It has been decorated to the hilt. His mother cannot bear to throw away anything which reminds her of her children, or her grandchildren, so every year the paper streamers he and Lola made when they were infants are brought out, repaired and restrung – even though the bright original colours have faded to a uniform grey – and Boo and Amy's latest creations are added to the collection. The tree, always at a drunken tilt, always too big for the room and always real (because real smells so much nicer and never mind the needles), is strung with home-made decorations: toilet-roll angels whose tissue-paper wings have faded to the colour of water over the years, and milk-bottle tops glittered and glued to the insides of yoghurt pots. Even the dangly decorations Lola laboriously sewed from the foil and cellophane wrappings of a family-size tin of Quality Street chocolates when she was eleven, because she said they were too pretty to go on the fire, are still on display. Sean hopes Belle finds a place for the scruffy glue-and-tissue masterpieces Amy brings home from school by the carrier-bag load. He pledges to help Amy make decorations on Boxing Day. There is a consensus that Christmas Day will take place on 26 December in the Scott household this year. Sean is grateful, but also, somehow, demeaned.

Now Sean's mother sends him out of the bedroom so that she can wrap his presents.

'You don't need to wrap them, Mum,' he says. 'I'm a grown man. I don't believe in Father Christmas.'

'Oh, don't say that. Pretend, for me,' she says, blurry with affection, giving him a squeeze and a kiss on the cheek.

Sean smiles and rubs his chin.

'Go and have another drink,' says Rosie. 'Cheer up. Get into the festive spirit. I want my number-one son to be happy.'

Downstairs, Grandma Vera is watching television in the living room and Sean's father, Darragh, is in the kitchen, standing at the sink in an apron and rubber gloves, preparing the vegetables for next day's dinner. The kitchen window is steamed up and there's a smell of poached apples. Darragh pushes his spectacles up his nose and nods in the direction of the fridge.

'I'll have a beer with you,' he says, 'and Lola's on the way over, so you'd better open another bottle.'

On cue the back door opens and Lola comes in, wrapped in a scarf; behind her, and six inches taller, is Boo, his shoulders hunched, his head held low. Boo is wearing low-slung jeans that reveal the top three inches of his boxer shorts, and a green hoodie. He has the hood up to cover the acne on his neck. When he sees his jilted uncle he colours in embarrassment and stares at the floor.

'Hello, darling, how are you?' Lola says, embracing Sean. Her cheeks are cold and she smells of peppermint. Sean feels a pricking at the back of his throat. He wants to hold on to his sister and cry like a baby.

'Good,' he says, 'great.'

Lola pecks her father on the cheek, unwinds her scarf, takes off her coat and pulls up a chair. She helps herself to a mug of wine, filling it right to the top. Darragh sighs but says nothing. Sean has to hide a smile. Lola has always got away with murder.

'Boo, I expect Great-grandma's watching telly. Go and be nice to her for a bit, would you?' she asks.

Boo pulls a face. 'I don't know what to say to her.'

'It doesn't matter what you say. Just mumble, like you normally do.'

'Oh, Mum . . .'

'Let him stay,' says Sean. Lola ignores him.

She leans back in her chair and squeezes her son's arm. 'Go on, Boo, I promise I'll come and rescue you in ten minutes.'

'Lola . . .'

'Give him a can of beer, Sean. You'll be all right, won't you, Boo?'

Boo grunts. Sean passes his nephew a can of Carling.

'Cheers,' says Boo. He slouches out of the room. Lola watches him fondly.

'Bless,' she says, and the moment the door shuts behind him she leans forward across the table and looks earnestly into Sean's eyes. 'So what's going on? Did you leave Belle off your own bat, or did she make you go?'

'No, nothing like that. Neither,' Sean says, picking a clementine out of the fruit bowl in the centre of the table, pushing his thumbnail into the fragrant skin and working it through the flesh.

'Why are you here on your own, then?'

'We're just on a break,' says Sean, pulling off a strip of orange skin. 'It's just temporary. Belle said she needed a little breathing space.'

'Oh. So she's with another man.'

'No, yes, well sort of. Bloody hell, Lo, how did you know?'

'Women always say they need a little space when they're shagging somebody else.'

'Lola, please, there's no need for vulgar language!' says their father, wagging a half-peeled carrot at his daughter. He spatters his apron with droplets of water.

'Sorry, Dad. Who is he? The man she's . . . seeing?'

Sean puts a plump segment of clementine in his mouth, pierces its skin with his teeth and sucks the juice. It's cool and sweet and clean.

'Her tutor.'

'What does he tute?'

'Creative writing. She was doing that degree course, remember? He's a proper writer. He's quite famous. He's been on television.'

'Sounds like an arrogant twat.'

'Lola!'

'Dad, I'm a grown woman!'

'You're still my daughter.'

Lola exhales and rolls her eyes. 'Sorry. Sean, is he older than her?'

Sean nods.

'Don't worry, it won't last.'

'That's what I think,' says Sean, relieved beyond measure that Lola concurs with his point of view. Lola is usually right when it comes to matters of the heart.

'Has it been awful for you?' she asks.

'No, I'm fine.'

'Yes, but really, has it been awful?'

Sean nods. He swallows. He has to concentrate to stop his lower lip from trembling as it used to when he was a child. He feels about five years old. He remembers the first time he realized that life wasn't fair, that you could play by the rules and be a good boy, and still be punished for something you hadn't done, and there was nothing you could do about it, nothing at all.

'You ought to have a little affair,' says Lola, 'nothing heavy, just a sweet fling with a nice woman. It would take your mind off Belle and, also, it would make her want you back.'

'Lola, really, that wouldn't be right on any level.' Darragh peels off his gloves and unwraps his apron.

Lola smiles down into her mug.

'There's nothing like a love-rival to make a woman see her man in a different light,' she says.

'Lola . . .'

'It's all right, Dad,' says Sean. 'I've had enough of love, for now.'

'Oh God.' Lola grins. 'That's a lyric if ever I heard one. You're writing songs again, aren't you?'

Sean nods. He grins under the gaze of his sister.

'Well, that's a good sign, I suppose,' says Lola. 'It's an indication that you've started the healing process.'

'Lo, you've got to stop reading those bloody pseudo-psychological self-help books,' says Sean. In reply, she pushes his shoulder and he pushes her back, and he thinks that maybe he will get through Christmas after all.

CHAPTER 13

Christmas Day is a beautiful, ice-white and sky-blue day, that starts with a perfect frost and a mist that hangs over the city, way below Crofters Road, so that only the spires rise up through it, like trees in a lake. From then on, the day works its way slowly towards a perfect sunset, the frost never melting on the grass that the sunlight does not reach, the air hazy with winter.

It is Fen's loneliest day.

She told her sister that she and Connor were spending the holiday with friends. She does not want Lucy to phone and hear the isolation in her voice; the last thing she wants is to spoil her Christmas. And it's true, there have been invitations, but she has turned them down with plausible excuses, because she doesn't want to intrude on anyone else's day and has persuaded herself that it will be good to be on her own, with Connor.

Fen tells herself a million times how lucky she is to have the liberty to spend the day exactly as she wishes. Connor has already enjoyed myriad Christmas-related activities at school and he is quite happy to have a low-key day at home. He likes having Fen's undivided attention, he is thrilled with the stocking at the end of his bed, the carrot stump on the doorstep that proves the reindeer came and the modest stack of presents piled beneath the little artificial tree in the living room. Fen thought a real one would be over the top. She thought it might remind her of her own childhood, and she can do without that.

After lunch, Fen takes Connor out for some fresh air on his new, second-hand, bicycle. It has a good pair of solid stabilizers. She takes off his Santa hat and straps on his helmet, his knee and elbow pads, and he stands beside his bike grinning proudly, like an Edwardian hunter, while Fen takes photographs on her phone. Up and down the street other children with protective headwear are out on skates, scooters and bicycles, or driving remote-control cars. Fen smiles at her neighbours and their extended families. She says, 'Hello, Happy Christmas,' and if they try to strike up conversations, she is friendly, but brisk. She doesn't want anyone to feel sorry for her. She says that it's lovely to see them, but she has to get on. She talks as if there is somewhere else she has to be.

Connor is a demon on the bike, fearless.

'Connor Weller, you've been having me on with this cerebral palsy malarkey,' says Fen, as he masters the pedals immediately.

Connor looks over his shoulder and laughs and Fen feels her heart swell with love.

'I want to go down the hill,' says Connor.

'Oh no, Connor. It's too steep.'

'Aw, Mum, please, I promise I won't fall off.'

Fen thinks: But you might. And then she remembers being a child and what it felt like to ride a bicycle downhill, her legs sticking out, the pedals spinning, the wind in her eyes and the rush in her ears, and she remembers how she swore to herself that she wouldn't make Connor afraid of life. So she says: 'Go on, then! But be careful, and keep your hand on the brake in case you need to stop!'

Connor sets off freewheeling down the hill, for once empty of traffic, and she has to run to keep up, and they're both laughing and she's soon breathless and happy and wondering how she'll ever get him back up again.

Most of the people who live on that side of Bath head up Solsbury Hill on fine bank holidays, but when Connor has had enough of his bike, he and Fen simply loop around the roads, up through the alleyway, into the garden and through Lilyvale's back door.

They watch a little television, an animated film, then they share a bath, Connor and Fen. Fen keeps topping up the hot water, to make the time go more slowly, and she talks to Connor, telling him stories. Connor lies beside her and rests his wet head on her chest, his damp breath cooling and warming her throat. He's so solid, so set in his body.

The rise and fall of his shoulder blades beneath her fingers is a validation of everything she has done to keep him. Fen kisses his cooling hair. The window is steamed up and, beyond it, the night is falling and there's another Christmas nearly over.

She climbs carefully out of the bath and wraps Connor in a towel that's been warming on the radiator. She puts on her dressing gown then takes the child into her room to prepare him for bed. She enjoys their little rituals, relaxing into his sleepy pleasure as she talcs him and helps him into his soft, fleecy nightclothes, the baby smells as soothing as Valium in her bloodstream. He's perfectly capable of dressing himself for bed, but it's something they both enjoy.

Downstairs she draws the living-room curtains, and sits with Connor on her lap, stroking his back. He is her anchor. He is all that stops her spinning away into deep, outer space, this heavy-eyed child with the fair eyelashes that are so like his father's.

He falls asleep, and she sits there still, until his weight makes her uncomfortable, and then she carries her son up to his little bed. She leaves the night light on for him, tucks him in, and he murmurs in his sleep and instinctively takes hold of his teddy and snuggles down into the bed.

Now she's alone, the ghosts of her past come to Fen. They tap on her shoulder and whisper in her ear. Quietly but persistently, they demand her attention.

She tries to push them away, but they will not leave her be, so she sits on the window ledge in Connor's room, stares at the shadows on the wall and lets the ghosts into her thoughts. Tonight it's not Tomas or even Joe at the forefront of her mind, but Emma Rees, Joe's mother.

Fen remembers a slight, tired-looking woman who always slipped into the background of any situation. She had mastered the art of self-effacement so successfully that Fen would find it difficult to describe her. She was always kind to Tomas and Fen. She was, in her quiet way, kind to everyone.

She had been widowed young and Joe was Emma Rees's only child. He must have been everything to her. He must have been her reason for living, as Connor is to Fen. She must have delighted in looking after Joe. Her heart must have leaped when she heard his voice in the hall, his voice calling her to let her know he was home. When he was out with Tomas, Emma Rees must have lain awake in bed at night, waiting for the sound of his key in the door. She would not have slept until she knew he was back safe.

Fen sighs. She looks down at her sleeping child, touches his forehead gently with the back of her fingers, and he moves a little in his sleep and murmurs something.

The last time Fen saw Emma Rees was at Fen's father's funeral, six or seven months after Joe died in the accident. Mrs Rees sat towards the back of the church. She looked shrunken, gaunt, a shadow of her former, shadowed self, and much older than she was. She was wearing a hat with a veil and you could see the shape of her jaw beneath the gauze. She sat there, on her own, perfectly still apart from her gloved hands, which twisted and twisted a lace-trimmed handkerchief on her lap. She took care not to look into anyone else's eyes.

Later, after the service, Fen's stepmother, Deborah, spoke to the woman, and the two of them were like mirror images of each other, Mrs Rees holding Deborah's chill hand between her trembling palms, trying to offer some comfort.

They were friends, Emma Rees and Deborah Weller, of a kind. Mrs Rees was devoted to Deborah and would do anything for her. Even after the accident she would go out of her way to please the wife of the headteacher of Merron College. But although Deborah always smiled when she saw Mrs Rees, although she had the clothes she no longer wanted dry-cleaned before she passed them on to the college's kitchen supervisor, there was a reserve to her friendship. Behind Emma Rees's back, and never in front of any of the kitchen staff, Deborah Weller would roll her eyes when she spoke of the woman and her 'funny little ways'. Although she insisted Mrs Rees was always welcome in her home, she complained about her every time Emma turned up looking for some company, or some sympathy. On the odd occasions when she did not have a convenient excuse at hand to avoid inviting Mrs Rees in for a cup of tea, Deborah said 'the Rees woman' always outstayed her welcome. She would mimic the other woman's voice, imitating her turn of speech, her accent, her nervous, continuous apologies. Deborah felt duty-bound to appear to be kind to Mrs Rees, especially because of the circumstances of Joe's death, but her graciousness was not heartfelt. Everyone knew how Deborah felt, except Mrs Rees, whose adoration of her employer's wife was unconditional.

Fen is certain that Mrs Rees will have been to church today. She won't have missed the Christmas service. Probably it is the only thing she will have looked forward to over the holiday, the only crack in the infinite ice of her loneliness. She will have tucked herself into a corner at the back of the church, dabbed a tissue at the corner of her eyes when the children in the choir sang 'Once in Royal David's City', and gracefully received the kind words of the congregation, the vicar's friendly handshake. Then she will have visited Joe's frost-hardened grave. She'll have brought some holly in a jar, perhaps a small gift. She'll have lit a tea-light in a glass jar with tinsel at its neck. She'll have had a quiet little chat with her only child.

'I'm sorry,' Fen whispers, her pain making her curl into herself, like plastic in a flame.

She drifts downstairs to switch off the lights and lock up. She does not want to put the television on; she does not want sentimental, nostalgic programmes to remind her of her isolation. She does not want to think about her sister with her swollen ankles, or her poor father, or Deborah, who now lives in Australia; and she definitely doesn't want her thoughts to return to Mrs Rees or Joe or Tomas.

So she chases her ghosts away. She fills her mind with thoughts of a different man, a new man, and thinking of Sean brings her only pleasure. She wonders what he is doing, whether he has thought of her at all today; she thinks that, probably, he won't have. She bought him a small gift, a little soapstone statuette of Ganesh to watch over him and keep him safe. He thanked her for the gift when she gave it to him and slipped it, unopened, into the pocket of his bag, and she suspects that he will have forgotten it is there.

Lilyvale feels empty without Sean. There is too much space, too little noise. And the neighbours on either side are away so there is nobody around and the quiet is deafening. In the silence Fen can hear the mechanics of the fridge and the ticking of the timer on the central heating system. She double-checks that the windows and doors are locked. She draws all the curtains. She feels jumpy, nervy. It's too quiet. She wishes there were somebody she could ask over, but nobody else she knows is entirely on their own.

It's her fault. She has kept herself to herself. She has not made many friends.

Sean will be back in a few days' time, but those days, right now, feel like forever.

Fen goes back upstairs and pushes open the door to Connor's room. Carefully, she lies down beside him on his bed, and listens to his breathing until Christmas Day becomes Boxing Day and there's a touch of light in the sky beyond the window, then, turning her face into the pillow, she sleeps, at last.

CHAPTER 14

Sean is standing on top of the Lady Chapel roof, in the rain, wearing a safety harness and gloves. He is taking photographs of the Victorian cupola, which is much larger from where he stands than it looked from the ground.

Two days previously, during a storm, a chunk of masonry fell from the roof and shattered so violently that the concrete of the path below caved and cracked. It is obvious, from Sean's vantage point, that the cupola is unsafe. Water has found its way to the steel rods which pin the structure together so the rods are corroding and, as they swell, they are putting pressure on the fine limestone blocks from the inside; now the stone has begun to concede and crack. Sean walks around the cupola and counts the visible fissures. He checks the condition of the roof. Frost-blackened weeds choke the guttering; there is a filthy mess of feathers and bird-shit; that's probably a seagull's nest crouching by the rear wall; some of the leading is loose or missing. It's clear that nobody has been up here to carry out any maintenance for some years.

Sean records a verbal summary of what he can see

into his phone, and then he gets back into the basket of the cherry picker, where the chapel's caretaker is waiting. He's a small, slight, chipper man, pale-eyed and grey-haired. He reminds Sean of a little terrier dog. He shakes his head as the basket goes down and says: 'I told them the cupola needed looking at. I told them a thousand times. What's the damage?'

'It's dangerous. It has to come down,' says Sean.

'Permanently?'

'No. It's fixable. Some of the stone will need replacing. It's hard to say until we've bought it down and had a proper look at it.'

'That'll cost a bob or two.'

'It will,' says Sean. 'But it's your best option in the long run. In the meantime –' he unhooks the safety bar as the basket reaches ground level – 'we need to fence off the area in front of the chapel. You've got temporary barriers?'

'I'll have a look,' says the caretaker, taking off his hat and scratching his head.

'You want to cordon off this whole section, all the way round, and put up some warning signs, in case it all comes down. Are you all right with that?'

The caretaker nods.

'What I'll do,' says Sean, 'is go back to the office now. I'll call . . . what's his name?'

'Mr Lamprey.'

'Yep, I'll give him a call and tell him my immediate thoughts and concerns, and I'll get a report and recommendations over to you and him by the end of the week.'

'Right,' says the caretaker. He does not look happy.

'It's not worth the risk of leaving it like it is,' says Sean briskly. 'Some punter gets hurt and you'd never forgive yourself.'

'I told them it'd come to this,' says the caretaker. 'They can't say I didn't tell them.'

Sean takes off his glove and extends his arm to shake the man's hand.

'I'll call you later,' he says.

In the car, he turns on the engine to warm up the heater and jots down notes in his pad. He finds it best to do this straight away because; lately, his brain hasn't been working as well as normal. He has forgotten important pieces of information; he has forgotten to do things that needed to be done. He can be thinking about a problem, where to source a certain kind of marble, for example, when his thoughts will suddenly drain away, like water disappearing down a plughole, and he knows he won't be able to retrieve them. They'll have vanished into the complex, underground pipe-ways of his mind to be replaced by thoughts of Belle.

The state of separation does not hurt quite as much now as it did at first, the sharpness of the pain has muted into a dull ache, but it's still there, all the time, the loneliness and the shock. He still finds it hard to believe that this thing has happened to him. That Belle, his Belle, who always said that trust was the only essential in any close relationship, has deceived him so badly.

He remembers a day last year. It was winter; they were with Belle's parents in a country pub in the Cotswolds. It was a low-ceilinged, oak-and-woodsmoke place with a menu that featured all manner of game but had no vegetarian option. Countryside Alliance notices were taped to the walls, and a stuffed fox posed, one paw in the air, in a glass case suspended over one of the fireplaces. The fox held a car-crash-type fascination for Amy. She looked like Alice in Wonderland in her white tights and blue dress, standing on tiptoe to get a better look at the dead animal.

Belle's mother squeezed Sean's hand affectionately. She hadn't thought much of Sean when he and Belle first met. She thought he wasn't good enough for her daughter. But as time went by, and his devotion to Belle was consistent, his salary increased, they married and bought their beautiful home, then gave her a beautiful granddaughter, she had grown fonder of him. She tried to compensate for her former sniffiness by praising and complimenting Sean at any given opportunity.

'Well, Sean, I don't know what it is you're doing for Belle,' she said with a suggestive edge to her voice, 'but I've never seen her look so happy. She's positively glowing.'

Sean smiled and looked over to Belle. He caught her eye for a second, but she looked away quickly.

'We've been wondering how you do it,' Amanda

continued. Her face was close to Sean's. She was wearing dark pink lipstick which seeped into the feathery cracks around her lips. 'Because honestly, Sean, our friends' children's marriages seem to be falling apart all over the place, but you two, you're steady as a rock.'

'Mum, please,' said Belle. 'Stop it.' She scraped back her chair, scrunched her napkin onto the table, picked up her handbag and called to Amy, who left the fox and returned to her mother's side, questions on her lips. Sean watched them head off conspiratorially towards the cloakrooms. He smiled.

'There's no secret,' Sean said to Amanda. 'If Belle's happy, I'm happy. That's all.'

It wasn't me, he thinks now. I wasn't making her happy. It was the Other.

'There you go again,' he says out loud. 'You're always thinking about her. What is the point? You have to stop.'

He closes the notebook and starts the car's engine. He'll put some music on loud. That usually does the trick.

Sean goes into work through what is known as the tradesmen's entrance, the rear fire-escape door where the smokers congregate in ever-decreasing numbers for their cigarette breaks and gossip, no matter what the weather. He uses this door because he does not like clocking in through the security-heavy front door, partly because of its cameras and codes but mainly because he has lost

116

his swipe card and therefore gaining entry is a time-consuming performance. The back door takes him, via a short service corridor, into the reception foyer, where Lina sits.

When Sean joined the company, the reception area was businesslike, befitting a small, specialist construction outfit. It looked like the sort of place you'd sit while waiting for your car to be MOT'd: masculine, scruffy, slightly untidy. Now it's all black faux-leather sofas self-consciously arranged to look informal, a water cooler, a coffee machine, and glossy magazines on a glass-topped table. Flowers, always fashionable varieties that Sean doesn't recognize, sprout out of big square vases half full of glass beads and gel; huge, framed prints of recent projects – the photographs taken at artful angles and tastefully lit – dominate the white walls. Lina, glamorous, neat, pinkly lipsticked, smiles at Sean from her glass-topped desk. He salutes her.

'How are you, Mr Scott?' she asks.

'Mustn't grumble.'

'Pleased to hear it,' says Lina, tapping a pen against her teeth. 'Nobody likes a grumbler.'

Sean grins and slots coins into the drinks machine.

'Cappuccino? Two sugars?'

'Please.'

He takes the coffee to Lina and sinks into one of the sofas beside her desk. She bites the end off the sugar wrap and sprinkles the granules onto her coffee froth.

'Anything exciting happen while I was out?'

'Errrmm . . .' Lina stirs her coffee and stares up at the ceiling. 'No.'

'Are there any messages?'

'No, but your wife called,' says Lina.

'Was anything wrong? Did she say?'

'She sounded all right. She didn't say it was urgent or anything.'

But Belle never calls him at work.

'I'd better call her back,' he says.

'You don't need to. She said she'd try again later.'

'Still . . .'

'Sean, leave it. Make her wait.'

'It might be something important.'

Lina shakes her head and rolls her eyes. Sean stands up, speed-dials Belle's number – his number, their home number – on his mobile, holds the phone close to his ear and walks away from the reception foyer, back out into the fresh air. It takes a while for Belle to answer.

'Hi,' he says. 'It's me. Is everything OK?'

'Yes, everything's fine.'

'Amy's all right?'

'Amy's fine. Everything's fine.'

'So what's so urgent?'

'Nothing's urgent. I didn't ask Lina to get you to call me back.'

'No,' says Sean. 'You didn't. I just thought . . .'

'Well, don't. There's nothing to worry about.'

There's a pause. 'Anyway,' says Sean, 'I've called you, so you may as well tell me whatever it is you were going to tell me.'

118

'OK . . .'

He hears Belle take the sort of deep breath that usually precedes a mental girding of her loins, and he prepares himself for something he won't like.

'I was just wondering, *we* were just wondering, if you could look after Amy the week after next.'

'Of course,' says Sean, his hackles rising. *Look after Amy* . . . like he's the childminder or something. 'She's my daughter; I don't need to be asked to "look after" her. I do that anyway.'

'You'll be able to get the time off?'

'If not I'll drug her while I'm out and hide her unconscious body in the wardrobe.'

'Sean,' Belle exhales wearily, 'you never used to be this childish.'

'And you never used to be this patronizing.'

There is a silence.

'What are you doing?' he asks. 'Are you having a holiday?'

'We're going to a writers' retreat in Cephalonia. Lewis has been asked to help with the course. It could . . . well, he's hoping it will lead to more work along those lines.'

'More European travel, more retreats in the sun. It's a hard life,' says Sean.

'I'm not sure how I'll fit in. I've never done anything like it before.'

'I expect you'll cope.'

'I didn't mean—'

'You love Greece,' he reminds her. 'It's romantic.

That's why you chose it for our holiday the year Amy was conceived. Remember?'

'Sean . . .'

'Sorry. That was insensitive.'

There is a pause while they each take stock.

'OK,' says Belle, obviously committed to keeping the conversation civil, 'well, look, I'll send you an email with the exact dates.'

Sean scratches his head. The phone stays connected, but there is silence again at both ends. He knows Belle well enough to know that there is something more on her mind, something she wants to tell him, something she wants to have out in the open, have done with.

'Is there something else?' he asks.

'There is something . . .'

'What?'

'It's not important. It can wait.'

Sean's heart beats in his chest.

'What is it?'

She sighs. 'I shouldn't tell you over the phone.'

'Tell me what?'

Another pause.

'Lewis has asked me to marry him.'

'Oh.'

There is a long silence as if it is a competition to see who can hold their breath the longest.

'Sorry,' she says.

'Why are you sorry? It's what you want, isn't it?'

'I'm sorry because if Lewis and I are to marry, it means you and I must first get divorced.'

'I suppose it does . . . What if I don't want to?'

'I know it's going to be difficult, Sean, but if you think about it, it will make things better for you in the long run. You'll get your share of the collateral from the house and you'll be able to get out of that poky rented room and buy somewhere of your own. You'll be able to draw a line under this, make a new start.'

'Oh, thanks,' he says, imitating the sympathetic tone of her voice, 'you're doing this for me?'

'Sean . . .'

'Why do I always have to do everything you say? Why is it all on your terms? And the room's not "poky", by the way.'

'We've been separated for seven months now. It's about time we—'

'We've been married for eleven years, Belle.'

'I know.'

More silence.

'I shouldn't have said anything,' she says quietly. 'We need to get together and talk about it face to face, sensibly.'

'Well, not right now, eh, Belle? Because I don't want to talk about it or look at your face or be sensible. I'll call you when I'm ready.'

'Sean . . .'

He disconnects the call. He walks back into the car park. He kicks the tyre of his car, hard. He doesn't like himself. He doesn't want to be this angry, mean person. It's not him. But it is what he has become.

CHAPTER 15

Fen asks: 'Are you all right?'
    He says: 'Yep.'
    'Aren't you going to fetch Amy?'
'Nope.'
'Isn't she coming down this weekend?'
'No.'
'Oh. Is something wrong?'
'No.'
'Are you hungry, Sean?'
'No.'
'What are you looking for?'
'Is there anything to drink?'
'There's some wine in the fridge.'
'No, proper drink. Vodka? Whisky? Beer?'
'I don't think so.'
'I'm going to the pub, then.'
'OK.'
'I'll tell you now, Fen, I'm going to drink until
I fall over.'
'Oh. All right.'
'Don't wait up.'
'I won't.'
Sean takes his jacket from the peg by the front

door, hooks it over his shoulder and slams the door so hard behind him that the displaced air causes the curtains in the living room to float like ghosts, and Connor, who hates loud noises, bursts into tears.

CHAPTER 16

He walks – strides – down to the sports bar facing the London Road. It is packed with men and he immerses himself in male company and male conversation and the football highlights on the big-screen televisions, and drinks beer and then vodka shots.

He tells his troubles – a condensed and humorous version of his troubles – to a lorry driver with an accent he can't place, and in return the lorry driver tells Sean some pornographic jokes. Sean thinks: Fuck you, Belle, I'm in the sort of pub you hate, getting paralytic with a misogynist lorry driver, listening to the most un-fucking-politically unfucking-correct jokes you could ever imagine and I'm having the time of my fucking life.

'Where are you from, mate?' he asks the lorry driver.

'Barry.'

'What are you drinking?'

'Whatever you are.'

You see, this is how it is, with men, thinks Sean;

it's easy. It's uncomplicated. You ask a simple question, you get a simple answer.

He stays in the pub until closing time.

Sean realizes he has had too much to drink when he bumps into both sides of the door on the way out, but that's all right because that was the whole point of the exercise.

'Mission successful,' he says to the lorry driver, only that doesn't sound right.

'It's mission fucking accomplished, mate,' says the lorry driver, slapping him on the back, and Sean feels drenched with testosterone and affection.

He falls over twice on the way back up the hill. Once he simply misjudges the distance between the road and the kerb, and the second time he is startled to see a badger walking down the pavement towards him from the direction of the church. He has to hold on to a lamp post and narrow his eyes to check it definitely is a badger, not a more likely dog, cat or fox, but it *is* a badger, quite a big one, in fact quite a big, aggressive-looking badger. Badgers, Sean knows, are nasty buggers, with big teeth, strong jaws and rough arses. He peers forward. This one looks like it's up to no good. It must be a new sub-species: urban, feral badger. Sean has a feeling the badger is out to get him, it reminds him of the sinister rabbit in *Donnie Darko*, so he turns and tries to run but stumbles and falls. He tears a hole in the left knee of his jeans and the palms of both hands are grazed. Feeling like the hero of an action film, he staggers to his feet and tries again. He does not look behind him because action heroes don't. They make a decision and they stick to it.

It takes him a long time to get back up the hill because the pavement keeps tilting, trying to tip him off. Sean doesn't give up. He perseveres.

Crofters Road seems to have become even steeper since the evening began, and Sean is panting by the time he nears the top. He stands on the pavement and stares at the front of Lilyvale. The hall light is still on, and the outside light, but Fen's bedroom light is off and her curtains are drawn.

Sean has a feeling he owes her an apology, but he cannot remember why.

It takes an inordinately long time to get his key successfully into the correct slots in both the outer and inner doors. He holds his finger to his lips to 'shhh' himself when the key misses the lock and taps on the glass for the several-th time. The first thing he does, when he manages to make his way through, is go upstairs on his hands and knees (he does not want to risk falling backwards) and into the bathroom, where the relief of emptying his bladder is so great that he gives thanks to God. He splashes and makes a bit of a mess because Connor's plastic trainer seat is still slotted in place on top of the normal lavatory seat, considerably reducing the target area, so he mops both seat and floor with a towel, and it's only after he's done this that he realizes he has used Fen's towel, not his.

She won't like that, he thinks. And there's no chance she won't notice because women's noses are always disproportionately sensitive when it comes to the smell of inappropriate urine. Sean decides to put the towel in the washing machine.

He climbs down the steep stairs carefully, holding tightly to the banister, and goes into the kitchen, but the washing machine has finished its cycle and is full of clean laundry. Sean feels a little sorry for himself. Even the washing machine is conspiring against him. He looks for a place to hide the damp towel and eventually decides on the bread bin. It's empty and so there's no reason for Fen to look in there and he'll put it in the washing machine in the morning.

After all this, Sean decides what he really needs is another drink. He's already established that there are no spirits in the house, but there is wine in the fridge; even better, there is half a bottle of wine with a screw-top lid. Sean tells the wine bottle to 'shhh' as it clanks on the counter and he doesn't trust himself with one of Fen's nice glasses, so he unhooks a mug off the rack beneath the kitchen units.

Then he has another good idea. He'll take some wine up for Fen, lovely Fen, who is so gentle, who is so devoted to her son, who works so hard. She'll like that. It will make up for whatever it was he did earlier that is making him feel vaguely guilty.

He slots the mug over the top of the bottle, puts the bottle under his arm and goes back upstairs.

He stands outside Fen's door and whispers: 'Fen!'

There is no answer. So he taps on it with his knuckles. Still no answer, so he opens the door and goes in.

He knows he won't find his way to the bed without the light on, so he pats along the wall until he finds the switch. When he turns it on, the room is filled with brightness, and he catches sight of Fen's sleep-tangled hair disappearing under the duvet, its cover patterned with faded forget-me-nots. He has never been in Fen's room before. It is smaller than his, warm and untidy with female clutter: a hair-dryer, bottles of moisturizer and cosmetics, mirrors strung with belts and beads, Connor's drawings tucked into their rims, a baby shoe, a collage of photographs, magazines, sewing paraphernalia and a dressmaker's dummy wearing a sparkly silver dress and a hand-knitted scarf.

'It's me,' he says in what he hopes is a whisper.

He hears her sharp intake of breath.

'Tomas?' she asks, leaning forward, shielding her eyes from the light.

He goes over to the bed but sits down a little too heavily so that he falls backwards onto Fen's legs.

'Oops,' he says. 'No, it's me, Sean. Sorry. Shhh.'

'Sean . . .' Fen sighs and slips back beneath the duvet. 'I think you're drunk.'

'I think I'm drunk too,' says Sean, manoeuvring himself up into a sitting position. 'So that's good, we have something in common.'

Fen puts the top half of her face above the covers, and squints.

'What are you doing?'

'I brought you some wine,' says Sean, feeling pleased with himself. This was a good decision. It will clear the air. He holds the neck of the bottle over the mug, and tips it.

'I don't want wine. I was asleep. I brushed my teeth ages ago.'

'Oh,' says Sean. He looks at the bottle in his hand, poised at a tilt, and the empty mug. 'It's empty anyway.'

'It's not empty,' says Fen, wiping her hair out of her eyes. 'You've still got the top on.'

'You see, I knew,' says Sean, 'I knew from the first moment I saw you that you weren't just a pretty face.'

Fen smiles and wriggles further up the bed. She sits up.

'Here . . .'

He passes her the bottle and the mug, which she fills and gives back to him, then she puts the top back on the bottle, and the bottle beside the bed.

'Are you pissed off with me?' he asks.

She shakes her head.

He reaches out his hand, meaning to touch her shoulder, but misses and gets her chin. She winces and backs away a little.

'You see,' he says, telling himself to concentrate because this has to come out right. 'You may not realize this, but you are actually getting the best of me, Fen Weller.'

'Am I?'

'Oh yes. Because one of the reasons, and there were many reasons, but one of the predominant reasons why Belle stopped loving me was because of my lack of empathivity.'

'Oh?'

'Yes. She said I never knew what she was thinking. Are you with me?'

'I think so.'

'So now I have improved. Because I put myself in your position and I thought: If I was Fen, I would probably be pissed off with me.'

'If that was an apology, thank you.'

'I'm tired,' says Sean. 'It's been a long day.'

He lies his top half down on the bed. Fen strokes his hair. Her light, warm hand on his forehead feels very nice, comforting.

'Can I stay here tonight?' he asks very quietly and the last word he remembers hearing for a long while is Fen saying: 'Yes.'

CHAPTER 17

He lies on his back, on top of the duvet, his hands folded on his chest, his eyes open, staring at the ceiling, and he talks. Fen lies beside him, beneath the covers. Her face is turned towards him and she sees him in silhouette. The diffused yellow light of the street lamp on the pavement filters softly through the curtains and, in the darkness, the shape of his face is outlined against them. Sean tells Fen how he met Belle, how he knew from the very moment he saw her that he would ask her to marry him. How, right from the beginning, he never doubted her, or their future happiness. He talks about the good times they shared. He describes Belle to Fen in loving detail.

Fen is half-listening, but he keeps repeating himself, and she suspects his more sentimental memories are coloured by alcohol-induced nostalgia. She does not particularly want to hear about Belle. Sean's marriage is none of her business; it's a private matter so she pays little attention to what he says. She is enjoying sharing a bed with Sean, though. She wants to remember every moment of this night.

She watches his face and she is infused with warmth and affection towards this beautiful, gentle, well-meaning man. She wonders, for a moment, what he would do if she were to kiss him . . .

Oh, but he does not think of her in that way, she's certain of that. At no point in all the months he has lived in Lilyvale has he looked at Fen with anything more than friendliness in his eyes. To him, she thinks, she is just part of the furniture.

Sometimes this makes her feel frustrated, but not now. He's lying on her bed. He's confiding in her. His mind may still be full of Belle but it's Fen who lies beside him.

'Then she met the Other,' he says slurrily, 'who, of course, is *very* good at asking Belle how she's feeling, the slimy-tongued bastard, and how she was feeling was that she had fallen out of love with me.'

'I don't think such a thing is possible,' says Fen.

'What do you mean?'

Fen draws one hand from the warm cave of the bed and touches Sean's cheek very gently with the back of her fingers. His cheek is cool and bristled. He does not seem to notice. He concentrates on her words.

'If you *really* love someone, then you never stop loving them. It would be impossible.'

Sean blinks.

'It's not a temporary thing,' she says, 'it's integral. If a person's love for someone else is sincere, it's with them forever. It changes them. They can never go back to how they were before.'

'Like a cooked egg?'

Fen has to think about this for a moment.

'Yes,' she says, when she recognizes the analogy. 'Exactly. Once the egg is set, there's no going back.'

'So either she still loves me, or she never really loved me at all?'

'Well . . . yes.'

'She never really loved me . . .'

'If that's the case, she's an idiot,' says Fen.

Sean moves his head slightly in her direction. His cheek rests on her fingers. Being so close to him, his skin on her skin, is thrilling. Fen feels him in the core of her being. She exhales shakily.

'Why?'

'Because any woman who had the chance to love you, but didn't, must be a fool,' she says quietly.

Sean smiles. She feels his lips move against her fingers. He is so close to her, so close, only inches away, and she knows that if she reached out . . . if she touched him . . . if she showed him how she felt . . . She wants him so badly, she can't understand how he cannot sense it. Can't he hear how she is breathing? Can't he feel the heat of her? Isn't her desire lighting her up like a firework?

Apparently not.

'Thank you,' he mumbles, 'for saying what you just said. You are a very kind person.'

'You're welcome,' she whispers.

Then he sighs and scratches his armpit and turns from Fen. He turns right away and curls his back towards her; in seconds his breathing becomes gruff and in minutes he is fast asleep.

Fen lies awake.

She thinks that if this is to be the only night she ever sleeps with Sean, then she wants to remember every moment.

She has not shared a bed with anyone except Connor since the night her son was conceived.

She feels the weight and warmth of Sean's body beside hers. She feels his sadness and confusion seeping into the cool night air, and she prays to a God she has not believed in for a decade that she will find a way to make him happy.

She is woken by her telephone ringing downstairs. It stops before she is properly awake. It's early still, not yet light. She rubs her eyes, and becomes conscious of the way the mattress feels, how it's different, and then she remembers, and turns and looks sleepy-eyed at Sean.

He is still lying on top of the duvet, fully dressed. He is lying on his front, with one arm dangling off the side of the bed. He reeks of alcohol, his jeans are torn and bloody, but what she can see of his face looks peaceful. There is a dark saliva stain on the pillow. Fen smoothes his hair with her finger-tips. She leans down and kisses him very gently, secretly, on his forehead. She watches him for a moment; it's the second time she has watched him privately, and the intimacy of this fills her with tenderness. She notices a little scar just beneath his left eye which she never noticed before. She notices his eyelashes, the shape of his earlobe.

Tomas comes into her mind unexpectedly. He used to sleep at unpredictable times. Sometimes she'd come home from school and find him in her bed, and she'd set out her homework on her table, listening to his breathing as she tried to muster an interest in whatever it was she was supposed to be studying. Even asleep he was present. He was always present. When he woke he would smile at her sleepily and he'd scratch his arms. He liked her to sit beside him and stroke his head. He said it made him feel like a cat, like all he had to do was lie there and be stroked, until it started to get close to the time when he needed his next fix and then he'd become all jumpy and anxious and he'd be off again.

Fen slips out of bed, and carefully covers Sean with her half of the duvet, folding it over him and smoothing it straight. He mutters in his sleep. She smiles at him, then turns and picks up her clothes and goes out of the room, closing the door.

In the kitchen, she picks up her phone from the counter. The missed call was from Lucy and Alan's landline. Fen wriggles into her dressing gown, presses call-back, but now the line's engaged.

She tries again, and again, each time receiving the same signal. She fills the kettle, plugs it in, hops into a pair of socks, tries again.

There's a stink in the kitchen, but Fen can't work out where it's coming from. It's neither the fridge nor the waste bin. She tries the line again, then makes a cup of tea. She hears Connor talking to himself upstairs. She presses redial, and this time the phone rings and is answered, immediately, by Alan. Fen hears the excitement in his voice and she relaxes. Everything is all right.

'It's a boy,' says Alan, 'the most perfect, handsome, amazing baby boy ever to come out of Wales. Not counting Connor, of course.'

Fen smiles, she goes up the stairs with her tea, the phone tucked between her ear and her shoulder.

'How's Lucy?'

'A little shell-shocked, but over the moon. She should be coming home after they've done their rounds, or whatever it is they do, this morning. You should be able to speak to her this afternoon.'

'Oh good,' says Fen. She goes into Connor's room, sits down on his bed and touches his shoulder. 'So how heavy is he? Does he have a name yet? Who does he look like?'

'Seven pounds something or other, not sure; name – William or Ben. And I have to say, if he looks like anyone he looks like my father.'

'Really?'

'We're hoping he'll grow out of it.'

'I'm sure he's beautiful. Was it a long labour?'

'Not too bad. Lucy wasn't sure if it was the real thing for ages so we rather left it to the last minute before we went to hospital. We got there just after two this morning and the baby arrived at three-thirty.'

'I'm so happy for you all, Alan. Congratulations a million times. Give Lucy my love and tell her I'll call this afternoon.'

'I will do. Oh Fen, there are some photos, they're up on the school website.'

'OK,' says Fen.

They end the call and Fen holds the phone to her chest.

She feels the warmth of her son's skin beneath his pyjama top. She makes a bracelet with her thumb and finger, and slides it down his arm. He smiles up at her sleepily. He's still so little, his bones are still so fragile. He is still her baby.

'I should be there,' she says to Connor, who is staring back up at her with his heavy, early-morning eyes. 'She's my only sister and she's waited a lifetime for this baby, and I'm not with her.'

'Are you sad?' Connor asks.

'No, I'm not sad, darling boy. I'm happy. You have a cousin, Connor. A boy, just like you! How good is that?'

After they have washed, dressed and breakfasted, Fen starts getting things together for going into Bath, to the library, so that she can use one of the communal computers to go on the internet and look at the pictures of her new nephew, but the library won't be open yet, it's still too early. Connor is happy watching his programmes on the television, and it's raining heavily. Fen looks out of the diningroom window. It's streaming with water and outside looks awfully dark and miserable. Inside, the house is warm and light. Fen does not want to expose her son to the elements, but she really does want to see the pictures of Lucy and the baby.

There is an alternative. Sean has a laptop with a wireless internet connection.

She goes upstairs and quietly opens her bedroom door. Sean is now properly in the bed, under the duvet; his hair is sticking up and he is snoring. The air in the bedroom is rank and sour. Fen closes the door, goes into his room, picks up the laptop from where it has been charging on top of the chest of drawers, and runs downstairs with it, without giving herself time to think. She perches on the edge of the settee, next to Connor, opens the lid of the machine and goes online.

'He owes me a favour,' she whispers to Connor. 'Don't tell him, will you?'

Connor shakes his head and snuggles into her side.

It takes her just a few moments to navigate to where she needs to be. The screen fills with thumbnail images and she opens one, and sighs. There is Lucy, pale in her hospital gown and looking vulnerable and naked without her spectacles, and in her arms is a lopsided baby, wrapped in a pale blue blanket, squinting up at his mother, one eye open, one closed, his fists next to his cheeks and an expression of puzzlement on his little red face.

Fen has never seen her sister look so peaceful.

She nudges Connor, and turns the screen towards him.

'Look, Connor! Look at the baby! That's your cousin!'

Connor points at the image. His finger leaves a wet smear around the outline of the baby's face on the screen.

'That's Auntie Lucy's baby?' he asks.

'Yes,' says Fen, 'that's baby William-or-Ben. Isn't he lovely, Connor? Isn't he just perfect?'

Connor pulls a face. 'He's yuk,' he says. 'He looks like a potato.'

'Well, a bit,' Fen concurs. 'He hasn't had time to grow into his face yet.'

Fen looks at all the pictures. She wishes she were there, in the hospital, looking after Lucy, looking after the baby while Lucy rested. Fen has always been good with babies; she's never been afraid of their vulnerability and she doesn't understand people who are afraid to hold them. In Fen's mind, there are few things less complicated than a warm baby held to the shoulder, its little back like a spiny loaf beneath the fingers, and its requirements so very simple and easy to manage.

She smiles down at Connor.

'He's not as good-looking as you were, Con.'

Connor grins. 'I was a good baby,' he says.

'You were. You were a perfect baby. The best baby in the whole wide world.'

Connor smiles and wriggles a little closer to Fen. He likes hearing tales of when he was little.

'Baby William-or-Ben's OK,' says Fen, 'but he's not a patch on you.'

Fen puts Connor's breakfast plate and spoons into the sink, squirts in some liquid and fills the bowl with hot water. She swirls the water around listlessly, staring out of the window over the back gardens. Now the rain has thinned to a drizzle, the outside colours are lovely in the soft spring light. Wild daffodils are rioting down the alleyway at the back, nodding in cheerful groups among smaller, deep-blue flowers, and all the miniature apple trees in the gardens are sweet with pink and white blossom. The Ford RS in the lower garden is covered with blossom petals; it looks beautiful, as if somebody has gone to great trouble to paint it with flowers.

It is a good time of year to be born.

Fen plays with Connor in the living room for most of the morning. At lunchtime she takes a mug of tea up for Sean. He has migrated back to his own bed.

'Thanks,' he mutters as she places the tea on his bedside table.

'Would you like some toast or something?'

'Mmm.' He shifts up onto his elbow, squinting into the light. 'God, I feel like death.'

'Ibuprofen?'

'You're an angel.'

He drops his head heavily back down on the pillow and closes his eyes. Fen pushes her hair out of her face. Out of habit, she picks up the dirty clothes he took off and dropped on the floor and she takes them downstairs, the jeans and the shirt and the T-shirt he wears as a vest, the boxers and the socks. She holds them to her face and she smiles to herself as she thinks: Last night we slept together, Sean and I.

In the evening, she calls Lucy.

Her sister's voice is thin and watery, yet full of elation.

'You didn't tell me giving birth hurt that much,' she says with sibling petulance. 'You said, and I quote: "It's a walk in the park."'

'I didn't want to scare you. Are you OK?'

'More or less. Bit stitched and achy.'

'It's quiet there. Is the baby sleeping?'

'No, he's here on the breast, and that hurts too. I am so sore.'

'Oh, Luce, I wish I—'

'Shhh, you've got enough on your plate. We'll see each other soon enough.'

Fen holds the receiver close to her cheek.

'Give your new son a kiss from his auntie,' she says. 'Give him all my love.'

CHAPTER 18

Sean walks up Solsbury Hill to watch the sun go down.

The hill is steep and its slopes are muddy. His boots sink into the soft mud and squelch as he lifts them free. Cows have been grazing the fields which cover the lower edge and the holes left by their hoofs are filled with water or a mixture of water and cow-piss. The mud seeps into the fabric of his jeans, while his boots become heavier and heavier. He still feels shaky and hung-over but he ploughs on uphill, working up a sweat, trying to eliminate the residual alcohol from his bloodstream. He showered when he finally left his bed, but his skin still smells of drink. It's a smell he associates with unhappiness, a smell of poison in the blood.

His sleeve catches in the brambles as he skirts the edge of a field to avoid the worst of the mud. Thorns scratch his wrist and little jewels of blood ooze through the tears in his skin. He is on the brink of taking the lazy option and immersing himself in self-pity, but he ignores the blood and hopes the exercise will tip him the other way.

Reaching the top of the hill, he stands still, as everyone does when they reach this point, and gazes out over the city flanking the slopes below him. Two crows flap lazily across his field of vision and extend their claws to settle on the branch of a shrubby little tree. Sean is surrounded by air and there's a haziness in it that makes him giddy. Lights are coming on in the windows of thousands of houses, little oblongs of warm yellow amid the dull grey. The faces of the buildings which look towards the west are tinged pink by the dying sunlight. Traffic curls along the main roads a long way below: streams of red and white light. He hears the noise of the traffic and wishes it would go away. He yearns for silence.

Sean thinks of Peter Gabriel. He thinks that when he goes back he'll find some early Genesis on You Tube. He takes a drink from the bottle of water he's carried with him.

Last night he crashed out in Fen's bed. He doesn't remember the details; he just remembers going into her room because he didn't want to be on his own, and how comfortable he felt on her bed. It's not that his is uncomfortable, but there's something cosy about a woman's bed. He liked the sweet, private smell of her linen, the smell of her washing powder and her shampoo. He remembers talking to her, but he can't remember anything that either of them said.

She was acting strangely earlier, before he left the house. She was shy, quieter than usual. He hopes he didn't say or do anything inappropriate, and he's annoyed at himself for waking her up. He hopes he has not offended her. He was so fucking drunk. And she doesn't deserve any trouble; she's too gentle, too sweet, and has enough on her plate.

Sean leans down. He puts his hands on his knees and blows out his breath.

Something has changed. He doesn't know what it is but today he feels a little more detached from Belle. He isn't experiencing the usual physical tug that he feels whenever he thinks of her. Today, for some reason, he is capable of accepting that Belle and he are no longer together. The fact doesn't fill him with desperation, as it normally does.

He stands up. He drinks some more water.

He thinks: Was that all I needed to do to get over her? Did I just have to get out of my mind to exorcize the woman from my heart?

It seems to him that it was.

CHAPTER 19

Fen has made asparagus soup. The saucepan is on the hob, keeping warm, and the smell is wonderful. Sean tears a piece of bread off the top of the loaf that's on the counter, dips it in the soup and sucks. He hears her footsteps on the stairs and she comes into the kitchen, smiling, with that dreamy, sleepy expression she always wears when she's put Connor to bed.

'This is fantastic,' says Sean, caught in the act of stealing the soup. 'It's delicious.'

'Help yourself,' says Fen. She sticks her hands into the back pockets of her shorts and looks at her feet. 'There's some cheese and onion flan in the fridge. It's only a supermarket cheapo one but I could do a few potatoes, maybe? Some salad?'

'Have you eaten yet?' Sean dips some more bread in the soup.

She shakes her head. She's still looking down, tracing the outline of the pattern of the vinyl on the kitchen floor with her toe.

Sean clears his throat. 'I was thinking . . . what if I were to buy you a takeaway, to say sorry for the other night?'

Fen looks up at him and smiles. 'You said sorry already. Loads of times. I didn't mind, Sean, honestly. You were sweet.'

'Fen, I was paralytic. But . . . well, I remembered some other stuff. The towel in the breadbin . . .'

Fen laughs. 'Oh that! It went a bit rusty. I put it out for recycling.'

'God! I'm sorry. I'll buy you a new one.'

'Oh, forget it. It doesn't matter.'

Sean looks at her. She genuinely does not appear annoyed or upset or irritated or disgusted.

'There are worse things in life,' she says.

'The thing is,' he says, 'I was at my nadir. That night was a turning point. I appreciate that it probably wasn't the best night of your life, sharing your bed with a drunken pig, but it was good for me. I'm on the way back up again.'

'I'm glad. Really.'

'I was worried I might have –' he pauses, looks at the ceiling, scratches his earlobe – 'said something inappropriate.'

'No, you didn't.'

'Phew!' He grins. 'Well, that's something!'

Fen looks away. She bites her lower lip and blinks.

'Anyway,' says Sean, 'I'm going to go out and buy us some dinner. It's the least I can do. Would you prefer Indian or Chinese? Or fish and chips? Or a pizza?'

'Anything,' says Fen. 'I don't mind.'

'OK,' he smiles, 'I'll find something nice for you.'

★   ★   ★

146

He picks up his wallet, then goes out through the front door and up the steps, turning right down the hill towards the shops at Larkhall.

It's a beautiful evening. Spring is setting in, making itself comfortable in the city. Children are playing outside and people are out in their gardens. There's a chime of an ice-cream van in the distance and it reminds him of the day last summer when he left home. The thought bothers him so he puts it from his mind. He quickens his step and does something he hasn't done for months. He whistles.

When he returns, Fen has put a small table outside in the back garden, and two folding chairs, side by side, facing out over the valley. There's a candle in a little glass pot, two plates, two glasses. She looks different. She's done something to her hair and she's wearing make-up.

'I know it's getting cold, but I thought we could sit outside for a while,' she says. 'We can watch the sun set as we eat.'

'How romantic!'

'Oh, I didn't mean—'

'I know you didn't.'

Sean sets the brown paper carrier of food on the table. He takes out the foil cartons.

'It's a good idea,' he says. 'It's nice out here. Why don't we sit out more often?'

'We never sit out together,' she says.

'No. We should, now the weather's getting warmer.'

147

Sean passes her a carton of rice, and she peels off the cardboard lid.

'My wife has asked for a divorce,' he says.

'I know. You told me the other night.'

'Oh. Did I talk about Belle a lot?'

She nods.

'Was I boring?'

'Not really.'

'I was, wasn't I? I bet I went on and on and on about the same old things.'

'A bit.'

'Oh Christ.' Sean sighs. 'I am *so* sorry. But you know what, Fen? It's got her out of my system.'

Fen licks her fingers and smiles.

'Good. Can we *not* talk about her tonight, then?'

'Not talk about who?'

Fen laughs and shares the rice between the two plates while Sean takes the wine from the carrier.

'Red or white?' he asks Fen.

'You bought both?'

'I didn't know which you preferred,' he says.

Sean is hungry, the food is delicious and, as his belly fills and the wine runs through his bloodstream, he relaxes. The sun performs beautifully, slipping off to the west with just the right level of drama and tension, leaving behind a sky stained pink so that the clouds high above the city are coloured from below. When it has gone completely, the temperature drops, and Fen fetches a jumper from inside then tucks up her feet beneath her, but still they stay outside, drinking the second bottle of wine and watching the candle flickering. Fen cradles her wine glass, sipping from time to time. She waves a moth away from the candle. A full moon rises, lights twinkle in the city and bats flit across the alleyway. A tentative breeze whispers in the leaves of the copper beech. Fen hugs herself. Sean says: 'You're very quiet.'

'I'm always quiet.'

'We don't know much about one another, considering we've shared the same house for so long.'

'I know a lot about your marriage.'

'That doesn't count. Where should we start?'

Fen smiles. 'With something simple. The basics.'

'Go on, then, ask me a basic question.'

'What's your favourite colour?'

'Ummm . . .'

Fen bites her lip.

'. . . Green,' he says. 'No, blue. Turquoise.'

'OK,' says Fen. 'Now you ask me a question.'

'What's your favourite Beatles track?'

Fen stares up at the sky. He notices the way her jaw seamlessly smoothes into her throat. '"She's So Heavy".'

'Christ,' he says, 'I wouldn't have guessed that in a million years. I'd have had you down as a "Norwegian Wood" sort of girl.'

'What's yours?'

'"Dear Prudence".'

'I like that too,' says Fen. 'But I like "Heavy" because it's my brother's favourite.'

'You're very close to your brother, aren't you?'

'Yes.'

'Have you heard from him lately?'

'It's my turn for a question, not yours. Tell me something about you that your mother doesn't know.'

He laughs. 'Where do I start?'

'Nothing heavy,' says Fen.

'When I was about ten,' he says, 'my friend Mark Watts and I burned down our village cricket pavilion.'

'Sean!'

'Not deliberately. It was an accident. We had a den at the edge of the cricket field. We were messing about with cigarettes and matches. It's what boys do. They all go through a pyromania phase. You wait, Connor will be the same.'

'What happened?'

'I can't remember exactly. One or other of us dropped a match. Or maybe we were trying to set a little fire. It was towards the end of summer and the grass caught and the fire ran – it literally ran across the dry grass. We were stamping on the flames, but they moved so quickly and next thing the hedge was on fire.'

'Oh no!'

'There was no stopping it. It caught light and there was all this black smoke coming off it and the fire was travelling along the hedge. At which point Mark and I realized we were in deep shit. So we did the sensible thing . . .'

'You called 999?'

'No, we ran away.'

'You ran away?' She's laughing.

'Yep. We got on our bikes and pedalled away from the crime scene as fast as we could. We went back to our respective houses and I made a big show to Lola, my sister, about how I'd been in my bedroom all afternoon, as an alibi you see . . .'

'Mmm.'

'And about two minutes later, we heard the fire engines going by. And Mum was saying: "What on earth's happened? Go and have a look, Sean."'

'She didn't!'

'She did! So I had to get back on my bike and go down to the cricket pitch, and by now the whole hedge was on fire and it had spread to the historic pavilion.'

'Sean!' Fen has her hands clasped over her mouth.

'And there were three fire engines and all these people had come out to see what was going on, and they were all horrified, and there I was, the culprit, and I felt as if I had the word GUILTY printed in big letters on my T-shirt. I almost wet myself. It made the regional TV news, you know, the fire. It was on the front page of the *Evening Post*.'

'And did anybody ever find out it was you?'

Sean grins. 'No, we got away with it, Mark and me. They blamed a cigarette end thrown from a car. The insurance paid up and the pavilion was restored and the captain of the county cricket team came along to cut the ribbon at the reopening.

People talked about it for ages. It was a long time before I'd go and play on the field again.'

'Don't you think your mum suspected?'

'Not a thing. She's not the sort. She thinks her children can do no wrong, no matter what the evidence to the contrary.'

'I don't think you should blame yourself,' says Fen. 'It wasn't really your fault. It was an accident.'

'No,' Sean agrees. He takes a big drink. 'What about you? What's the worst thing you've ever done?'

A shadow passes over Fen's face. He sees it clearly, and says: 'Nothing heavy.'

Fen sucks her lower lip, runs her finger around the edge of her glass and, after a few moments, a mischievous smile creeps onto her lips. Sean thinks that when Fen is not being introspective, she is a very nice-looking woman. He wonders why he did not notice before.

'Oh, Sean,' she says, glancing up at him, and away, 'If I tell you . . . no, I can't.'

'What? Why can't you tell me?'

'Because you might be offended.'

'I'm not easily offended.'

She blows breath between her lips.

'Is it something to do with me?'

She nods. She puts her hand over her mouth to contain her smile.

'What?' he asks.

'I can't.'

'Go on,' he gives her a nudge, 'just say it quickly.'

'I can't.'

152

'You have to, that's the rules of the game. I told you about the pavilion. It can't be worse than that.'

She shakes her head.

Sean leans forward and takes her left hand in his.

'Go on,' he whispers, squeezing her hand. It's small and cool.

She looks up. 'I saw you in the shower,' she whispers back. Her eyes seem suddenly very dark. She holds his gaze for a moment, and then looks away. She takes a sip of her wine. Her upper lip is stained ruby red and its wetness catches the candlelight. Sean feels something. He feels a flicker of desire. He ignores it.

'It was ages ago,' she says. 'Before Christmas. I didn't mean to spy. I thought the tap had come on by itself and I looked in to see and . . .'

'You saw my bare arse?'

'More than that.'

Her hand presses into his. It's an involuntary action. She swallows and looks up into his eyes again. Her lips are parted now, he can see the bottom edge of two teeth.

'Oh Christ,' he whispers. 'I wasn't . . . was I?'

She nods. She gives a little sigh and says quietly: 'You were beautiful. It was lovely and . . .' She pauses as if she's afraid that she's already gone too far, and Sean feels that tug of desire in his stomach again, a pang of longing, and he too sighs. She continues: 'The thing is, I've been thinking about you all the time, ever since. I mean . . .' She hesitates again, unsure of how to articulate what she wants to say, but it doesn't matter because Sean feels the atmosphere change: the air between them, the space, is charged now, he feels the change with his heart, his groin, his head. Fen isn't laughing any longer. She holds on to his hand and gazes down at it and her face flickers in the candlelight.

'Fen . . .'

She turns towards him and it is as if it was always meant to be. He reaches out to her and they kiss and something ignites inside him, that's how it feels. It's like throwing a match into a field of dry grass – no, more than that, a sea of oil. There's a huge, intense longing blazing inside him. His hands cup her face. He kisses her and she kisses back and it's tender and sweet and he knows, he can feel, how much she wants him, how much she has wanted him for months, and her desire arouses him almost beyond anything he's known before. She kisses him with honesty, her lips are gentle but she does not try to disguise the depth of her feeling, and Sean is turned on almost to the point of unconsciousness.

Her breathing is heavy, that deep, shaky breathing of a woman on tenterhooks. He moves away, licks on his lips the salty taste of her, then he takes both her hands, her cool, small, slender hands.

'Come with me,' he says.

He puts the candle on the mantelpiece, and in its light he lies Fen down on the old settee that's covered with mismatched, cheap throws, and he

154

unbuttons her shirt, watching her face, not looking at her body, holding her eyes.

He parts the front of her shirt, and leans down to kiss the space between her breasts. Her fingers are light on the back of his skull and she murmurs: 'Please.'

She wriggles out of her shorts and pants; he unzips the fly on his trousers, and then pauses. She's shaking like a leaf.

'Are you OK?' he asks.

She nods.

'Are you sure?'

'Yes.'

'Thank God,' he says, for he does not know how he could stop now.

She lies back gazing at him and he strokes the cup of her belly with the back of his fingers and she is taut as a drum beneath his hands. Her skin trembles and her hips are arched, very slightly, towards him.

'God,' he whispers, 'you're lovely!' And he is full of the newness of her, the slightness, the way her fingers touch her lips, the sweetness of her. She is as tentative as a virgin and she keeps trying to hide herself with her hands, her fingers; she is a mystery to him, different, unknown.

He climbs onto the settee and looks down at her, smoothes back her hair, and again she says: 'Please.' He kisses her again, and she lies there, trembling, as he uses his hand to make a way between her thighs and to find the right place.

It is the sweetest, gentlest, quickest fuck. She comes in an instant, almost on the first stroke, and her response is so unexpected, so thrilling, that the moment she comes he is flooded with the sex rush, the rise in the bloodstream, the tingling in the nerves and the urgency in the groin, and he comes too. He puts his lips on her shoulder, and he comes and he comes and he comes, holding her tight, feeling the aftershocks inside her. The unaffected, unselfconscious release of her fills him with tenderness. He rests his forehead on the cushion beside her and she says: 'Thank you.'

Afterwards she cries. Or she laughs. He can't tell which.

She lies beneath him on the settee and he does not want to lose the intimacy, so he stays above her but takes his weight on his elbows, and he wipes away her tears with his knuckles.

'I'm sorry,' she says. 'I'm just so . . . it's just too . . .'

'I know,' he says gently. 'I know.'

They make love again, more slowly. She is bolder, he takes his time. He feels the shape of her, the inside and the out, the way the muscles cleave beneath her skin. His fingers explore her, the shape of her chin, her ears, her breasts, and her fingers work their way around his body too. They are a mystery to one another. They fit one another very well.

The candle flickers, Fen shivers. She covers her breasts with her elbows.

'You're amazing,' says Sean.

He helps her into his fleece. He turns on the gas fire set into the far wall and it makes a reassuring whumph as its line of flame gradually thaws from blue to red and the room warms. He does not know how to thank her. He could not begin to explain how her desire for him has restored so many of the parts of himself that he thought he had lost forever. He feels alive again. He feels powerful and potent. He feels like a man.

He pulls his guitar out from behind the settee, and takes it out of its case.

He sits beside her, naked, and curls over the guitar. His feet cross at the ankles, his knees are wide apart. He plays a chord.

'Do you know what that is, Fen?'

She shakes her head. She pulls her knees up to her chin and wraps her arms around her legs.

'That's D. What about this?'

'No.'

'E minor. My favourite chord.'

He plays a little show-off tune. Fen smiles. She is twirling her hair.

'Do you know why guitars are so sexy, Fen?'

'Because you play them with no clothes on?'

'There is that. But also, a guitar is both woman and man.'

Fen laughs.

'It is so. We have here, you see, the up-thrust of the neck, which can only be described as proudly, majestically phallic, contrasting with the female

157

shape of the body. The hourglass, see?' He strokes the outer edge of the guitar, its perfect curves.

She nods.

'To make beautiful music,' says Sean, putting on a mid-European accent, 'both the male and the female parts of the guitar must operate harmoniously. One hand –' he holds out the relevant hand – 'slides up and down the neck, which is grasped by fingers applying various pressures to the different frets and strings. This, I believe, is a process with which madam is familiar?'

Fen smiles. She bites her lip.

'The fingers of the other hand, at the same time, work the strings over the sound hole, like so. Erotic, no?'

'Yes.'

'The beautiful noise is achieved by the vibration of the strings, controlled by the fingers, echoing in the sound board. Male and female working together. Beautiful.'

He plays more music. She rests her head on his shoulder and they stay there, together on the settee, until the sky beyond the curtains begins to turn pale, and then they wrap themselves in each other's arms, and he waits until she sleeps so that he can watch her. He spends a while enjoying the warmth of her beside him then, sometime during the early morning, Sean too drifts into sleep.

CHAPTER 20

Everything has changed.

Fen knew things were getting better and she thought she was all right, but she wasn't, not compared to how she is now. Now the world is a wonderful place, every moment of every day is filled with potential; she is entirely grateful to be alive, to be living in Bath, to be working in the bookshop and living in Lilyvale, to be Connor's mother and Sean's lover. She looks at herself in the mirror and she realizes that she is pretty. She thinks how lucky she is to be healthy and still young and pretty. She has a new energy with her son and she thinks of new ways to help him with his speech and his motor skills. She has more fun with the boy; he has a great sense of humour which Fen wasn't bringing out in him before. It was a kind of neglect and she is ashamed of herself.

She is enjoying her life – all of it, or almost all of it. Only her memories interfere with her happiness.

Sean has not just made a difference to her waking hours; she's now sleeping better too. Before, Tomas and Joe were often in her dreams, and mostly, strangely, they were good dreams, dreams of how it was when they were younger, and they would be out in the fields playing football or fishing in the river or they would be queuing outside the cinema or sometimes even fighting. Or she would dream of Tomas as he was just before he left, and he was OK, he was his normal, sarky, self-deprecating, funny self, not the prowling, scratching, secretive person he was when he was taking drugs. And Joe, Joe was always fine, fit and well in her dreams, always laughing, sometimes draping his arm around Tom's shoulder, sometimes leaning his face towards Tom and the two of them sharing an intimacy that was exclusive.

Whenever Fen dreamed of the two young men in a good way it was as if Joe had never died and Tomas had never gone away, and she would, in her sleep, chide herself for her anxiety. Then, when she woke, she'd be confused for a while. She would not remember whether the dream was real or not, and she'd have to experience anew the horror of confronting the reality that Joe was dead and Tomas was gone and that she was responsible. It was as if she could never come to terms with the situation and so had to keep reliving it in her dreams. A million times she thought the accident had never happened; a million times she had to wake up and accept that it had. And this emotional see-saw exhausted her and coloured her every waking moment. Always Joe and Tomas, Tomas and Joe at the front of her mind.

It's different now, and although Fen feels slightly

guilty and disloyal, these days she craves the erotic, happy, flying, swimming and dancing dreams that suffuse her sleep, and neither Tomas nor Joe is in these dreams.

Now when Fen wakes, the blood is already streaming through her veins and her heart beats in anticipation of the pleasures of the day ahead. She cannot wait to be up. She looks forward to drawing the curtains and going in to wake Connor, but the first, most intimate thing she does is listen to hear if Sean is already out of bed, moving about in his room or running the taps in the bathroom or downstairs, making tea.

Sean makes tea for Fen every morning and he brings it up to her, then kisses her before he leaves for work. He kisses her on the lips, like a lover, not on the cheek, like a spouse. He always squeezes her hand. Sometimes he reminds her of some small commitment: 'Don't forget I'm going to be late,' or 'Could you pick up some stamps for me, if you have time?'

They are still respectful of each other's privacy, but they are comfortable with each other, the two adults. Their familiarity has bred content. On evenings when neither has anything to do, they sit together in the living room. Sean has become proprietorial over the television remote control. He no longer asks Fen whether she minds if he changes channels. In other people, Fen would have found this lack of consideration annoying, but she is so grateful to him for bringing her back to life – and for being with her in her life – that everything he is, and says, and does, is beautiful in her eyes.

Once Sean fell asleep on the settee, his head on a cushion on the arm, his legs tucked up behind him, and his socks, thick, woolly, working-man's socks, filled Fen with a pang of tenderness so exquisitely sharp that she had to double over to contain it.

Every day she knows him a little better, every day she loves him a little more. She has slept with other men, of course, but they were all a long time ago, before Connor, and she has never been in love with a man before. She is finding the whole process intoxicating and enchanting. It is the most wonderful, natural thing she has ever experienced. It colours every single aspect of every moment of her life. It has changed every molecule in her body. It affects everything. And Fen appreciates it, she realizes how lucky she is; she knows some people go through their lives without knowing how it feels to love somebody as she loves Sean and to be, apparently, loved back.

She finds everything about him erotic, from the little scar beneath his eye to the way he stands with his legs just slightly apart and his feet square on the ground. The smell of him turns her on, his voice, his eyelashes, the mud on his boots.

He relaxes with her now. He comes in from work and he talks about his job. He tells her where he's been, who he's spoken to, what he's done. He explains the ins and outs of restoration, the chemistry of composites, the physics of load-bearing structures. He washes his hands in the sink and as she watches the soap slipping between his palms, and the lather as he brushes the dirt from beneath his fingernails, inwardly she sighs and swoons with pleasure like the heroine of a romantic novel.

And it's not just that. No, it's the things he does for her. He looks after her, in big ways and small. Nobody has looked after Fen since she was a child. Yet Sean drives her to the supermarket, pushes the trolley, packs the bags and refuses to let her pay, or else he drops her off outside Sainsbury's and takes Connor and Amy to look at the quirky shops in the old Green Park station so she can shop in peace. He carries her bags. He puts out the bins. He goes back to his old house and comes back with the car loaded up with gardening tools. He mows her lawn and digs up the old flower beds, which have, for years, grown only weeds. He plants potatoes. He puts up two lines of canes and Connor helps him start the beans off in little pots. He comes home from work one day with a tray of seedlings: tomatoes, courgettes, peppers, salad.

What gives Fen the most pleasure is to see how Sean is happier too.

She checks under his mattress every now and then, but he has written nothing in the notebook for weeks.

He hardly ever mentions Belle and the shadows have left his eyes.

★　　★　　★

She hasn't told anyone what's happening. In truth, she wants to talk about Sean all the time because she wants the whole world to know that she is in love. She would like to wear a T-shirt, carry a banner, charter a plane trailing a streamer, shout it out across the city, but she says nothing at all, to anyone. She is afraid of jinxing the situation. She believes – oh, it's superstitious madness, she knows – but still she believes that while their love is a precious secret then nobody else can come between them. No one can damage it.

Besides, there isn't really anyone she can tell.

Fen does not think about the future. She doesn't know what's going to happen; neither of them has spoken of it. They have fallen into this intimacy almost by accident. They have never been out together, they've never had a date as such. Neither of them has attempted to categorize or analyse this precious closeness they share.

Fen does not think of Sean as her boyfriend or her partner.

He is far more to her than either of those words would imply.

He is her lover.

He is the man she loves.

And this loving has changed her so fundamentally that already she knows there is no going back.

CHAPTER 21

Sean walks into Membury services and immediately something is different. Usually Belle and Amy are waiting for him in the foyer. More often than not, Amy is looking at the comics in the rack outside the newsagent's and Belle is standing beside her, checking her watch and watching, but not really watching because her mind is already on the weekend ahead. Today they aren't in the foyer, but Sean knows they are somewhere in the services because Belle's little gold Mazda is in the car park. He parked beside it.

He hangs around in the foyer for a while, looking at the headlines and the pictures on the front pages of the newspapers. Some minutes pass, with no sign of Belle or Amy, so he wanders into the restaurant . . . and there they are: Belle, Amy and a casually dressed older man who has to be the Other, sitting at a table together, like a proper little nuclear family. Sean's immediate instinct is to turn and leave. He'll get in his car and drive. He'll just go. He'll phone Belle later and say there was an accident or something – he'll think of something. She'll be angry, sure, but . . . but it's too late.

165

'Daddy!' Amy calls, and there is such joy in her voice that Sean has no option but to try to make his face look normal and walk towards the table. Amy is already weaving through the other tables to greet her father. She throws herself into his arms. Her greeting is so dramatic and so much more emphatic than normal that it must be a show for the benefit of the Other. Sean is hopelessly grateful. He vows never to deny Amy anything she desires ever again. He picks her up and she wraps her legs around his waist and her arms around his neck, and kisses his cheek. Her lips are sticky. Her hair smells of the inside of Belle's car. Sean gears his anxiety down a notch or two and relaxes into the now familiar state of dislocated existence. Here is another situation over which he has no control, which he did not know was coming, and in which he has no idea how to react. Should he punch the Other's well-groomed, leathery old face or shake his well-manicured, leathery old hand?

At the table, Belle is using handfuls of paper serviettes and making a big deal out of mopping up the milkshake Amy has just spilled. The Other looks intensely uncomfortable, which gratifies Sean.

'Wow,' says Sean, standing beside the table, Amy still clinging to him as tightly as seaweed to a rock, her breath hot on his neck and her fingers knotting themselves in his hair. 'A delegation. To what do I owe this pleasure?'

He knows this is an arsey thing to say but it comes out of his lips anyway.

'What?' asks Belle, frowning.

'What's going on?' says Sean, scratching his chin.

'Nothing, we just . . .' says Belle.

The Other stands up. He holds out his hand to Sean. That hand has touched Belle. Those fingers have touched her most private places. Sean cannot touch them. He'd rather cut off his own. He ignores the extended hand and looks at Belle. She looks back calmly.

'Hello, I'm Lewis,' says the Other. Sean ignores him.

'Just what?' he asks Belle.

'Lewis and I, we wanted to speak to you about where we go from here.'

'That's easy,' says Sean. 'East to London, west to South Wales.'

He doesn't know what's wrong with him. Why does he keep talking rubbish?

'Sean,' says Belle, 'can't you just sit down for a minute? Can't we just—'

'No,' says Sean. 'No, we can't. You didn't warn me there was going to be an ambush.'

Belle shakes her head. 'It's not an ambush. For God's sake, Sean, this isn't a war, don't be so—'

'I'm in a hurry,' says Sean. 'I've got things planned for this evening. Where's Amy's bag?'

'In the car.'

'Come on, then.'

He turns on his heel, still carrying Amy. She burrows her face further into his neck as he strides out of the services. Belle is trotting behind him.

'Sean, I know it's difficult but—'

'No, Belle, you don't know what it's like at all.'

'I'd like us to be adult about this. There are things to sort out.'

'All right,' he calls, 'let's be adult, let's sort things out, get divorced, whatever you want.'

They are outside now, in the car park. Sean is still walking very fast, very powerfully. Belle is half-running in her heels to keep up. Amy is clinging so tightly that he has no need to support her. She gives him strength. She makes him strong.

Belle catches him at the car. 'What did you say?'

Sean unlocks the boot of his car. He flips it open and steps back.

'I said OK, let's get divorced. Do we *need* to talk about it? No doubt you've already decided what you want. Can't you get your solicitor to write to my solicitor or whatever?'

'It will be cheaper and . . . friendlier if we work together,' says Belle. She takes Amy's bag out of her car and passes it to Sean. He avoids touching her but takes the bag and puts it into his boot, and slams it shut.

'I don't want to work with you, Belle.'

'Sean . . .'

Sean peels Amy's limbs from his body, slides her into the car seat, fastens her in and closes the door.

Then he turns to his wife. He speaks quietly, so that Amy won't hear.

'Belle, I've finally taken your advice. I have stopped hoping that one day you will change your mind and

168

ask me back. I have stopped blaming myself for what has happened. I am getting on with my life. One day I'm sure we'll be able to be civilized together, you, me and that pervy old Lothario back there, but not now. Write me a letter. Tell me what you want. We'll take it from there.'

He gets into the car and starts the engine, and Belle has to step out of the way as he reverses out of the space, then he heads noisily out of the car park and back to Bath without another glance in her direction.

Sean calms down as soon as he pulls out onto the motorway, and when Massive Attack come loud and moody out of the stereo he feels more like a man again. He turns to smile at Amy, who is sitting very straight with an anxious look in her eyes.

'It's OK, honey,' he says. 'Everything's OK.'

'You shouted again.'

'I know and I'm sorry. When we get to Bath I'm going to call Mum to apologize.'

Amy relaxes and sighs. 'I don't like Membury.'

'Me neither.'

'It always makes you cross.'

'Yes,' says Sean. 'Yes, it does.'

CHAPTER 22

'Please, Fen, slow down. You're giving me a headache,' says Vincent.

Fen has taken it upon herself to give the bookshop a proper clean, the first in a long while. She has already brushed the ceilings and shaken the cobwebs out into the yard, where the homeless spiders scuttled for shelter in the cracks of the cobbles and the wall. Now she is working methodically, shelf by shelf, taking down the books, dusting them, and cleaning the woodwork. So much dust has been displaced that they've had to prop the door open, and the sounds and the smells of the city in summer freshen the musty air.

'What's got into you?' asks Vincent. 'I preferred you how you were before. All quiet and introspective.'

Fen thinks: You should be asking *who*'s got into me.

'Oh Lord,' says Vincent, reading her face or her mind. 'You're not in love, are you?'

'A little.'

'Dear girl!' Vincent leaves his desk and comes over to Fen, taking her hands in his and leaning

170

forward to kiss her. 'Thank goodness! And about time too!'

A gaggle of students come into the shop, speaking a language Fen can't place. She carries on with her work and Vincent withdraws and attends to them. When they have left he says: 'It's not that lodger of yours, is it?'

'Yes.'

'I thought as much. It's obvious every time he comes in that he holds a torch for you.'

'Don't say anything to anyone, will you, Vincent?'

'Of course not. It's nobody else's business. But he's a good sort, is he? He treats you well?'

'Yes, he does.'

'Well,' says Vincent, rubbing his hands together, 'I think we should put the kettle on, don't you? To celebrate?'

'By "we" you mean me?'

'You make coffee so much more nicely than I do, Fen.'

Fen smiles. 'You sweet-talking charmer, you!'

She goes into the kitchen, and while the kettle boils she rummages through the cluttered, doorless cupboard until she finds what she is looking for. She makes Vincent's coffee in the *Man and Superman* mug and hers in *Great Expectations*.

CHAPTER 23

It's a perfect Wednesday.

Sean and Fen have both taken a day off work, and they are making the most of every precious minute of their time without children or responsibilities. Fen feels like a teenager again, like she did before everything went wrong; she feels fresh and new and sexy. They left the car parked on the verge of a lane and walked for miles along overgrown paths full of brambles and nettles and tiny moths and shafts of sunlight. And now here they are, just the two of them, and it is like a place in a fairy tale: a secret glade beside water that ripples in the sunlight's glare, that's smooth and oily and cold and clear, so clear that you can see the fish in the reeds, the pebbles at the bottom and the freshwater oysters. Millions of tiny insects, like dust motes, shimmy above the water and the leaves in the trees rustle as a little breeze skips through the branches. It is a perfect day. It's one of those days, Fen knows, that she will never forget – a day that will come into her mind when she's lonely or frightened or old, a day that will always bring a smile to her lips.

'We should do this more often,' says Sean. 'Let's go away. Let's have a holiday. We can catch a plane and go somewhere warm.'

'I don't have a passport,' says Fen.

Sean squints up at her. The sunlight refracts from the tiny droplets of water caught in the hairs that cover her body, making her dazzle like an angel.

Sean is lying on a towel in the long grass of the meadow beside the weir. Fen sits beside him, rubbing her arms with a towel. They have been swimming in the river, and now the blood is fizzing in her veins and her body feels hard and sinewy and strong.

'How can you not have a passport?' he asks. 'Everyone has a passport.'

'I don't.'

He pulls a face.

'There are lots of things I don't have,' she says. 'You know that.'

'I know you don't have a computer or a car or a screwdriver. But a passport?'

'Stop looking at me like that,' she says. 'I've never needed one.' She shakes her hair, spraying Sean with tiny droplets. 'God, that water is cold!'

Sean lazily reaches up his arm, takes her wet hair in his hand and pulls her face down to his. He reaches for her with his lips and they are warm, and his mouth tastes of beer.

His finger hooks under the leg of her swimsuit and works its way around from the back.

'Stop it,' she says, but already she is sinking like

the *Titanic* into what seems to her to be a bottom-less ocean of desire. She shifts a little on the rug to make her body more available to him, and as she does so a breeze parts the leaves of the tree canopy above them and sunlight dazzles her eyes, burns her retina.

He rolls her onto her back, kissing her so hard she can hardly breathe, and she pushes him away with her hands.

'We can't,' she says, 'not here. Anybody could come by.'

'What are you talking about?' He is panting, his breath hot as flame on her cold neck. His hand is down inside his shorts. 'We're miles from bloody anywhere! I want to take you to Paris,' he tells her, tugging at her costume. It's wet and sticks clammily to her skin. She feels the goose pimples everywhere. She smiles up at him lazily, like a cat, she thinks, who is about to have the cream.

'I want to take you to Venice and Rome and Madrid and Bordeaux. I want to sail you down the rivers, I want to swim you in the seas.'

He takes her hand and guides it down and she holds him, strokes him with her fingers.

'I want to fuck you all the way through Europe.'

She reaches up for his lips and they kiss again, and as he covers her she can feel the ridge of her spine and the wings of her shoulder blades pressing into the hard ground beneath the rug, and she has to half close her eyes against the sunlight.

'I'll get you a passport and I'll get you a suitcase

and I'll buy you a big bottle of sunscreen and nothing will stop us,' he says.

He tilts his head back so she can see the underside of his throat, where the tiny hairs darken the skin and there is a red flush, and he finds her and sighs deeply.

'You're so cold on the outside, and so hot on the inside,' he whispers.

She measures his back with her hands, the pressure of his muscles, his gentle strength as erotic as anything else. Over his shoulders, she sees two white butterflies dancing together, going round and round one another, spinning in the sunlight, and she thinks: It has always been like this – it was no different for the first people who evolved, it was no different for people ever – this is how every woman feels, this is how it feels to have a man you love inside you, and nothing else really matters.

She tries to bring her mind back to the sex, but Sean is too far gone now, so she wraps her legs around his waist to help him and he comes in a moment and drops his lips to her shoulder, as he always does.

'Oh God.' He sighs. 'Oh God, that was lovely.'

Fen smiles to herself and strokes the hair around his ear. She listens to the water splashing down the weir; it's such a good sound.

'You know,' says Sean, 'for a while, last summer, I didn't think I could ever be happy again.'

'Mmm . . .' she says, too lazy to speak, too happy in her own moment.

Sean props himself up on one elbow and she shifts a little for he's heavy on her hips. He picks a piece of grass and sketches her nose, her eyebrows, her chin.

He smiles.

'But you know what?' he asks.

'No.'

'This is as good as it ever gets. This is amazing. I want to feel like this forever.'

'Good,' she says, smiling, but from nowhere a sadness seeps into her belly and behind his back she crosses her fingers to ward off bad luck; just in case.

CHAPTER 24

The weather is set fair so Lina suggests they all get together for a picnic in the park. She puts a notice up on the board in the reception area at work, and everyone Sean speaks to seems to be going; they have had impromptu parties in the park before and they've always had a great time.

Sean has avoided mass social gatherings for some time now, but he knows Amy will enjoy the party so he accepts the invitation with good grace. He's making the most of his daughter because, after the weekend, he won't see her again for a while. After the success of the Greek retreat, the Other has been invited to co-host a similar event in the south of France. Belle told Sean she is going to help by providing refreshments to the students and tutors throughout the day and cooking meals for them in the evening. Sean was surprised by this. He was surprised that Belle agreed to take on the role of caterer. He asked if she wouldn't rather be doing the writing herself; she said she would learn more about the human condition by observing than by participating. Sean can't remember when she started talking like this. It sounds, to him, as if something isn't quite right.

He told Belle that the retreat didn't sound like much fun for Amy, and Belle said it would be OK because it was a much bigger, more established event than the Greek one and there would be a children's club with activities every morning and afternoon.

Sean imagines Amy in her little ruched swimsuit and her cotton hat standing barefoot on scratchy, south of France grass, squinting up at the children's club team leader – some nice, sensible French teenager – through her baby sunglasses. He imagines her running around with tanned French kids, learning some words. He imagines her in the swimming pool, in her armbands and her float-belt, splashing with her feet, the cold water sparkling in the sunlight. It's a part of her life that she will never forget and that he will have missed completely.

Lina comes into Sean's office and asks if he'll meet her in Sainsbury's on the morning of the picnic, so that they can load up his car with food and drink. Freddie will bring the chairs, the rugs, the barbecue and the coals in their car, but they won't have room for everything and she'd appreciate Sean's help.

'Of course,' says Sean.

'Bring Fen with you,' says Lina.

'OK.'

Lina pauses at the door, tapping an envelope against her thigh. Sean looks up.

'It'll be OK, you know,' she says. 'I know it'll be your first time on your own without Belle but everyone knows now and . . .'

'Yeah, yeah,' says Sean, 'I'll be fine. Thanks.'

She closes the door, and he drops his head into his hands.

He doesn't know what he's going to say to Fen. He hasn't told anyone at work that they are together. The opportunity simply has never arisen. Sean has never been part of the drinking crowd, and since the break-up with Belle her has avoided invitations to social and sporting events, mainly because they all take place at weekends and that's the only time he has with Amy. People don't ask about Belle because they know his marriage is a sore point; they avoid conversations about women and Sean is not the sort of person to make announcements. He doesn't quite know how to explain all this to Fen.

On the way back to Lilyvale he stops off at the florist's and buys a bunch of yellow roses.

Fen is barefoot in the kitchen. The back door is open. Connor is sitting on the doorstep eating sandwiches. A pan of new potatoes is steaming on the hob.

'Here,' says Sean, passing the roses to Fen. 'These are for you.'

'Thank you,' she says, a blush of pleasure seeping onto her cheeks. 'They're lovely.'

She runs two inches of water into the sink and

stands the roses in that while she finishes preparing the meal.

'What are you doing on Sunday?' asks Sean, leaning against the counter.

'Nothing,' says Fen.

'Wrong. You're coming to a picnic in the park.'

Connor looks up at Sean wide-eyed.

'Is Amy going?'

'Con, don't talk with your mouth full,' says Fen without even looking at him.

'Yes, Amy's going.'

'Can I go with Amy?'

'I'm sorry, mate,' Sean says, 'you and your mum will have to make your own way there. Amy and I are going to help Lina with the food.'

'Doesn't she know about us?' asks Fen. She picks a boiled egg out of a plastic bowl and taps it against the edge of the counter.

'I thought *you* might have said something.'

'I haven't seen her in ages,' says Fen.

'I keep meaning to tell her but we've been so busy lately, I haven't been in the office much. I've been out on site,' says Sean. It is the truth.

Fen peels the brown shell from the egg. The smooth, exposed, congealed white glistens in the palm of her hand.

'Don't you want your colleagues to know about us?'

'Oh, Fen, no. It's nothing like that. It's just . . . I haven't had the chance to say anything. I don't know how to tell them.'

180

He puts his hand on her shoulder and kisses the top of her head. She concentrates on the egg. He leans over and steals a slice of cucumber from the salad bowl.

'Did they all really like Belle?'

'I don't know. We don't talk about women – we're real men.'

He feels her shoulder relax beneath his hand and she looks up and smiles.

'You talk about sport and cars?'

'Exactly.' He takes another slice of cucumber and a lettuce leaf.

'Stop it,' she says, waving him away. 'There'll be nothing left.'

Sean kisses her temple.

'Come on, you,' he says to Connor, 'finish that sandwich because we need to put in some practice at rounders.'

The Sunday of the picnic is the sort of day that's made for England. Little white clouds wisp across a perfectly blue sky, and between the pavements and the clouds long-winged birds soar, while a breeze that's perfect for taking the edge off the heat breathes affectionately through the leaves of the trees on the hill.

Amy is wearing shorts and a T-shirt, with her fairy wings over the top. The wings have been worn so many times that they are distorted and the gauze is distinctly grubby. She skips as she holds Sean's hand on the way into the supermarket.

Lina is already there, with a deep trolley, and the three of them fill it with beer, fizzy drinks, burgers, sausages, rolls and wine, and miscellaneous goodies that catch Amy's eye: black olives ('Mummy likes them'), buffalo mozzarella ('Mummy likes that'), salted pistachios ('they're Mummy's favourites'). Sean is trying not to place undue significance on the fact that Mummy has featured far more predominantly in their conversations since Amy woke from a nightmare one night and found Sean in bed with Fen.

Once the car is loaded, they drive to the park, and, miraculously, find a space close to a nice spot towards the bottom end of the hill, below the Botanic Gardens and above the play area. Sean helps Lina and Freddie set up the barbecue while Amy lies on her stomach on the grass pulling the petals from daisies and telling herself a story. Soon other people arrive, a couple of families, a few couples, and the picnic area expands, blankets next to blankets, grey smoke curls skywards and children's laughter puts smiles on the faces of the adults.

Freddie declares himself head chef – he has a comedy hat and an apron – and Sean, designated sous-chef, quietly follows his orders. He has been given the role of Freddie's assistant out of kindness, so he will not have to sit on his own, doing nothing. He is grateful to Lina and Freddie for their thoughtfulness, but at the same time he feels intensely uncomfortable because now Fen will be sitting on her own. The longer he says nothing about her, the more difficult it becomes to broach the subject. He realizes that she has been on her own for so long that it is assumed, among the people who know her, that it is her natural state. It does not cross their minds that she might be with someone. He tries to think of a way to bring her name into the conversation casually, but Freddie is talking about global finance markets and other people are joining in with their opinions; there's nothing Sean can do.

He peels sausages out of their greaseproof paper and onto the tines of the barbecue, where they smoke and spit. He pokes them with his fork and turns wooden skewers heavy with chunks of vegetable. Freddie drinks beer from the can and waves away the smoke. Lina has taken off her shoes and kneels on the blanket, unpacking salads and quiches with the other women.

'Freddie,' says Sean, 'there's something I need to—'

'Look,' says Freddie, pointing with his tongs, 'there's your landlady.'

Sean glances across the park, and in the distance he sees Fen struggle to manoeuvre Connor's pushchair through the gate. He moves the sausages to the edge of the barbecue where they won't burn.

'I'll go and give her a hand,' he says to Freddie. 'Keep an eye on Amy, would you?'

He trots down the path and as he comes closer to Fen it's clear that there's trouble. Connor is not happy. Snot and tears are smeared all over his face and his clothes are all out of place. Hair is stuck to his forehead.

'He wanted to go with you and Amy,' says Fen, 'and he was in a bad mood because he couldn't and then when we left the house he ran into the road. Then he wouldn't hold my hand or sit in the buggy so we had a big fight.'

Connor's body is at an awkward angle. He scowls up from behind his hand and spits, which is his latest thing.

'Oh, come on, Connor,' says Sean. 'That's not very manly.'

He unbuckles the harness and swings the little boy out by his arms.

'Got a wet wipe, Fen?'

'Here.'

'Right,' says Sean, cleaning Connor's face. 'See that smoke over there? That's our dinner, and if we don't hurry up it's going to be burned!'

He picks Connor up and hefts him onto his shoulders, holding him tightly by the waist. Connor squeals with delight. He is light, much lighter than Amy; there is nothing to him, really. Sean breaks into a pretend gallop, and Connor screams. Fen follows behind with the pushchair.

When they come close to the picnickers, Sean lifts Connor off his shoulders, turns him upside down and carries him the last few yards by his ankles. Connor is wriggling and laughing, his T-shirt falling over his chin, his little bare tummy on display.

It is crossed by a pale scar that Sean has never seen before. Sean lays him down on the rug, and Amy comes over and takes charge of the boy. The status quo has been restored. Sean waits until Fen has joined the group and Lina has embraced her and pulled her down beside her, then he returns to the barbecue.

'How do you get on with Fen?' Freddie asks, passing him a beer.

'We get on very well.' This is the perfect moment. Sean takes a breath.

'Always found her hard work myself,' says Freddie. 'Bit odd. Doesn't say much, does she? Most of the time she seems away with the fairies.'

Sean looks over at Fen. She is listening intently to something Lina is saying.

'She's great when you get to know her,' he says.

Freddie squeezes half a lemon liberally over the tail-on king prawns that are cooking, speared in groups of half a dozen on wooden skewers.

'And how well have you got to know her?' he asks, with a nudge.

Sean pretends not to have heard. He can think of no way to answer this question honourably.

The meal lasts for hours. Sean and Freddie cook the food a little at a time, and the women organize the drinks and the cold food. In the pauses before new batches of hot food are ready to eat the adults drink, or play with the children. They play French cricket, Grandma's footsteps, tag.

Other families join in. The boundaries of the group are blurred and it's very sociable.

Lina sits between Freddie's legs, resting her head on his chest; her arm strokes his big calf, smoothing the gingery hairs, and his hand is on her belly, just below her breasts. Sean glances at Fen. She sits apart, hugging her knees, her sunglasses holding back her hair. He tries to catch her eye, but she is casually ignoring him. She picks at a salad with her fingers, a slice of cucumber, a shred of lettuce, and watches the children. Amy is chasing Connor around in circles, pretending that she can't keep up with him. Connor is screaming with laughter and the anticipation of being caught. Sean squeezes the smoke out of his eyes and turns chocolate-stuffed bananas, wrapped in aluminium foil, with his tongs. A little grey-muzzled dog is sitting politely a few feet from the barbecue, alternating his brown-eyed gaze from the last of the meat, to Sean's eyes. He's not a stray; he's a clean, well-groomed old thing with a nice collar.

Later, they douse the barbecue coals with water and pack away what little food is left. They take off their shoes and play rounders with a tennis ball. Jumpers mark the bases. Fen plays with Connor, holding his hand and sometimes hefting him on her hip. Lina can't hit the ball and keeps leaning over, with her hands on her knees and her skirt wrapped around her thighs, laughing. The men are stupidly competitive, even with the children. Still they let Connor win and Connor's face nearly cracks with happiness. The other children are suspicious. Airidas's daughter stands on tiptoe to ask her father if the game was rigged and Sean doesn't hear what he says, but the child is appeased. She nods and smiles and leans against her father.

Some of the adults take the children down to the playground, while Sean, Freddie, Lina and Fen tidy up the detritus. The party has spread itself across a large area and children's jumpers and socks, plastic cups and paper plates are scattered.

'How do you two know each other, then?' Sean asks, gathering up a stray crisp packet. Fen has hardly said a word all afternoon. Every time he's moved closer to her, she has tensed. When they are alone they are perfectly at ease, but they have never been together in public before.

'We went to the same school,' says Lina.

'Merron College?'

'No!' Lina laughs. 'It was a church school on the other side of town. Girls only. Lots of singing and praying and discreet religious fundamentalism.'

'It wasn't that discreet,' says Fen. 'We had to wear horrible coats.'

Sean raises an eyebrow.

'No, really, they were awful: great ugly, clumpy things,' says Lina. 'The whole uniform was designed to make us look ugly. It was the school's version of a burkha only nowhere near as glamorous.'

'It didn't seem to do either of you much harm,' says Freddie.

187

'Huh,' says Lina meaningfully. 'You don't know the half of it.'

'So you've always been friends?' asks Sean.

'We lost touch,' says Lina, and she hiccups and giggles, then picks up a plastic bottle of lemonade and takes a good swig. 'After school finished. We hadn't seen one another for years and years. Then we met at the hospital . . .'

'The Royal United?'

'Mmm. I'd broken my wrist and had gone in to have the cast taken off and Fen here was massively up the duff.'

'Lina!' says Fen.

'Well, you were. Like a barrage balloon. And it turned out she needed somewhere to live and Lilyvale needed a tenant.'

Fen picks up some sandwich papers, screws them into balls and puts them into a carrier bag.

'It was like we were destined to meet, wasn't it, Fen?'

'Yes,' says Fen. 'You were very kind to me.'

Lina hiccups again and takes another drink. 'Shit,' she says, 'I hate having hiccups. People will think I've had too much wine.'

'As if!' says Freddie.

Fen brushes down her skirt. 'I ought to go and see if Connor's OK.'

'He'll be fine,' says Lina. 'They'll look after him.'

'I'll be back in a minute,' Fen calls and she sets off trotting down the hill in her bare feet.

'God, she's such a worrier,' says Lina.

'She manages very well,' Sean says quickly. 'She's amazing.'

'Oooh,' says Lina, 'you leaped to her defence there! Is there anything we should know?'

'Actually—' he says and at exactly the same instant Fen, halfway down the hill, stops, hops and then sits down on the grass and holds her foot.

'She's trodden on something,' he says to Lina.

Lina slaps his thigh gently. 'Well, you'd better go and sort her out, then.'

She passes him his trainers and he puts them on, then jogs down to where Fen is sitting, pale-faced, with her foot cradled in her skirt. A shard of glass is stuck in the meaty part of her sole.

'Let me have a look,' says Sean.

Gingerly Fen extends her leg, and he takes the foot between his hands, cradling it at the heel and taking its weight on his knee. The displaced flesh is pressed close around the glass, holding it tight. He glances at Fen. She is staring at her foot.

'Look at that!' he cries, pointing over her left shoulder, and as Fen turns her head to follow his finger, he grasps the shard and tugs hard and, although it resists, it comes out.

'Ow,' says Fen and then she laughs and relaxes. She lies back on the grass and covers her face with her forearms. 'Thank you,' she says. 'Is there much blood?'

'You'll live,' says Sean, dabbing at the wound with the hem of his T-shirt. 'Did you see the size of it!'

Fen props herself on her elbows and admires

the shard. It is diamond-shaped, more than a centimetre long.

'All that was inside me?' she asks, then she colours a little and adds, 'As the actress said . . .'

Sean laughs. He spits on a clean patch of his T-shirt and cleans around the cut. Fen's foot is grass-stained from the rounders earlier. He puts it gently down, back on the grass.

'Do you want to keep this,' he asks Fen, offering her the shard, 'as a souvenir?'

She shakes her head. Her hair is tangled. She pushes it back behind her ears. The sunglasses have gone.

'I'm sorry,' he says, 'sorry if it's been a bit awkward today.'

'It's not just you.' Fen smiles. 'We don't have to make an announcement,' she says. 'People will realize, won't they? They'll realize gradually.'

Sean leans forward and kisses her very gently on the lips.

'Of course they will,' he says.

CHAPTER 25

Fen gets to the pub first and she buys a bottle of rosé and picks up two glasses. She takes them outside and finds a bench in the shade of the trellis, which is hung with clematis. She picks at a packet of salted cashews until Lina arrives, clip-clopping across the paving stones in a slim, sleeveless black dress and gladiator sandals.

'You always make me feel scruffy,' Fen complains, standing to kiss Lina's cheek.

Lina sits down and artfully crosses her legs. The hoops in her ears catch the sunlight. Her hair is pulled back into a tight ponytail.

'And how come you're so tanned? It hasn't been that sunny.'

'It's fake,' says Lina. 'What's this?' She picks up the bottle. 'Wine at lunchtime? What are we celebrating?'

'Nothing. I thought you might like it.'

'Oh, come on,' says Lina. 'I might have been a little tiddly at the barbecue but I wasn't blind. There's something going on between you and Sean, isn't there?'

Fen pours the wine. 'Sort of . . .'

'I knew it!'

Fen feels the blush rising from her neck.

'Sean's been a lot . . . chirpier these last weeks. I thought either Belle was being nicer to him, or he'd met someone. So have you actually—'

'Lina!'

'Everything?'

'That's none of your business.'

'I see. And how long has this been going on?'

'A while.'

Lina swirls the wine around in her glass. 'Go on,' she says, 'tell me. All the gory details.'

Fen looks up and smiles. She does not know where to begin but the relief of being able to talk, at last, about Sean overwhelms her.

She starts to speak and the words come quickly, they fall over themselves in the rush to explain how she feels, how wonderful Sean is, how happy he has made her. 'It started a couple of months ago. It just sort of . . . happened. And God, Lina, it's like he's taken over my world and changed it and everything is so much better now and he's so amazing and . . .'

Something in Lina's eyes stops her.

'What?' she asks. 'What is it?'

'Nothing,' says Lina, chasing an ant off the table with her fingernail. She pats Fen's hand. 'So you have feelings for him . . . you like him a lot?'

'Yes.'

'It's not just a little fling? Not just a way for you to get back in the saddle?'

'What do you mean?'

'Sorry. I didn't mean it to come out that crudely but . . .'

A sort of ache is forming in Fen's belly. It's a kind of dread. 'Aren't you pleased for me, Lina?'

'Of course I am.'

'What then? Is there something about Sean that you haven't told me?'

Lina sips her wine. 'I'm guessing you haven't talked much about your future.'

'It's a little early for that.' Fen laughs nervously. 'And it's not important. All that matters is now.'

Lina nods. She helps herself to a nut.

'Why are you being like this, Lina?' asks Fen. 'Why are you being so negative?'

'I don't think I've said anything negative.'

'You've been telling me for ages to find a man and now I have and you . . .'

Lina looks Fen straight in the eyes and squeezes her hand. She says: 'I don't want you to get hurt, Fen, that's all. You've been through too much already.'

'I won't. Sean wouldn't hurt me.'

'No, I know he wouldn't. Not deliberately. But maybe he's approaching this relationship from a different perspective to you.'

'What do you mean?'

Lina sighs. 'I don't know if I should say anything. I could be completely wrong.'

'About what?'

They are interrupted by the barman. He says:

'Excuse me, ladies,' and places two ploughman's lunches on the table in front of them.

'Lina . . . ?'

'Look, I'm going to tell you what he said to me after Christmas. It might be absolutely nothing but . . .'

'What did he say?'

Lina unfolds her paper napkin very slowly. She smoothes out the creases with the palm of her hand. She places it on her lap. 'He said he was going to have a nice, uncomplicated little affair to make Belle jealous.'

'Oh.'

Fen lays her fork back down on the table. She exhales.

'He said,' says Lina, with the resigned air of somebody who thinks they might as well be hanged for a sheep, as for a lamb, 'he'd talked about it with his sister, and she'd said it would be good for him, because it would build up his confidence and it was the most likely route to making Belle see him in a new light. She told him to find a sweet woman who would treat him well but who wasn't in quite the same league as Belle. Of course, he might feel differently now.'

The words are like a physical pain in Fen's belly. But she trusts Sean. She thinks he would not be capable of such a manipulative act.

'He might have said that but that's not how it is with me and him. And anyway he wouldn't. He's too honest.'

'Has he told you he loves you?' Lina asks.

'He hasn't actually said those words, but he's not good at talking about emotional stuff.'

Lina shrugs.

'He doesn't need to say it,' says Fen, 'because I know.'

She is aware that she sounds naive, gauche, but what else can she say? She and Sean, they are not complicated. If you know somebody loves you, if it's perfectly obvious, then why should they have to tell you? Maybe it's difficult for Lina to understand, but it is clear to Fen.

'What did he say at the beginning? When you first got together?'

'It was me who started it,' Fen says quietly, 'not him.'

'Oh,' says Lina. 'Well.'

'Lina, please, it's not like that.'

'He's a lovely man,' says Lina. 'I'm sure he'd never . . . you know, use you or anything. But if it was in his mind to have an affair, and then you let him know you were interested, well, you have to admit, it's convenient.'

'No.' Fen shakes her head. 'Please stop talking like this, Lina, I know you mean well but you're wrong. Really you are.'

It is hateful for Fen to hear anybody doubting what she and Sean have. They are connected, she knows they are; they are together and they fit together as closely and perfectly as the teeth in a zip. Fen knows she's not experienced in love but she cannot imagine feeling this connected to any other person. She would know if Sean didn't feel the same. She would be able to sense it. How could she feel so attuned to him, how could his happiness be so important to her, if he were keeping anything from her? He is the most open person she's ever known. In the night he holds on to her like a drowning man clings to a lifebelt. He makes her feel happy, and their being together is so right, it's natural; their whole is greater than the sum of their parts.

She knew that they should have kept their love to themselves. They should have kept it hidden. She feared that as soon as they let the world in, it would no longer be safe, and she was right. Together they are perfect, and she cannot bear for this perfection to be doubted, or tarnished, or seen in the wrong light.

'You're wrong, Lina,' she says again.

'I'm sure I am,' says Lina cheerfully and briskly as if talking to a child. 'All I'm saying, Fen, is be careful with that heart of yours. OK?'

The barman brings a little china pot of mayonnaise. Lina thanks him, spears a cherry tomato with her fork, and dips it in the pot.

Fen stares into her plate. If she says anything else, Lina will think she's protesting too much, but she can't bear for Lina not to believe in Sean's love for her. Her lack of conviction has somehow cast a shadow over everything.

CHAPTER 26

Sean's parents, Lola and Boo come to Bath for his birthday. They book into a bed and breakfast just outside Cold Ashton because Sean's father wants to walk some of the Cotswold Way while they're here. Sean says he'll meet them in town for lunch.

He asked Fen to go with him. He told her he'd like his family to meet her. He said they'd love her, especially Lola. Fen said no. She said she thought it would be better if he went alone. When he asked why she didn't want to come, she said she just wasn't ready to meet his family yet. She wasn't being straight with him. He knew she wasn't but she wouldn't elaborate; she said she'd already promised to take Connor to the beach and that's what she's going to do.

Amy is with him for the weekend. Half an hour before they're due to meet the family, he stands in the kitchen looking at his daughter. She looks odd. It's her hair. Sean still hasn't mastered the art of bunches. Amy's parting zigzags one way and then the other, a good deal of hair is still loose and sticking up and there is a disproportionate amount of dark hair in the left bunch.

Sean looks out of the open back door. Fen is in the garden with Connor. She stands with one arm across her waist, the hand supporting the opposite elbow. She is covering her mouth with her fingers so that Connor won't see her smile. He is swinging a little plastic golf club and has not hit the luminous green ball once, despite a dozen attempts and his deep concentration. Fen keeps offering encouragement.

She glances up, catches Sean's eye and immediately looks away.

She has done this a lot, lately. Sean has caught her watching him through windows or across the room, a spacey look in her eyes, and when he's asked her what she's thinking she's always said: 'Nothing.' Now, his gaze pressing on her, she glances up again and smiles with her lips, but not her eyes, then looks away.

He goes to the door and leans out.

'You couldn't give me a hand, could you?' he calls. 'With Amy's hair?'

'Sure,' says Fen. She leans down and whispers something into Connor's ear, and then trots up the back steps. She laughs when she sees Amy's hair, but covers up the laugh so as not to offend the child.

'Hmm,' she says, 'that's an interesting look.'

'It's supposed to be Hannah Montana but ended up – I don't know, St Trinian's meets plucked chicken,' says Sean. Fen laughs again. The laugh is a little artificial.

Fen indicates for Amy to climb onto a kitchen stool so that her head is at a workable height, and she unravels the elastic bands that hold the bunches, taking care not to pull, rolls them up onto her wrist and smoothes out the child's soft hair.

'Change your mind,' says Sean. 'Come with us, please.'

'No,' she says, gently.

'Why not? It's my birthday. You're supposed to indulge me.'

'I'll indulge you later.'

'Go on, Fen,' says Amy quietly. 'We'll have a nice time. My nana and grandad are very nice.'

'I'm sure they are, Amy,' says Fen, 'only I'm taking Connor to the seaside.'

'He won't mind coming with us if I ask him.'

'Not this time.'

Sean takes hold of Fen's elbow and squeezes it affectionately.

'I haven't done anything to upset you, have I?' he asks.

She shakes her head, and he holds her eyes and he knows something is wrong.

'Please . . .' he mouths.

'No. I'm sorry. I just can't.'

He lets go of her elbow.

'So what did you get Daddy for his birthday, Amy?' Fen asks.

Amy smiles up over her shoulder.

'Mummy and me went into Oxford and we got him a new guitar strap from both of us.'

Fen nods. 'That's lovely.'

'It was exactly the right one. Mummy remembered that Daddy looked at it ages ago and she remembered that it was the one he wanted.'

'That was nice of her.'

'She said she wanted to give him something nice.'

Fen nods to Sean to indicate that he should pass her the little pink hairbrush on the counter. He does, and as he gives it to her their fingers touch and a tiny electric shock passes between them, but it's just physical energy from the nylon of the brush, the hairs on his hand, the hem of her sleeve.

'Have *you* got a present for Daddy?' Amy asks.

'Mmm.'

'Have you given it to him yet?'

'Not yet.'

Sean watches as Fen parts Amy's hair using the brush handle. Amy is fidgeting with her bracelet. It's made of little round sherbet sweets, threaded on elastic. Her head is at the same height as Fen's chest. Fen is wearing a blue T-shirt with a scoop neck. Sean can see the lace trim of her underwear, the darker space between her breasts where he likes to kiss her. He looks away, looks back. Fen collects Amy's hair in her hand to make the bunches, she runs it through one palm, then the other, making it smooth and tidy, and rolls the elastic bands down her wrist.

'There,' she stands back. 'There, how's that?'

'A huge improvement,' says Sean. 'Thanks, Fen.'

He leans across, over Amy's head, and kisses her cheek.

The kiss catches Fen off guard. Her fingers go to the spot where his lips touched her.

'Go and fetch your shoes, Amy,' Sean tells his daughter.

He follows Fen's gaze out of the open back door to the garden, where Connor is still trying to hit the golf ball.

'Fen,' says Sean, 'please come. I'd like to show you off and my parents are great, they're easy, they'd spoil Connor rotten, and Lola would love to meet you, she'd think you were perfect, she'd think you were the best thing that could possibly have happened to me right now.'

'Right now?'

'Yes, of course. When else?'

Fen turns to go back out into the garden.

'Fen? What is it? What's the matter?'

'Nothing,' she says.

Sean sighs. He rubs his chin with his fingers.

'If you won't tell me what's wrong,' he says, 'then how can I put it right?'

She looks back at him over her shoulder.

'It's nothing, Sean, honestly. Please have a nice time. I'll see you later.'

'OK,' he says. 'All right.'

He hears his family before he sees them. They are at the far side of the recreation ground, admiring the views up to Pulteney Bridge and over to the

201

Parade Gardens, on the other side of the river, which are just coming into their full glory. Rosie's in a patchwork dress and high-heeled boots, Darragh's wearing his walking boots with his shirt tucked into his trousers, Lola has her arm hooked through Boo's, and Boo's face is now almost covered by two curtains of dark hair. The sight of his family puts all discord from Sean's mind. The three adults are arguing about something; he catches only stray words.

'Here they are!' cries Rosie, her face lighting up as she sees Amy. Grandmother and granddaughter run towards one another, their arms outstretched, and meet in an embrace of sheer joy.

'Oh, it's lovely to see you!' Rosie cries, holding Amy to her.

'Hello, old man,' says Dad.

'Hi,' says Boo.

'Sean, you fat bastard, you're getting a beer gut,' says Lola.

They eat in Garfunkels and it's a long, extended feast of a lunch. Amy has taken a shine to Boo. She sits on her hands and stares at him with quiet adoration. When he moves, to clear the hair from his face, or to run his fingers over the Braille of his spots, her eyes widen a little further. If he ever actually looks at her, or speaks, she turns into a giggly little bundle of coyness, wriggling in her seat, blinking her eyes. Boo is embarrassed beyond belief but the adults are charmed.

Darragh tells Sean, in great detail, about the

innovative waterproof coating on his new walking boots and Sean maintains an interested expression. Rosie shoots Sean sympathetic glances, but is too fond of her husband to interrupt him or change the subject. Her loyalty touches Sean. He loves his family. Nothing would keep them from him, he realizes. They would stick with him, every one of them, through thick and thin. No matter what he did, no matter what happened, they'd be there for him. A cynic would call it genetics. A romantic would call it unconditional love.

This thought pings a distant memory in the back of his mind, but he can't retrieve it and forgets about it instantly as the waiter brings a cream, strawberry and sponge cake to the table, ablaze with candles and a sparkler. Amy's eyes open wide and she says: 'Oh!' Everyone, the whole restaurant, sings 'Happy Birthday' to Sean.

'I love you guys,' he says, blowing out the candles.

'You must be pissed,' says Lola. 'Wish that was my cake. How come I never get cake?'

'You're not going through an emotional crisis and living far from home,' says Rosie. 'And you're always telling me you're on a diet.'

'My life is one long crisis,' says Lola. 'That's why I comfort-eat. It stems from being the least-favourite child.'

'Daddy,' whispers Amy anxiously, pulling at his sleeve and glancing to and from Boo's face to make sure he isn't listening, 'I need a wee.'

'OK,' Sean whispers making eye contact with Lola over Amy's head.

'I'm going to the Ladies,' says Lola. 'Anybody want to come with me?'

Amy slides off the chair and slips her hand into her aunt's.

'I really do love you guys,' says Sean, trailing his fingers through Lola's as she walks away from the table.

'I have to say,' says Darragh, 'that you're looking better, Sean. You looked awful at Christmas . . .'

'Thanks, Dad.'

'Well, you did, didn't he, Rosie? You were all hunched and grey and middle-aged-looking. And now you're not.'

Rosie dabs her lips with a napkin, and refreshes Sean's glass.

'We were so worried about you, darling. Are you getting used to things now?'

'I'm OK,' says Sean.

'Do you talk to Belle?'

'A bit. It's getting a little easier.'

Rosie sighs. 'So you haven't talked about getting a D-I-V-O—'

'Yes,' says Sean. 'We've talked about it. Well, she has. It's up to her, really. If she wants to set the ball rolling, it's fine by me.'

He scoops some cream on his finger and sucks it.

'And your lodgings are all right, are they? You are comfortable? It's just . . .' Rosie trails off. Sean guesses that she was going to mention the unfair disparity between his situation and Belle's, but doesn't want to sound critical of either of them.

'Yes, they're great.'

And suddenly Sean misses Fen. He misses her with a physical pain. She should be here, with him. She should be here. It is as if she has become part of him, as if he is not fully functional without her. She may not say very much, or take up much space, but without her there is a roaring silence, a gaping chasm.

He looks out of the window, hoping she'll be on the other side with Connor, peering in, trying to find the courage to come through the door. He imagines taking hold of her hand, finding a chair for her, ordering a drink. He imagines her – his slight and graceful Fen – slipping into her seat, smiling shyly. And his parents would see her and their hearts would lift because they would see how much she means to Sean. They were hurt too, by Belle's betrayal. They were hurt on his behalf, hurt that anyone could do what she did to their beloved son. They would see that Fen would never hurt him that way. That would be enough to make them accept her. And she'd fit in very well. She'd like his family. She wouldn't mind their ways, his parents' eccentricities, Lola's obscenities, Boo's hair. They wouldn't get on her nerves, like they used to irritate Belle. It would be easy with Fen, as everything with Fen is easy.

'Mum,' he says, 'something has happened. I've met someone . . .'

But Rosie isn't listening. She is staring awkwardly down at her shoulder. Darragh has fallen asleep, his head resting against her. His mouth is hanging open and saliva is staining the sleeve of her dress. Rosie slides down in her chair a little so that his position is more comfortable. She strokes Darragh's head.

'He never could handle his drink at lunchtime,' says Rosie fondly. 'We might have to take him back to yours for a lie-down.'

'We aren't allowed back in the B and B until teatime,' Boo explains.

'Funny woman runs it,' says Rosie. 'She's very suspicious.'

'"Don't think you can treat this place like a hotel,"' says Boo in a camp imitation of a woman's voice. '"And breakfast closes at nine o'clock prompt."'

'I ask you! What person in their right mind has break-fast before ten at the weekend?' asks Rosie.

'Shocking,' Sean agrees.

Lola returns with Amy skipping at her side. Boo immediately puts his face away.

'We were saying we might have to go back to Sean's so Dad can have five minutes,' says Rosie.

'Oh, good,' says Lola. 'That means we can meet the landlady. What's she like, Sean?'

'She's nice.'

'So she's – what? Middle-aged divorcee? Bit heavy on the old make-up? Heels? Too much wrinkly décolletage, that kind of thing?'

Sean snorts. 'No, not at all! She's younger than me. She's . . . lovely.'

'Lovely?'

'Yes.'

'Oh my God!' cries Lola. 'You're sleeping with her!'

'I am not!' he protests, but he feels his cheeks burn.

'You so are! Look at your smug face! Tell me more! Tell me everything!'

'She's called Fen,' says Amy in a weary voice. 'She's got a little boy. He's called Connor. He's five and he goes to school on a bus and he's got a funny hand and he doesn't walk properly.'

'Cerebral palsy,' says Sean.

'And Daddy . . . likes her. He kisses her.'

'No! Do you?'

Sean shrugs. 'Oh, you know.'

'Oh, Sean, that's wonderful!' says Rosie, her eyes filling with tears. 'That's made me so happy! And she's good to you, is she? She treats you well?'

'She's perfect,' says Sean. 'She's just so . . . easy. Easy to be with, I mean. She's lovely.'

'So where's the boy's father?' asks Lola.

Sean shrugs.

'Don't you know?'

'It's not my business, is it?'

'Christ on a bike,' says Lola, polishing off her drink. 'What's wrong with men? How can they go through life without *talking* to anyone?'

'We do talk,' says Sean, 'only not about rela-tionships.'

'What else is there?' asks Lola.

CHAPTER 27

Fen sits on the beach at Weston-super-Mare looking out over the water. Connor is standing barefoot beside her, in his pants and T-shirt, meticulously spading sand into his bucket. Fen likes the hot, dry smell. She draws a circle with her finger. She puts a smiley face into the circle and Connor steps back and rubs it out.

'Hey, you,' says Fen, pulling the back of his shirt, 'watch where you're putting those great feet of yours.'

Connor squeals and sits back down on her lap. She kisses his hair; it smells of the seaside, of sun protection cream, salt and sun and sweat. Fen covers his ears and neck with kisses.

'You great lovely smelly sandy boy,' she murmurs into his neck, loving the weight of his bony little buttocks against her thigh. He wriggles. She takes a cotton sunhat from her bag and pulls it down over his head.

'Can we make a sandcastle, Mum?'

'The sand's too dry.'

Connor stares at her.

Fen scoops a handful of sand and lets it trail

between her fingers. 'It won't stick together, Con, not unless it's wet.'

Connor sensibly looks towards the sea. It is a long way out. It's hard to tell how far, but the people who have already set out to find it are just tiny black silhouettes in the distance, like spent matchsticks, fragile as insects against the expanse of glaring sand which is reflecting the sun back to itself like a huge mirror.

'It's a long walk . . .' Fen warns Connor.

'More than a mile?'

'About ten miles, I'd say. Are you up for that?'

He grins and nods and she pushes herself to her feet, then he puts his hand in hers and they walk down to the sea.

The sand cools and becomes firmer as they walk. A long way to the right and behind them is the silhouetted pier, and beyond that are the donkeys trailing patiently around their circuit. The beach is busy with holidaymakers and day trippers but the further out towards the sea they walk, the fewer people they meet.

It's just them and the sunlight and the patterns on the sand and seagulls wheeling overhead.

Connor is singing a little tune to himself. Fen looks down at the top of his hat, his narrow shoulders, his long feet, and she is filled up with love, as she always is with Connor.

She dusts off her memories of his father in the rhythm of her footsteps as she and her son cross this massive expanse of warm outdoors, a gentle breeze blowing her hair into her eyes.

Connor's father's name was Connor. It was almost all she knew of him and the only thing of his that she could give to his son. Fen and he weren't together for long, just a few hours, but they were a good few hours. It was the second night of the festival, Saturday. It was wet. She had become separated from her friends and he took her back to his tent. She was intensely exhausted, but chemically high and as bright as the lights in the sky. The inside of his tiny tent was damp, the nylon dripping condensation, but it was cosy, cave-like; he had made a nest of blankets and sleeping bags. There was just enough room for the two of them and everything smelled of wood-smoke, damp fabric and rain. They were both cold. They huddled together with their clothes on in the not-quite-perfect darkness, listening to the rain on the oversheet and the footsteps and voices of passers-by beyond, people humming snatches of songs.

Every now and then somebody tripped over one of the guy lines and the canvas would lurch and they would both laugh.

Connor was thin and slightly built. He spoke with an Irish country accent. He was missing a front tooth. He had a cough. Fen remembers he coughed long and hard into his fist. He asked if she wanted anything to eat; he had some pasties in a carrier bag hidden beneath a corner of the airbed and she laughed because it was funny that food was in such short supply that it had to be hidden, even out-of-date Ginsters' pasties. She was not eating anything much at the time, but it was nice of him to offer to share. She was talking a lot, too much; she can't remember what she was saying but she remembers the boy's cold lips on hers, and his tongue finding a way between her teeth, and him whispering: 'Will you shut the fuck up?'

And that was the beginning of the beginning of Connor.

The sand is hard underfoot now. As her feet press down, the perfect shallow indentations fill with water. She looks over her shoulder, and sees a double trail of footprints, hers and Connor's, side by side.

A wet black dog with a red collar and three legs hops by, its tongue hanging from the side of its mouth, its feathered tail held low, but happy. It pauses to grin broadly at Fen and Connor and then carries on its way.

Connor cannot believe it.

'That dog, Mum!' he cries. 'What happened to its leg?'

'I expect it had an accident,' says Fen.

'I want a dog like that,' says Connor.

Fen can see where the sea starts now. It is as calm as glass. The fierce, fast-rising estuary tide seems like a myth in these flat shallows where the sea is so placid it can't even be bothered to break into waves. The sand has turned to darkish mud.

Fen has heard of accidents, children getting stuck in the soft, containing mud-sand when the sea was subdued and still and harmless, like this, and nobody panicking, because there was no obvious danger, and adults trying to dig the children out and the tide quietly turning while they struggled with the mud, and then, by the time they realized that the water was hurtling in, it being too late to summon help. Terrible stories. She holds tightly to Connor's hand. They reach the water's edge.

She stayed in the boy's tent all night, pressing herself against him, and they were both bony and their skin was cold. He coughed into his fist, and then he wrapped her in the damp blanket and held on to her, and the tops of her thighs were pressed together, hot and slippery.

Neither of them slept.

In the morning gloaming, she lay on her back under the blankets and wriggled back into her pants and her jeans.

'Where are you going?' asked the boy.

'Toilet. Can I borrow a jumper?'

'Sure,' he said. He squinted at her with one eye. 'You are coming back?' he asked. 'Aren't you?'

'Yes, of course,' whispered Fen.

She remembers squatting on her heels while she leaned over to kiss him and him putting his hand in her hair, pulling her head down, and how she felt a little sick and giddy, dry-mouthed, but also how she wanted to fuck him again, to have him

212

inside her with his weight on top of her and her hip bones sticking into him. She liked sex. It was all that stopped her feeling lonely.

'Bring me a mug of tea, would you?' he asked. 'And some fresh orange juice and a bacon sarnie and some hot toast and jam.'

'Yeah, sure!' she said, laughing, for these things were the stuff of festival fantasies.

She unzipped the front of the tent and sat down to put on her boots, then she zipped the canvas flaps together again and stood and stretched, gazing out across the site.

It was huge, a city of multicoloured tents – the hues soft in the early morning mizzle beneath a wide, low sky – with the great cathedrals of the stages dominating the central area.

There were curls of smoke here and there; people with carrier bags flat on their heads to keep off the rain squatted and poked at tiny, ineffectual fires, and others emerged from tents, yawning, stretching, rubbing their eyes, their hair all messed up, wearing layers of jumpers over pyjamas. They drank from plastic water bottles, lit cigarettes, brushed their teeth, hawked and spat.

It was like being part of an army on the way to battle, part of a huge army: everyone on the same side, everyone with the same goal.

Connor's little blue and green tent was in the middle of the field, packed close to its neighbours. Fen was careful to notice the long, triangular flag featuring the red dragon of Wales, which hung like a beacon from a pole on a nearby tent. She would use it as a point of reference. She fully intended to come back. She liked the boy, Connor. She planned to stay with him for the rest of the festival, maybe longer.

Picking her way between the tents, stepping carefully over the guy lines, it took her ages to find a proper path, and she wove such a circuitous route that she was soon disorientated. But she kept looking back over her shoulder, keeping an eye on the pointed flag.

Most of the site was still asleep, but as she came closer to the toilet blocks there were more and more people heading the same way.

Fen did not have to queue. She took a breath, pulled the neck of the boy's big jumper up over her mouth and nose, closed her eyes and went into the portable toilet.

Afterwards, she tried to find her way back to his tent, but she couldn't. There were Welsh flags everywhere and she did not know which direction she had come from. She walked for ages. She searched high and low, but in the end she had to give up, and although she scanned the faces of the boys at the site for the rest of the festival, she never set eyes on Connor's father again.

Connor insists on filling the bucket himself. It takes a while. Fen stands in the shallow water and watches it cover her feet. She watches how the pale skin goes faintly green and mottled when it's

214

underwater. She wonders where the water came from, where it's been.

She shades her eyes and gazes out. The two bridges to her right, further up the estuary, are hidden by the Weston promontory. To her left, in the distance and forming the other arm of the bay, is the silhouette of the recumbent hulk of Brean Down and, further out to sea, the dark islands: Steep Holm and Flat Holm. She can't remember the legend exactly but the islands are supposed to be the exposed head and shoulder of a giant who drowned himself in the estuary out of grief. He accidentally killed his brother or something.

'Look, Mum.'

Connor holds up his little yellow bucket and sloshes a couple of inches of water back down his arm. He squeals and jumps.

'Here,' says Fen, taking it from him. 'I'll carry it back for you, baby boy. We need to go back to our things now, the tide is turning.'

'I'm *not* a baby.'

'No, no, you're not.'

'Is it ten miles back as well?'

'At least.'

'Whoah!'

CHAPTER 28

'Fen, hi, it's me. Listen, would it be all right if I bring the family back to Crofters Road for a couple of hours?'

'Yes, of course.'

'Only they want to see where I live and . . .'

'Sure.'

'Mum's dying to meet you. I've told her all about you and she's really pleased for me. Well, us – she's pleased for both of us. She'll probably ask you loads of personal questions.'

'Oh, I—'

'You'll like her.'

'But I'm not at Lilyvale, Sean. I'm in Weston-super-Mare.'

'Oh.'

Something, some genuine disappointment in his voice touches her. It soothes the sore part of her heart.

'I told you I was going out for the day,' she reminds him gently.

'I know, I just thought that maybe you'd be back by now . . .'

'I'm sorry,' she says.

'Don't worry. There'll be plenty of other times for you to meet them.'

Fen sucks her lower lip. She looks down at Connor and smiles.

'Maybe we could go up for a weekend sometime? Would you like that?'

'Yes,' she says. She takes a breath. 'Say "hello" to them from me. Your family. Tell them I'm sorry I missed them.'

'I will. Fen . . .'

'Mmm?'

'I missed you today. I wish you'd been there.'

'Oh . . . I . . .'

'I mean I *really* missed you.'

Fen breathes very slowly.

'I don't know what's going on,' he says, 'but stay with me. Please . . .'

Fen says nothing.

He draws a breath. His voice changes. 'Well, look, have fun at the beach.'

'OK.'

'I'll save you some cake.'

'Thank you. Sean . . .'

'What?'

'Oh nothing. I'll see you later.'

She disconnects the call and holds the phone to her heart.

'What?' asks Connor. They are sitting on the promenade wall, eating hot dogs.

'Nothing,' says Fen. 'Just that everything is going to be all right. I shouldn't have worried. I should have known better.'

She leans down to squeeze and kiss her son.

'Oh, Mum . . .' He wriggles away. 'Stop it! Get off!'

CHAPTER 29

Connor is fast asleep in the buggy, his head to one side, his mouth slightly open. Fen looks tired. There are freckles on her cheeks and across her nose, her cheeks are pink and even her hair looks a little fairer. A tatty old straw hat slides down her back, its elastic loose around her neck. Her shoulders are sunburned. She smiles at Sean, and shakes her feet out of her flip-flops.

'Did you have a good day?' she asks as Sean helps lift the buggy into the hall.

'I did,' says Sean. 'It was great. Did you?'

'Yes.'

'Fen, I . . .'

'I got you this,' says Fen, passing him a white envelope with his name on the front.

He takes it and smiles.

'An Eastern European birthday card?'

'How did you guess?'

'Is there a cheque inside?'

'You'll have to open it and find out.'

'Thanks,' he says. 'Fen . . .'

'Yes?'

He takes a breath.

Fen blinks.

'I'm not very good at this . . . relationship stuff,' he says.

Fen looks at his hands as they turn the envelope.

'I know something's wrong and I don't know what it is but I don't want you to go and take up with some sweet-talking older man just because of something I said, or didn't say, or—'

'Sean, I will never stop feeling like I do about you,' she says simply.

'Oh.' He scratches his head. 'Wow. Thank you. But . . . what is it, then? Why wouldn't you meet my family?'

Fen looks at her feet. She is very gauche. Sean's heart rushes with affection.

'Lina said something . . . She wasn't trying to cause trouble, she just wanted to warn me . . .'

'About what?'

'She said that your sister told you to have an affair to make Belle jealous.'

Sean exhales. 'Yes, she did, and I did tell Lina, but that was before *us* . . . Oh Christ, Fen, you *know* it's not like that. You *know*.'

She nods. 'It's just . . . well . . . I didn't think I deserved to have anyone like you . . . I couldn't actually believe that anyone could like me that much, especially you . . . and when Lina told me, it sort of made sense . . . I thought—'

'Stop it,' he says.

She stares down at the top of the buggy. 'It's just

220

that we don't ever talk, do we? We're not the kind of people to say what we want or how we feel . . .'

'We don't have to. We know how we feel. Don't we?'

'Yes.'

He thinks for a while. Then he says: 'When I said I missed you today, well, it was the truth. It was like . . . um . . . it was like Sky Sports on Saturday without Jeff Stelling! That's how much I missed you.'

Fen looks up at him through her hair. She is smiling.

'You are a bloody idiot,' he says.

Later, in her bed, he combs her hair with his fingers and he puts his mouth close to her ear, so that the stud in the rim of its curl presses into his lip, and he whispers: 'Fen . . .'

'Mmm.'

'I've been thinking . . . It shouldn't be all about my family. What if I were to drive you to Merron? You and Connor? You can introduce me to your sister and the baby and show me around the city's fleshpots.'

'There are no fleshpots in Merron.'

'Don't be pedantic,' he says. 'I'm sure Connor would like to meet his cousin and we'll take photographs, and you and your sister, you'll both probably cry and—'

'Lucy won't cry.'

'You're doing it again. You'll definitely cry and

it'll all be lovely and then we'll find somewhere to go, on the coast maybe, and we'll have a little holiday, just the three of us. I'd obviously rather take you to Paris but, as you don't have a passport, it's the best I can come up with.'

She sighs.

'I don't know . . .'

'Oh, go on, let me take you. We don't have to stay long. We don't even have to stay overnight.'

'I suppose . . .'

'What's the worst that could happen?'

She thinks: Oh, if I told you that you wouldn't want to take me there.

'I've never been that far into Wales,' says Sean.

She turns in his arms, wriggles down the bed and he holds her close.

'Is it all ladies wearing lacy collars and pointy hats and fields full of sheep and men called Dai saying "boyo"?'

'Yes, that's exactly what it's like.'

He kisses her hair.

'I can't wait,' he says.

He closes his eyes and is at the point of sleep when the phone trills on the bedside table beside him. Fen groans. He turns over and picks up the phone and he can see from the number on the illuminated screen that it's Belle.

'It's Belle,' he murmurs.

'Aren't you going to answer it?'

'It's the middle of the night.'

'It might be important.'

Sean presses the green key.

'Belle? Are you OK?' he asks.

Fen slips out of the bed, switches on the light, unhooks her dressing gown from the back of the door and leaves the room.

Belle says: 'Yes, I'm fine. I just wanted to wish you a happy birthday.'

'At this time of night?'

'It's only eleven-thirty. When did you start going to bed before midnight?'

Sean smiles to himself. He squints his eyes against the light and touches the warm dent in the pillow where Fen's head so recently lay. He picks up a long fair hair and draws it the length of his lower lip.

'It's been a long day.'

'Was it a good one?'

'Yeah, it was great. The whole family came. And thanks for the guitar strap.'

'That's OK.'

There's a pause.

'Are you on your own?' Sean asks.

'Yes. Lewis is away.'

'Teaching?'

'Mmm.'

There is another silence. Sean hears Belle take a drink. He hears her swallow.

'Sorry,' she says. 'I'm a bit tired and emotional.'

He knows she is waiting for him to prompt her to tell him what's wrong. At the end of the hallway, the lavatory flushes. Fen puts her head around the door, sees he's still holding the phone, and disappears again.

'Belle, I appreciate you calling but . . .'

'I know. It's late,' she says. 'You've obviously got more important things to do than talk to me.'

'Belle . . .'

'I'll see you tomorrow afternoon,' she says, and Sean thinks he hears a sob in her voice. 'Membury, six o'clock.'

'Belle . . .'

It's too late. She's disconnected the call.

CHAPTER 30

F en checks her watch as she queues at the till. She looks at the dress folded over her arm – it's a pretty, dark blue, ankle-length sundress – and she smiles and touches the material. She can't wait to wear it. She pictures herself out walking with Sean and the children, she's wearing the dress, and the four of them, together, make a lovely picture in her mind.

It's the first time in a while that Fen has spent money on herself. Usually she relies on Lina's hand-me-downs and charity shops for clothes. The garments that end up in Bath's second-hand shops are generally of a very high standard, but still it's good to buy something new, something nobody else has ever worn. When she tried the dress on, Fen saw herself in the mirror as Sean sees her. She knows she's not as beautiful as Belle, she's nowhere near as striking, but she's all right. She has a nice body, her hair is better now she's had it cut, and her face is fine. Sean likes it. He smiles when he sees it. That's all that matters.

The girl behind the till smiles at Fen when it is her turn to pay.

'This is lovely,' she says, folding the dress on the counter, slipping it into a bag. 'I was looking at these the other day. I think I might treat myself.'

'You should,' says Fen. She thinks everyone should treat themselves. Everyone should be happy. Everyone should see the world for the beautiful place that it is.

With the bag in her hand, Fen threads her way back through the city.

She knows something is wrong as soon as she turns the corner into Quiet Street. Vincent is standing by the door of the shop, looking out for her. She's not late, she certainly hasn't been gone an hour. She quickens her pace.

His face, gaunter than ever, is hung in an expression of pure concern.

'What is it?' she asks as she trots along the uneven pavement.

'You forgot your phone,' he says. 'Now don't panic, but your sister called the shop when she couldn't get you on your mobile.'

'Lucy? What's happened? Is the baby OK?'

Vincent frowns. He opens his mouth but he says nothing.

'Oh my God! He's not . . .'

'He's in hospital. That's all I know.'

'Oh no! He's only a few weeks old! Oh, Vincent . . .'

'Hush! We don't know what it is; it's probably nothing to worry about. We mustn't think the worst.'

226

Fen allows him to guide her into the shop, and he passes her the telephone. She goes into the tiny kitchen, where there is a modicum of privacy, and calls Lucy's mobile. Her hands are trembling so badly that it takes her three goes to dial the right number.

'Lucy? It's me. Are you OK? How is William?'

Lucy's voice is tired and fragile and hoarse with worry.

'We're at the hospital. They're doing tests. They think it might be meningitis.'

'Oh God! What happened?'

'He was a bit hot last night but he slept OK. He slept all night and then this morning I went in and he was burning up and he had a rash and . . .' Her voice trails off into a sob.

'I'm coming up, Lucy,' says Fen. 'I'll be there this evening.'

'They aren't sure,' says Lucy. 'It might be nothing. They say it's hard to tell with little babies and he . . .'

'Lucy, darling Lucy, just try to keep positive. I'll see you later.'

Fen cuts off the call. She takes a deep breath. She dials Sean's number.

He takes a while to answer, and when he does his voice is low and guarded.

'Hi,' he says. 'Fen, are you OK?'

Fen has never called Sean during working hours before.

'Sorry,' she says, 'sorry to bother you. Are you in a meeting or something?'

'Sort of. What's up?' He sounds furtive, as if he's trying to prevent somebody else hearing what he's saying.

'Sean, you know you said you'd take me to Merron? Well, could we go now? Right now? Lucy's baby's ill. It might be meningitis. I need to get there quickly. I don't know what to do about Connor. I need you, Sean, I . . .'

She hears him exhale.

'Fen,' he says, 'I'm not in Bath . . . I'm, hold on, let me go somewhere I can talk.'

He sounds stressed.

'If you're busy,' she says, 'don't worry. I'll get the train.'

'No,' he says, 'no, wait, I'll come and get you. I just need half an hour to sort things out here . . .'

'I haven't got half an hour,' Fen says, trying to keep the frustration from her voice. 'I need to go now. How far away are you?'

'Swindon.'

'Are you with Belle?' Fen asks. He hesitates. 'OK,' says Fen, and he starts to speak but she disconnects the call and turns off her phone.

She does not have time to think about Sean. She takes three deep breaths and then she goes back into the shop and tells Vincent she has to go back to Merron.

He passes her a sheet of paper. 'Train times,' he says.

'Thank you.'

'All you have to do,' says Vincent, 'is call Connor's school and tell them Sheila and I will be looking after him for the next day or two.'

'Oh, Vincent, I couldn't ask you to do that.'

'You didn't. Go on, call them quickly. Leave me a key so we can pick up Connor's things. If you go now, you might make the three-thirty.'

'Vincent . . .' says Fen, but she can't finish the sentence because she is overwhelmed with gratitude and sadness.

'It's all right,' he says, 'I understand. Just go.'

There is no time to think, so the panic attacks that in the past have always forced her to turn back do not stop Fen this time. She goes to the station and catches the train and now the train is going under the Severn estuary.

She sits in the carriage, her forehead resting against the window. She feels the great weight of the water above her, the miles and depth of it, the immense, unstoppable expanse of it. The river has the second-highest tidal range of any river in the world. The estuary water is funnelled into the narrower channel of the river, invisible forces tug and suck it, and long after people have gone from the world, and when there are no trains and the tunnels have flooded and the bridges have collapsed, the water will still rise and fall and, on certain tides, the bore will still race up the river and elvers will turn the shallows black, as they used to.

The water weighs heavily on Fen. Only when the tunnel ends does she realize she has been digging her fingernails so hard into her palms that there are four perfect crescents of red gouged into the middle of each hand. She leans her head back, and exhales. If she narrows her eyes a little, she can stare into the reflection of her own face in the glass of the train window with the geography of Wales playing out behind it like a film.

Sean was in Swindon. He was with Belle. He didn't say he was going to see her. He didn't mention any plans or problems.

But he was in Swindon, with Belle.

And then Fen squeezes her eyes shut and hates herself for her self-centredness.

Baby William is in hospital, Lucy is worried out of her mind, the child might be very seriously ill, he might even be in a coma or something by now, and she's thinking about her own selfish heart.

The sky is still light when the train pulls into Merron station over the raised section of line that gives the best views over the city that Fen used to love. Still she almost does not get off the train. She almost stays put and travels on. She is afraid she will meet somebody who remembers her. She is afraid she will have to look into the eyes of Emma Rees.

Merron is a small city, made wealthy from silver and now in gentle decline. Its location and its lack of amenities mean it has never been a popular spot

230

with holidaymakers or second-homers or incomers seeking work, so the population is largely indigenous, a people set in their ways, and their ways set in solidly hard-working, religious foundations. They are intensely proud of their heritage, the kind of men and women who boast of never having taken a penny from the state, who would rather go without than humiliate themselves by asking for outside help. Their children are imbued with good manners, taught the difference between right and wrong at an early age. The young people don't go to church any more, but no matter how much they try to convince themselves, there's always the niggling doubt that God might exist, and might be watching. Generally, this keeps them in check.

A river that is smaller, politer and far more conservative than the Severn winds through the city beneath stone bridges topped with fancy ironwork. It has only flooded once in living memory, an uncharacteristic aberration that is still often discussed. The particular circumstances of the flood are the benchmark by which measures of contemporary rainfall are judged, memories of its inconveniences bring relief that nothing has ever been so bad since. The river is flanked by brick-built terraced cottages and factories that are derelict now because no investors have come along to convert them into fashionable apartments or unique office spaces. There's nobody to buy the flats or work in the offices anyway so birds nest in the old chimneys and plants self-seed in the cracks and crevices, and all the windows are broken and the factories have a kind of resigned elegance about them, as if they don't mind weathering away. They are as much a part of the natural landscape as the trees.

The cathedral still stands proudly in a city centre, and around it are the narrow shopping streets, although the shops are the usual mixture of discount stores, cut-price supermarkets and charity outlets. Merron College, where Fen's father used to be headmaster and where Alan now teaches music, is situated in its own grounds beside the cathedral, and these two venues, together with a Victorian town hall, form the triumvirate of sights described in the mid-Wales sections of guide books as 'worth seeing' in Merron. The school, in particular, founded in the seventeenth century with money generated from the sale of silver mined in the surrounding area, and extended regularly ever since, is a glorious hotch-potch of buildings of various architectural styles, the only common thread being ostentatious ornamentation.

Beyond the centre are the main residential areas, but with a population of fewer than twenty thousand people the city does not take up much space.

Fen musters all her courage, every ounce of it, as she steps off the train and walks out of the station. Everything is the same as it was. She remembers the smell of the pink flowers on the bushes growing along the footpath that winds down the hill from the station. She remembers the colours of the taxi-cabs and the concrete litter bin outside the newsagent's kiosk, overflowing with lollipop wrappers and discarded copies of the *Merron Gazette*. Fen is shocked at how familiar the city still feels. She had forgotten what kind of place it was but now everything comes back to her and engulfs her in a tidal wave of memories. Her legs feel weak and her fingers are cold. In her panic, her heart beats furiously, like the wings of a trapped bird, and she says a little prayer each time she turns a corner or sees a tired-looking, middle-aged woman walking towards her. Please, she prays, please don't let me bump into Emma Rees.

At the bottom of the hill, Fen crosses the main road. She sits on the bench and keeps her head down so that her hair shields her face from the eyes of passing motorists. She holds her bag tightly on her lap and waits for the bus that will take her to the hospital.

She prays again, to no particular god.

'Please,' she whispers, 'please let the baby be all right. Please don't let anything bad happen to him.'

When she was young, Fen dreamed of leaving Merron, just as Joe and Tomas did, but her dreams were always vague. She was never one for making plans. She imagined, indistinctly, saying goodbye to her family as she boarded a train to Somewhere Else. She hoped she'd end up doing something worthwhile, preferably something rather glamorously dangerous. She imagined people talking about her in voices tinged with admiration and jealousy. They'd say: 'That Weller girl, do you know what she's up to now? She's rescuing South American street children!' or 'She's protesting against Amazonian deforestation!' or 'She's with Greenpeace, stopping the harpooning of whales!'

It didn't happen at all like this. After her father died there was no reason for Fen to stay in Merron, and plenty of reasons for her to go. She slunk away, saying goodbye only to Lucy and Alan. She didn't know where she was going, or what she was going to do. She never wanted to return. She thought it would be better for everyone, especially Mrs Rees, if she was not around: out of sight, out of mind. The reasons why she left are still valid. Fen is not sure if there will ever be a time when they don't matter any more.

Through the grimy windows of the bus she watches Merron city centre travel in a leisurely, stop-start fashion that is in keeping with its personality. Her memories are everywhere, lurking in the shadows on the pavements, tangled up in the railings, at the bus stops and in shop doorways. She sees small groups of teenagers, and they remind her of her younger self and Joe and Tomas. The young people are sharing chips from the paper, standing slouch-shouldered in the cinema queue and sitting on the steps outside the Spar, nudging one another, pulling at their sleeves and socks and hoods, their heads so close they share the air they breathe. She watches them. She feels a great tenderness for them with their brave insouciance and their shy bravado. She sees a group of boys in Merron College uniform, the grey trousers and blue blazers. They are carrying cricket bags and waiting for a coach. These boys stand taller. They are more privileged but no less vulnerable. She touches the glass of the bus window, but she can't touch the past.

Fen remembers her sister; she remembers why she's here. She wishes the bus would go faster, and at the same time she does not want to reach the hospital, in case she has to look into Lucy's face and see the worst.

She tries to be calm. She knows that babies are resilient. She knows that, mostly, high temperatures do not indicate serious illness. Only sometimes they do. She wishes Sean were with her; he is good at taking the logical, rational viewpoint while she is apt to imagine all kinds of terrors. He says she is an expert in dreaming up worst-case scenarios, and he is right, but he doesn't know that it's not her fault. She can't help it. She feels a twinge of pain in her heart.

Fen asks the driver to drop her at the hospital entrance, and she thanks him when the bus judders to a stop and she steps down.

An emaciated old man in striped pyjamas and a blue dressing gown is standing outside the doors

235

speaking to a girl who is wearing a green dress that strains at her waist and is stained under the arms. The man is attached to a drip. He is smoking a cigarette. As Fen passes he doubles over, wracked with coughs, and the cigarette burns between the yellowed knuckles of two fingers on the hand that clutches his stomach.

The automatic doors open. Fen steps aside for a man with a cast on his leg coming the other way.

'Sorry,' she says, 'sorry.'

It is getting late now, but still people are coming and going: a pale, acned teenager with no hair or eyebrows, a woman in a burkha holding the hand of a child, and two young men in combat gear, one of them weeping, the other rubbing his fist between the shoulder blades of his friend. Fen scans the area quickly but there's no sign of Alan or Lucy. There's no sign of Mrs Rees.

She crosses to the reception desk and waits for the attention of the woman behind it. 'Hurry up, hurry up,' she says to herself, but the woman takes her time.

'Yes?' she asks, after an age.

'I've come to see baby William Kelly. He was admitted this morning.'

'You're family, are you?' asks the woman.

'He's my nephew,' says Fen. Her palms feel clammy and her mouth is dry. She wishes she'd bought herself a drink at the station.

'Are you all right?' asks the receptionist. 'You're looking a bit pale yourself.'

'I'm fine,' says Fen.

'William Kelly . . .' The receptionist's face has a greenish tinge from the computer screen in front of her. 'You say he was admitted . . .'

'He came into A and E. I don't know what happened after that.'

'Ah yes. Here he is. William Kelly, Thomas House, Merron College. Oh . . .' she says. 'I'm sorry, dear, he's been transferred to the Special Care Baby Unit.'

Fen feels the blood drain from her. 'Oh my God,' she says. There are pins and needles in her fingers and her knees go weak. The hospital reception tilts suddenly and she holds on to the ledge beneath the window to stop herself falling.

'Sit down,' says the receptionist. 'Sit down, love. I'll call someone to come and look after you.'

CHAPTER 31

It's midnight. Sean stands in the living room, drinking coffee.

He cannot sleep.

There was a note on the kitchen counter when he came home. It was signed Sheila, and it said: 'Connor's with us. Food in fridge.'

Sean does not know who Sheila is. He does not know where Fen is, only that she's in Merron. He hopes to God that the baby is all right. He knows he has let Fen down and he is furious with himself for this, but he's also annoyed that she didn't give him a chance to help. He would have taken her to Merron, of course he would. She should have let him speak. If she'd let him explain, she would have understood. Now he feels lonely, he feels useless, he feels as if something has been torn from him. He does not know if he should drive to Merron anyway. He would find the hospital, but he is not sure if he would find Fen. Her family might regard it as wholly inappropriate if he were to turn up in the middle of their crisis. He doesn't know if they even know about him. He does not know what to do.

This is the first time since he has been lodging with Fen that she has not been here, at home at night. And it's weird. It's only a small house, but without Connor, without Fen quietly doing what Fen does, it feels like a mansion. It is full of empty space where Fen and Connor should be. It has dark corners and heavy hollows. It echoes like a cave.

Sean has called Fen a dozen times, but each time he has been connected to the digital voice of her answerphone, asking him to please leave a message.

He said: 'Hi, it's me. Hope everything's OK. Let me know if there's anything I can do.'

He said: 'Fen, please call me, please let's talk.'

He said: 'I could drive over and meet you, if you'd like me to.'

He said: 'I miss you.'

Her phone may not be ringing because its battery is flat. Fen's charger is still plugged into the socket behind the armchair in the living room, where she always leaves it. But Sean knows that's not the reason why the phone is turned off.

Earlier, he went for a run. He ran to release all the stress hormones from his body. He ran to get rid of the excess adrenaline in his bloodstream, to diffuse his anxiety, to make himself think straight again. He ran along the rim of the city, keeping to the roads that run straight along the

239

side of the hill that curves around the westerly edge of Bath. He ran past elegant terraces, past the backs of hotels where the maids still wear ankle-length dresses and aprons, past shopkeepers watering their newly planted hanging baskets, past groups of teenagers sitting on walls, talking self-consciously and spitting on the pavements. Sean ran all the way to the top of the golf course, and then he stood panting in the shade of one of the grand old trees, his hands on his knees, catching his breath. He bought a bottle of water, then sat on the grass and watched the families playing pitch and putt while expensive cars purred up the hill to the exclusive houses behind.

He jogged back more slowly, showered, and went to the pub for chicken and chips and a couple of beers.

He should be tired after all that.

But he isn't.

Everything goes round and round in his mind. He takes his guitar out of its case and plays a few tunes. More time goes by and eventually Sean dozes on the settee covered by his leather jacket, his legs curled up behind him and his face on a cushion.

He is woken by the trilling of his phone, and spends an age finding it in the pocket of his jacket.

'Hello?' he mumbles. 'Hello? Fen? You OK? Fen?'

There is silence at the other end, but there's somebody there, Sean knows there is.

'Fen . . . ?'

The person at the other end disconnects.

'Shit,' says Sean. He squints at the face of the phone, but his eyes are still sleepy and won't focus. After several attempts, each tetchier than the last, his fumbling fingers manage to find the call log. It doesn't help. The number of the last call received was withheld.

'Shit,' says Sean again.

He yawns, scratches his crotch and shambles into the kitchen, switching on the light and screwing up his face against its brightness. The back door is ajar, and moths speckle the outside of the light shade. Sean pushes the door shut and locks it. He pulls the window closed and locks that too. Then he draws down the blind.

The room is chilly. He switches on the kettle, and is leaning on the counter, his eyes closed, waiting for it to boil, when the phone rings again. This time it's on the counter, jumping with its vibrations. Sean stares at the phone. Number withheld, it says on the screen. He lets it ring five times and then he picks it up and answers but says nothing. There is silence at the other end too, but he can hear somebody holding their breath.

'Fen?' he whispers eventually and immediately the call is cut off.

Sean switches the phone off with his thumb and bounces it down on the counter. It spins on its face.

It was Belle. He knows it was Belle.

CHAPTER 32

The two sisters sit in the light and airy day room attached to the SCBU. Lucy is feeding William and Fen keeps her sister company, sipping lukewarm tea from a cardboard cup.

'Thank you for coming,' says Lucy, for the twentieth time. 'It means the world to me that you're here.'

Fen smiles. 'Of course I came.'

'I didn't think you would. I thought you'd have one of your turns and chicken out, like you always do.'

Fen looks away. Lucy does not know why it is so difficult for Fen to be in Merron. She thinks Fen is just being lazy, or awkward, or maybe even throwing some kind of drama-queen act.

Lucy looks up. 'Now you've made the journey once, you'll be able to come again, won't you? You'll be able to bring Connor to stay with us.'

'I don't know. Maybe,' says Fen. She changes the subject: 'Did you get any sleep last night?'

Lucy shakes her head. 'Not really.'

'Didn't they give you a bed?'

'There's a room for parents, but I didn't want to be in it, I wanted to watch over William. I thought if I took my eyes off him for a moment he might stop breathing . . .'

'You need to rest, Lucy.'

'I can rest at home. Honestly, Fen, I thought we were going to lose him.'

Lucy looks down at her baby. She touches his forehead with her fingertips.

'You can't imagine how frightened I was yesterday when he was so hot and ill. Alan kept telling me to stay with it, but my mind insisted on thinking the worst. I kept running through what would happen if it was meningitis, what the consequences might be, you know?'

Fen nods. She knows.

'And when they told us they were transferring him here, to the Special Care Baby Unit, I thought: "That's it, he's going to die." I was planning the music we'd play at his funeral.'

Lucy sighs.

'I was thinking about Emma Rees. I was thinking that I've only known William for a few months and already he is everything to me, and that poor woman had Joe for twenty-two years, and she didn't have anyone else, did she? I don't think I ever really understood before, how she must have felt when she lost him.'

Fen turns her face away.

'I mean I felt sorry for her, of course I did, but I didn't really get it. I was outwardly sympathetic at Christmas, you know, but there was a bit of me thinking: "Oh, come on, it's been ten years. Move on."' Lucy shakes her head. 'I should be ashamed of myself,' she says.

Fen wipes her eyes with the wrist of her sleeve. Lucy doesn't notice; she's engrossed in her son.

'William does look a bit better, though, doesn't he?' says Lucy. 'The nurse said his temperature's normal again. She said she thinks he's over the worst.'

Fen nods and manages a smile. 'He's looking much better.'

Lucy is sitting in a faded old wing chair by the hospital window. Fen can just see the baby's hand patting his mother's swollen breast. She can hear the contented little clucking noises he makes as he sucks. Through the window, she sees the shrubs and trees in the walled garden beyond, nodding and shaking in the wind. Little grey clouds are sketching across the blue sky and rooks are in the air.

Fen is wearing her sister's clothes: a pale green jersey dress that falls to mid calf and a lemon-coloured cardigan that smells of fabric softener. She should have picked up the dress she bought in Bath yesterday, but she must have left it in its plastic bag on the counter in the bookshop. She stares at the baby's hand and misses Connor. She misses Tomas. She misses Sean.

Lucy pushes her glasses up the bridge of her nose, and unhooks the baby with her little finger. 'Greedy little boy,' she says affectionately.

She sits the baby upright, his head lolling drunkenly between her thumb and forefinger, and rubs his back. The baby has a stupidly content expression on his face.

He burps and a bubble of milk forms between his lips. The bubble swells and glistens, and then it pops. His eyes roll.

Lucy leans down and kisses the baby's head. She wipes his mouth with the cloth she'd been holding beneath his chin, and picks at his cradle cap for a few moments with a sleepy expression in her eyes. Then she seems to wake up. 'How's your shoulder?' she asks.

Fen touches her back. It hurts where she fell in the hospital reception area and banged it. It's stiff and achy. It embarrasses her.

'It's OK.'

'You'll wait with me, won't you, Fen? Until the doctors come round? Then if they say we can take him home, we can go together.'

'Of course I'll wait,' says Fen.

She would rather be here, in the hospital, than outside on the streets or at the college. She wants to be with her sister, but also she feels safe here because the Special Care Baby Unit at Merron Royal Infirmary is the last place on earth where she would expect to see Emma Rees.

Lucy and Alan live in staff accommodation provided by Merron College. Their house faces the tree-lined street that connects with Aberaeron

Road at the front, and the back garden is separated from the college playing fields only by an old, red-brick wall.

It's not as grand as the house where Lucy, Tomas and Fen grew up when their father was headmaster, but it is more comfortable. It is lighter and has been refurbished within the last decade, so tastefully double-glazed windows and solar-powered roof panels now sit alongside the ornate cornicing and the fancy end gables. The carpets are plush and new and everything in the kitchen works efficiently and without fuss.

After William was discharged, Lucy called Alan, who fetched them home from the hospital. Now he has gone back to the school, and Lucy, who is exhausted, is running herself a bath. Baby William is sleeping in his carry-seat on the living-room carpet.

Fen wanders over to him and feels his forehead with the inside of her wrist; their blood is the same temperature. She smiles, and leans down to pull his blanket up to his chin then, left to her own devices, she wanders across the room to Alan's meticulously polished grand piano. She looks at the framed photographs displayed on top. There is one particular picture of her parents that Fen likes. Her mother is laughing, posing for the camera, while her father, Gordon, stands beside her. He is looking at Mari with the greatest affection and she, so much younger and so much more vivacious, seems almost oblivious to him. A few photographs track the years they had together. There's a picture of Mari holding a baby who looks just like William in her arms, and she's smiling down at the baby – Tomas – and Gordon, with his hand on her shoulder, is smiling down too. They both look very proud. Lucy, a curly-haired, chubby little girl with clips in her hair is standing next to Gordon with her thumb in her mouth, looking slightly sad.

Mari gave the children their names. Tomas after some Portuguese footballer she used to hero-worship, Fen after the part of Cambridgeshire where she first met Gordon, and Sky, which is Lucy's real name but from the age of about five Lucy flatly refused to answer to it, and told everyone that her name was Lucy.

Fen first makes an appearance in a school photo-graph. It was taken at primary school the summer after Mari left. Fen and Tomas are together in front of a paleblue canvas screen that is supposed to represent the sky. They are wearing matching, slightly grubby, white polo shirts and red jumpers, and are sitting head to head, grinning at the camera as if they don't have a care in the world. Fen re-members the teacher tidying her hair for that photograph and making Tomas take off his jumper and put it on again, because he was wearing it inside out. Fen is missing her top two front teeth and Tomas's teeth look too big for his face and have not been brushed in a while. There is a crust of sleep in the corner of his eye. Fen looks at the picture and smiles back at the two unkempt children with affection.

The next picture is a large photograph of Gordon and his revised family standing primly outside the grand arch at the formal entrance to Merron College. It was taken when Gordon was appointed to the role of Headmaster. Now the children are clean and immaculately dressed. Fen is wearing a blue coat and tights. She is skinny, slope-shouldered, nine or ten years old. Lucy's hair is cut in an unflattering bob. She looks shy and uncomfortable in her new glasses. Between his sisters Tomas is smiling proudly for the camera. Gordon's new, improved wife, Deborah, stands beside him holding his hand. Gordon looks imposing and confident. Deborah looks exactly as the wife of the headmaster of one of Britain's leading independent schools should look. She looks like an attractive, well-dressed, middle-class woman who is devoted to, and very proud of, her clever, much-respected husband and who is doing her best for his wayward children.

Fen puts the picture back on top of the piano. She wipes her hands on the side of her dress and looks out of the window for a few moments, watching the finches at the feeder. Then she crosses to the bottom of the stairs and calls up quietly, so as not to disturb the baby: 'Luce? Is it OK if I call Vincent?'

And Lucy calls down: 'Of course. You don't have to ask.'

So Fen phones the Gildas Bookshop and Vincent

says everything is fine and that Connor was no trouble whatsoever last night; the only problem is that Sheila is already besotted and might not want to give him back.

'Thank you both so much,' says Fen. 'I don't know how I'll ever make it up to you.'

'It's our pleasure,' says Vincent. 'Oh, and that young man of yours was in earlier, worrying about you. He wants you to call him. He said it was important.'

'Did he?' asks Fen, and she looks at herself in the mirror over the telephone table, and combs her hair with her fingers.

'I know it's none of my business but he looked, frankly, dreadful. He looked like he hadn't slept. You two haven't fallen out, have you?'

'No,' Fen says quietly. 'No, of course not.'

When she has finished speaking to Vincent, she takes a couple of deep breaths and then she dials Sean's number.

She is connected to his answerphone. She doesn't even have the pleasure of hearing his voice, just the virtual lady telling her to leave a message.

She apologizes. She says she's sorry for not speaking to him last night, then she summarizes William's dramatically improved health in a couple of sentences, and says she'll text him to let him know when she's coming back. She does not tell him that she misses him and wishes he were here with her.

★   ★   ★

In the late afternoon, after Lucy has rested, the two sisters go for a walk. Lucy pushes the baby in his buggy, and Fen walks beside her, one hand on the handle. Lucy has an old-fashioned notion that fresh air is what William needs. She believes it will do him good. They walk along pavements, past buildings that Fen has known all her life, along roads that are so intrinsic to her history she imagines they must be embedded in her DNA. They don't go anywhere near the suburbs where Joe used to live; Lucy and Alan's house is in a different neighbourhood altogether.

It is such a long time since Fen has been on her own with her sister that she finds the intimacy awkward. Although they speak of superficial, trivial things, Fen has an urge to unburden herself and to confide in her sister. She feels like a little child again and she has to hold herself back. She isn't sure if it would be appropriate to start being honest with Lucy now, after so many years of lies. She does not know where the boundaries are, whether complacency should trump propriety, or vice versa.

'How long is it since we were alone together, like this? Without it being somebody's wedding or funeral?' asks Lucy, reading Fen's mind.

'Ages. Not since before you went to university.'

'Twelve? Fifteen years, then?'

'I suppose.'

Lucy sighs. 'That's awful.'

They walk a little further.

'I feel like I've let you down,' says Lucy.

'Me? No! Of course you haven't.'

'I haven't been much there for you, have I?'

'You've always been so busy, Luce. You had Alan and your job and the school to look after.'

'And who's been looking after you?'

Fen shrugs. 'I don't need anyone to look after me. I've been fine. Mostly . . .' Then she tries to take the bull by the horns. She says: 'Only, we never really talked about the things that matter most, did we? You and me, I mean . . . We've never talked about the accident . . . about Tom and Joe . . . the accident . . . that night . . .'

Lucy turns to her sister and smiles. 'Alan and I, well, we always think it's best not to look backwards, not when the past is different to how you wish it was. Sleeping dogs and all that. There's no point opening old wounds, is there?'

'No,' says Fen quietly. 'Of course not.'

Lucy says: 'You should always turn your face away from darkness and towards the sun. That's more or less what the Bible teaches. It's not a bad philosophy, is it?'

'No,' says Fen. 'Only . . .'

'Deborah came over last month,' Lucy says briskly. 'Did I tell you?'

They both know she didn't.

'She's looking really good, for a woman her age, and after all she's been through. The Aussie lifestyle obviously suits her.'

'Mmm.'

'She asked after you. She said to give you her love.'

Fen watches her shoes.

'And,' says Lucy, 'you'll be pleased to know that Emma Rees went out there earlier this year and stayed for a month. She had a lovely time. Deborah took her out into the Blue Mountains and they went to the opera and walked over Sydney Harbour Bridge. Deborah didn't say as much but I'm pretty sure she paid for Emma's ticket.'

'That was kind.'

'It was,' says Lucy.

They walk along in silence for a while.

'Deborah's a good person,' Lucy says. 'She was the best stepmother we could ever have had. She did so much for Dad . . .'

'Yes, I know.'

'I don't think Dad was an easy person to love.'

'I *know*. I was there too.'

Lucy gives her younger sister a hurt look.

'Sorry,' says Fen.

'All right,' says Lucy, 'all right. Change the subject. What about you, then? Are we allowed to talk about you? What's new in your life?'

Fen picks a leaf off a shrub at the side of the road, crushes it and sniffs her fingers.

'Actually,' she says, 'I've met someone.'

'Goodness,' says Lucy, and then she adds quickly: 'Someone nice?'

'Yes, very nice. He's my lodger. He has a daughter a little older than Connor.'

'Single parent? Divorced?'

'Separated.'

'Oh.'

'It's all right, Lucy, he was separated before I met him. He's still getting over it, but he's much better now than he used to be.'

Lucy measures her words.

'Fen, are you sure it's not just a rebound thing?'

'Yes.'

'Darling, you don't have much experience of this kind of situation. How do you know?'

'I just do.'

'Fen . . .'

'If I try to explain you'll think I'm mad.'

'I won't.'

'You will. Because if somebody tried to explain it to me I'd think they were exaggerating . . . Or imagining the whole thing, or something.'

'Try me.'

'It's just that, when I'm with him, it's as if I'm where I was always supposed to be.'

Lucy leans over, squeezes Fen's elbow and kisses her on the cheek. 'There you are,' she says, 'you explained that very well.' She seems genuinely, deeply pleased. 'Still,' Lucy adds, 'you be careful. Marriages are complicated, messy things. Sometimes they look like they're over when in fact they're not; they're just having a lie-down.'

They walk a little further. Fen isn't concentrating on the route and when she raises her eyes and sees that they are on the street where they used to live, she is surprised at how ordinary it looks.

In her mind, whenever she remembers the last weeks in her father's house in Merron, she remembers a dark, gloomy, oppressive building on a long, cold street. She remembers wet pavements, black hedges, dark evenings and gloomy facades, pale-faced people in sombre winter clothes, their quiet, sad voices, one funeral after another, the volume on the radio turned down low. She remembers Deborah's damp handkerchief bunched on the dresser, the gentle foot-steps of the palliative nurse, the hair in the priest's nostrils and his habit of jingling the change in his trouser pocket. She remembers the smell of bleach and bedpans and flowers rotting in their vases, the air chilling around the damp fabric of coats hooked on the stand in the hall and the spatters of water droplets on the parquet beneath the folded umbrellas, the endless cups of tea and the steam on the windows. She remembers, one day after another, having to be brave for her father's sake and not mentioning Tomas, how she felt as if she were wearing a corset pulled too tight all the time, how she could not breathe, she could not properly feel because she was so constricted and . . . Deborah.

Deborah was always at her side, squeezing her elbow. Deborah was saying things like: good girl, well done, now make another pot of tea, it's important to be positive. Deborah was brisk, she was always busy, she never seemed to sleep and, sharp-eyed like an eagle, she watched Fen; she watched her and she chivvied her along and made sure she held herself together.

It didn't change the facts, though.

Fen's poor father was dying and she was unable to look into his face because all she could see was Tomas's face reflected back at her and, beyond that, her terrible, terrible guilt.

Now she's here again and nobody she knows has died in ages, years, and she sees that it's just another street lined with large, attractive, bay-windowed houses built in the 1930s. It's quite pretty with all the trees in leaf and flowers in pots in the small front gardens.

The sisters stop in front of the house where they used to live. It's been looked after and tastefully modernized; everything is neat and tidy and in order.

The hedge that Tomas used to hide behind has gone. The front garden has been paved to provide off-road parking. There's a child's tricycle parked inside the open, arched porch; a paper note is tucked under a glass milk bottle on the step; the same coloured glass is in the fanlight above the door.

Fen looks up to the window of what used to be her old bedroom. Football stickers frame the window. She remembers what it was like before the stickers were there, how it felt to be Fen, inside the house, looking out to Tomas, who was standing here, where she stands now.

It doesn't feel like the place where something terrible happened. It feels normal. She is amazed to find that there are no ghosts here.

It's this, this normality, which gives her courage. She turns to her sister and touches her arm. She says quietly: 'Lucy, what I said earlier . . . We never talked about the accident and I need to tell you what happened with Joe and Tomas. I need your help . . .'

'Our doctor lives there now,' says Lucy, moving her arm slightly to dislodge Fen's fingers, walking on so seamlessly that Fen honestly is not sure whether her sister heard what she said or not. Something about Lucy's posture, her demeanour, reminds Fen of Deborah. 'She's a specialist in mental health, she's very nice. Her husband has written a book about model railways. They have twins.'

CHAPTER 33

Sean walks up and down outside the railway station and watches the diggers and the men working on the redevelopment of the shopping centre; the old post-war, concrete shopping mall and the coach station were demolished months ago and now the foundations are being laid for replacements which will be more in keeping with the rest of the city. All the planners will need to do then, thinks Sean, is sort out the gasworks which dominate the western side of central Bath.

Wearing yellow hats, industrial gloves and boots spattered with concrete, the builders are working under artificial lights, to move things on. They seem to be acting independently, each focusing on his own job, but they've already moved so much, changed so much. Sean likes watching. He has enjoyed watching the mechanics of construction since he was a child. It's not his line of work, the deep-piling and the steel-framing and the concrete-pouring, but still it gives him pleasure to watch. A concrete-mixing lorry is churning away in the corner, but the long arm of the crane is motionless overhead now. In its monstrous shadow the men, with their rolled-up sleeves exposing their sinewy forearms, gesture to one another and spit the dust out of their mouths. It's like watching a film, but better, thinks Sean, because there's so much going on at the same time and it's real. It's construction; it's dynamic, creative. And all this activity takes his mind off Fen. It takes his mind off how he will feel when he sees her again.

After a while, an eastbound train rumbles in on the tracks behind him and stops at the platform with a screech of metal on metal. He tucks the newspaper he hadn't been reading into the bin and steps forward to meet Fen.

She is towards the back of the crowd coming off the train and he doesn't recognize her at first because she's wearing unfamiliar clothes – an ankle-length green dress and a yellow top – and she is walking awkwardly, limping, and her eyes are downcast. He holds up his hand and waves to her, and when she sees him her step quickens.

He is still not used to Fen. He would recognize Belle anywhere because he knows her so well. If she was among a crowd, no matter how big, his eyes would find her, they would seek her out, identify the contours of her face, the cut of her hair and the arch of her eyebrows.

Fen is still new to him. He had forgotten how slight she is. He had forgotten how young she looks, the length and fairness of her hair, the shape of her eyes.

She reaches him through the crowd and smiles.

He puts his arms around her and she leans into his shoulder. Her hair smells different. Somebody else's clothes, somebody else's shampoo.

'It's good to see you,' he says.

'And you.'

'You look knackered.'

She scratches her ear. 'I'm OK.'

'God,' says Sean. 'I wish you wouldn't go on about yourself so much.'

She watches her feet. They walk out of the station and along the street.

'You've been so self-obsessed you haven't even mentioned the baby.'

Fen relaxes against him. 'The baby's fine.'

'We had something like that with Amy when she was tiny. She was burning up. I drove to the hospital in the middle of the night and we had the car windows open, and that cooled her down so by the time we got to A and E she was perfectly OK and screaming for a feed.'

Fen says, 'It's what they do, babies. To keep you on your toes.'

'I guess.'

Sean exhales. 'So what's he like, this William?'

'Cute. Ugly-cute. Where are the children?'

'That nice lady from over the road, Mrs Amini, is looking after them. Connor was in bed before I left and she was teaching Amy how to play cribbage.'

'We ought to get back.'

'She's got my number,' Sean says, patting his

259

pocket, 'and she's going to call if there's any problem. I thought we could go and get something to eat.'

'Are you sure she doesn't mind?'

'I'm sure.'

'Only,' Fen says, holding out the skirt of the dress she's wearing, 'I can't go out in these clothes. I look like a case study from *The Watchtower*.'

'It's all right,' says Sean. 'Prim, but sweet.'

'Really? I feel like my sister.'

'I'm sure your sister's lovely.'

'She is, but in a . . . cardiganny sort of way. And also I'm wearing her shoes because I lost one of mine when I fell over in the hospital. And they're too small and my feet hurt.'

'You fell over in the hospital?'

'I fainted.'

'God,' he says, 'you're such a drama queen.'

He takes her to a little restaurant overlooking the river. They sit on the terrace holding their menus. Fen gives her order to the waiter and then, after sipping her water, she takes a deep breath and says: 'Sean, why were you in Swindon with Belle the other day?'

He puts down his beer and wipes his upper lip.

'It was Amy's school sports day. And when she saw us there together, Amy's teacher asked if she could speak to us in private. That's what I was doing when you called.'

'I'm sorry,' says Fen, 'I'm really sorry if I sound

like I'm being paranoid, but why didn't you tell me you were going?'

'I wasn't going to. Belle said she and Lewis were going together and then she called me that morning and the plans had changed. She was upset and I wanted everything to be good for Amy, that's all. I would have told you about it when I got back.'

'Sean . . .'

He holds his beer in his hand.

'I have to communicate with Belle,' says Sean. 'I have to be a team with her, for Amy's sake. Her teacher's worried about her. She seemed to be coping with the separation at first, but the teacher said that lately she's become very withdrawn and quiet. We've got to try harder with her. We've both let her down. We were in the classroom when you called and Miss Simpson, that's the teacher, gave me a filthy look when the phone rang as if I was failing to put my daughter at the top of my priorities again. If it had been anyone else but you, I wouldn't have answered.'

Fen understands. She understands and is flooded with selfish relief.

'What are you going to do, then, about Amy?' she asks.

'I'll take as much time off as I can during the school holidays. We can do things together, you, me and the children. We'll have some days out. Longleat, Cheddar, Wookey Hole . . . Christ, there are loads of places round here just waiting to take

261

our money off us. It'll be educational,' he says, wagging a finger at Fen and putting on an advertiser's voice, 'and fun!'

They eat grilled prawns with their fingers, watching the moonlight rippling on the water and bats hunting moths. As the evening wears on, Fen relaxes. She laughs, she fidgets, she is animated and sparky. Sean is as attentive as he can be. He does his best to make her forget about Belle. He tangles his fingers in Fen's soft hair and cups her cheek in the palm of his hand. The feel of her delights him. He feels her in his hand, and also in his belly, his brain, his toes. He feels her everywhere. He slides his hand down her cheek and she kisses it with oily lips, and then he leans forward and he kisses her. Her eyes are bright and sleepy, her smile lopsided from the wine and the relaxing.

'Do you know,' he says quietly, 'that you are a beautiful woman?'

'If that was true, you'd have noticed me ages ago. And you didn't. It took you months to realize I even existed.'

'I was blinkered,' he says. 'I was an idiot. And you didn't exactly make it clear that you were interested in me.'

'I wasn't.' She smiles coquettishly. She is slightly drunk. 'Not until I saw you in the shower.'

'Oh, please, can we forget the bloody shower?'

'It was an iconic moment.'

'If I'd known you were looking . . .'

'Sean, you couldn't have been any sexier. You couldn't have put on a better show.'

'Thank you.'

'My pleasure.'

'And mine.'

They smile at each other in a congratulatory way. They eat lamb with sautéed potatoes and summer vegetables and drink more wine. Sean holds Fen's hand in his lap and as he holds her hand he feels that he wants to look after her. He won't let people hurt her. From now on, he'll be there when she needs him.

After dinner Fen takes off her shoes and they walk along the river back into the city centre. The reflections of the fairy lights strung along the moored boats dance in the rippling water, and everywhere there seems to be music. Laughter comes from rooms whose doors are left open to admit the cooling summer air, from outside pubs and clubs, from upstairs rooms and from basement flats. There's laughter and music and light everywhere. Even the traffic seems to be cheerful tonight. The leftover warmth of the sun radiates from the pavements, walls and balustrades. The city is alive and beautiful.

She holds on to his arm.

'I'm tired,' she says. 'Will you carry my shoes?'

'Of course I will, Fen,' he says. 'Of course.'

They walk the usual route, up Snow Hill and along Tyning Lane past the health centre. They stop every now and then to catch their breath and to look back over the city, to see how far they have travelled, and also to make the walk last a little longer. Their fingers are linked.

Sean is amazed.

He is amazed at how easy everything is with Fen.

Everything is easy.

Mrs Amini is asleep in the armchair when they get back, her book face down on her lap and her spectacles on the chair arm. Sean is touched to see that she has had a little clean round, but doesn't thank her. He hopes Fen thinks he alone is responsible for the tidier-than-usual state of the house.

Mrs Amini refuses to take any money.

'They are such good children,' she says, holding her hands to her heart. 'Both so polite, so obedient. You must be very proud.'

'Are you talking about *our* children?' asks Sean.

Mrs Amini gives him a flirtatious little push to the chest.

'Oh you,' she says.

They watch her across the road, back to her own house, and then Fen locks the doors. Sean checks the windows quickly. Then he holds out his hand to Fen.

'Oh, Sean,' she says, 'I'm tired to the bones.'

'It's all right. I'm only going to wash your feet.'

She sits on the edge of the bath, her sister's skirt trailing in the water, its hem darkening, while he, sitting beside her with his trouser legs rolled up, cleans each of her feet in turn with the shower head. Every now and then he glances at her face and he sees that her eyes are heavy, she is almost sleeping. He works the soap between her toes.

'Filthy,' he mutters, leaning forward for a kiss. 'You can't get into bed with feet like that.'

He runs out the dirty water and goes downstairs to fetch the wine that he left in the fridge, and when he comes back she is standing, naked, under the shower. The curtain is drawn, so her lines are not clearly defined, but he sees the shape of her and the way her wet hair travels down her back. She is using her own shampoo, pulling herself back into her life, out of the past and into the present. He opens the window a fraction to let out the steam and pulls back the shower curtain. She is bruised on one side of her back, a blooming, spectacular bruise like a flower running from her shoulder to her spine. She can't have seen it, so he says nothing. He does not want to alarm her.

Instead he asks gently: 'Do you mind if I join you?'

'This is where it all started,' she says.

'Yes, I suppose it is.'

He does not undress. The desire to touch her is too strong. He climbs into the bath and steps under the shower fully clothed and she laughs, but only for a moment, for he finds her mouth with his, and he finds her breasts, all slippery and warm. His shirt is clinging to him, and they're both soaked and soapy and kissing, with water in their mouths.

He whispers, 'Can I?' into her ear and she whispers, 'Will you rinse my hair first?' so he does. He unclasps the shower head and rinses her hair carefully, and when the suds have run down her body and are all congregated around the plughole, he lifts her, still soaking wet, and carries her the short distance to her room and he lays her on the bed, on her unbruised side, her wet hair soaking into the pillow, and he climbs onto the bed beside her and stares at her and thinks: I cannot believe this beauty is all for me.

Then he stops thinking. He says: 'I will be so gentle you'll hardly know I'm there,' and she smiles and holds out her hand to him, and everything blurs into the hot, sweet, manwoman healing thing that is sex.

CHAPTER 34

He fetches a towel from the airing cupboard and rubs her hair, because she's shivering. He lifts the duvet for her and she wriggles beneath it. Then he climbs in beside her and holds her tightly, to warm her, his body knuckling into hers.

'Do you want to talk about it?' Sean combs her hair with his fingers.

'What?'

'Why you never talk about your family.'

Fen shrugs.

'Go on,' he says. 'Tell me.'

'I can't.'

'You can.'

'I can't. It would change us.'

'How would it?'

'Because you wouldn't feel the same about me.'

Sean sighs. 'Try me.'

Fen turns away from him a little. He feels her tense. Her fear is like a presence in the room, it's like somebody else is there, watching them.

'You don't know what happened to us,' she says.

'No, I don't. So tell me. It's your brother, isn't it?

Something happened to make your brother go away?'

She makes no sound but her head moves a little. It's a nod.

'What was it?'

'There was a car accident. Joe – Joe was Tom's . . . his best friend – and he . . . Joe died in the accident. Tom went away because it was the only way to protect me because . . . Oh, Sean, it was all my fault . . .'

'Hey –' her hair is cool as it slides between his fingers, cool and silky – 'come on, it can't have been all your fault. I know you, Fen. I know you would never do anything to hurt anyone. Not on purpose. Whatever you did, it can't have been that bad.'

'Oh, it was,' she says. 'It was the worst thing you can imagine.'

Sean holds his breath for a moment. 'Tell me,' he says.

Fen shivers. She thinks back to the previous day and how she wanted to confide in Lucy, and she remembers what Lucy said.

'No,' she whispers. 'I can't.'

They are both quiet for a long time. Sean says: 'What you're ready, you can tell me. Whenever that is.'

Fen says nothing.

'Are you tired?'

'Terribly.'

'I'll watch you,' he says, 'until you sleep.'

'Thank you.'

He kisses her and puts his head on the pillow beside hers so that his cheek rests on her hair and he waits. But later, when he looks again, her eyes are still wide open and she's still staring at the wall.

CHAPTER 35

Sean is walking through a tunnel, down the middle of a railway line, the tracks polished by wheels on either side shining in the light of his torch. It's pitch-black inside the tunnel, dark as death and strangely warm, the air static. It's a long, brick-lined, Brunel-designed Great Western Railway tunnel. It's more than a century and a half old, and soot from the furnaces of the old steam-engined trains has stained the interior a black that's deep and as plush as velvet. Sean flashes his torch on the arch-shaped walls as he walks and the project manager walks beside him, the two men stepping from sleeper to sleeper, as the manager explains about the seepage through the brickwork, and what kind of structural repairs are needed.

Behind them the engineers who were safety-checking the rails are clearing the track, ready for when it goes live again and the next train comes through.

'This is where the problem starts,' says the project manager. 'This is where it's really bad.'

Sean crosses to the wall, flashes his light up at where the water's coming through. The soot has been washed away, and there's slime on the brick-work which has eroded and loosened.

'That can be fixed,' he says. He checks his watch. 'How much longer do we have?'

'Twenty minutes.'

'I'll take some pictures but we'll need to come back next time the line's closed. When's the next possession?'

'Not for a couple of weeks.'

'Let me know. We'll do a proper survey.'

Sean finds his camera, angles it so that the water won't reflect back into the lens, and takes some pictures.

The manager's radio crackles. There's a testy exchange of words. Sean nods; he understands that they have to get out.

'There's a tunnel at Box,' says the project manager, 'and it's said that if you stand at the western end you can see the sunrise at the eastern end on Brunel's birthday.'

'Is it true?'

'Don't know,' said the man. 'But it's a beauty of a tunnel. Two miles long, perfectly straight. Thirty million Wiltshire bricks lining the inside. And all of it blasted by hand and the spoil taken away by horse and cart.'

'Blimey.'

'They don't know they're born, the labourers these days,' says the project manager.

Sean shakes his hand, then he goes back to his car and sits down to unlace his boots. He records a brief summary of the morning's events into his phone, then switches it to Bluetooth and throws the handset onto the passenger seat. He is on the A46, on the way back into Bath, when the ringtone broadcasts out through the car speakers.

It's Belle. Again.

'Hi,' he says.

'Hi. Sean, I wanted to apologize for calling you so late the other night. I was feeling a bit sorry for myself and wanted to hear a friendly voice and I know you were probably . . .'

'It's OK. Listen, I'm in the car, Belle. Can I call you later?'

'Oh,' she says. Her voice drops. 'Aren't you on hands-free?'

'Yes.'

'Well, that's all right, then. I just wanted a quick word.'

'Go on.'

She pauses. She gives a nervous little laugh. 'This is difficult,' she says, and then she takes a deep breath and continues: 'It's Amy's birthday next Saturday, as you know, obviously, and I . . . well, I thought it would be nice if we spent it together, all three of us, as a family.'

Sean holds his breath.

'I can't, Belle, I'm sorry but . . .'

'You hadn't forgotten it was Amy's birthday?'

'No, of course I hadn't. But I wasn't expecting to see her. You told me you were going to be in Cornwall.'

'Well, our plans have changed. Lewis is going on his own.'

'Oh.'

Belle sighs. There is a silence. Sean spots a lay-by, indicates, and pulls over. He turns off the engine. A magpie is picking at road-kill at the junction between the lay-by and the road. Lorry drivers and police officers in hi-visibility jackets are socializing by the burger bar. The traffic on the main road goes by.

Belle speaks again. 'She's going to be seven, Sean. This is an important birthday for her. I want her to have happy memories.'

'I know. But—'

'I've given up my week in St Ives. You can at least spare a day, can't you?'

'I'm doing something else.'

'Oh.' The hesitancy and warmth evaporate from her voice. 'So you've got something more important to do.'

'Belle,' he says, 'this is the first time in nearly a year that you've called to suggest something like this. I wasn't to know.'

'It's the first time since we separated that Amy's had a birthday.'

'And you told me you were taking her to Cornwall. I'm sorry, but I've promised to do something.'

'With your new girlfriend?'

'Yes.'

'And her child?'

'Yes.'

'How am I going to explain that to Amy?'

Exasperation rises in Sean like bile. Somehow he is in the wrong again. Somehow he has found himself in the role of uncaring father, selfish ex-husband, bastard man.

'Belle, you're twisting things,' he says, and although he can't justify this statement he knows he has been unfairly out-manoeuvred.

Belle replies in a calm, measured voice. 'Honestly, I'm glad you're moving on, really I am, Sean, but after everything that was said at the school, now that we *know* our daughter has problems, don't you think she should come first? Especially on her birthday?'

'What were you thinking of?' Sean asks slowly.

'We could do something special, something she'll always remember. Maybe spend the day at the zoo?'

Sean sighs. He looks at the reflection of his eyes in the glass of his car windscreen. Amy is his only child. His only chance.

He pushes his hair back with the flat of his hand.

'She'd be devastated if you didn't make the effort for her.'

This he feels like a fist in his belly.

Belle is silent. She knows she has achieved her goal.

'I'll sort something out,' he says. He ends the call. He turns off the phone.

He gets out of the car and goes to stand at the

side of the road, staring through the traffic at the countryside beyond, the lovely Cotswold hills and valleys. The air smells of exhaust fumes and fried onions. The men at the snack van, standing like cowboys with their legs apart, hold the paper-wrapped burgers with their two big hands as they chew their meat and watch him.

He was going to take Fen and Connor out into the countryside. He was going to walk with them alongside the Kennet and Avon canal. He was going to show Connor the narrowboats, maybe take him for a ride on one, and watch Fen's face as she marvelled at the beauty of the valley below Limpley Stoke, sunlight dappling her hair. They were going to pack a picnic and a blanket, and after a while they'd leave the canal and walk by the river instead, and perhaps find somewhere where they could swim and Connor could paddle. He had believed he would not see his daughter on her birthday, so he had planned an alternative that would help keep his mind off what he was missing. He had promised Fen another perfect day and now he must let her down.

CHAPTER 36

Fen nibbles around the edge of a sweet-corn cob. A line of butter glistens down her chin.

'When I was little,' she says, wiping her chin with her hand, 'I saw a film and these children were playing hide and seek in a maize field. I thought it looked like the best fun. And then we were on holiday and there was a maize field there so I went and hid in it and it was horrible.'

Sean raises an eyebrow.

'Tomas and Joe were supposed to come and find me but they didn't, they just wanted to get rid of me for the afternoon. They were fed up of me tagging round after them. But I couldn't get out of the corn. Because what you don't realize is that in real life you can move up and down the lines, but you can't get in between the canes; they're like trees. I was too small to see over the top and I was disorientated. I couldn't remember which way I'd come in.'

'What happened?'

'Huh?'

'How did you find your way out?'

'I can't remember. I must have done.'

'Well, you're here now.'

She puts her feet on his lap. 'Yes I am.'

'More wine?'

'I thought you'd never ask.'

He plays with the little silver chain around her ankle. Traces the daisy-chain tattoo with his fingertip. He has been quiet all evening.

She senses more than hears him take a deep breath and she thinks: Uh-oh.

'Belle called today,' he says.

'Again?'

'Yes. You know it's Amy's birthday next week?'

Fen wriggles with pleasure at the thought of what they have planned. 'They're going to Cornwall, aren't they?'

'There's been a change of plan.'

'Oh.'

'I'm sorry, Fen.' Sean holds her calf with his hand. He says: 'We're thinking of going to the zoo. Belle thinks it's important to give Amy some quality time. She's given up her holiday so we can be together, as a family, for Amy's sake.'

She adjusts immediately. She says brightly: 'Amy will like that. It's a good idea.'

'Fen . . .'

'We can walk the canal another time.'

He says: 'I know this is shit, I know it's a mess, but it will sort itself out. We'll get to some kind of status quo and then—'

'It's OK. I understand.'

'You don't have to be so understanding all the time. If you want to be angry that's fine. Scream at me, shout at me, tell me not to go.'

Fen looks up at Sean, and then down again.

'It's Amy's birthday,' she says. 'Amy needs you.'

'What about Connor?'

'I haven't made any promises to him.'

Fen takes her feet off Sean's lap. She begins to stack the plates.

Sean looks up at her. She smiles back brightly but inside she feels the old anxiety wake and stretch itself. What can she do? She can't ask Sean not to spend the day with Amy. She can't tell him about the fear that's nagging away at her, the instinct that's warning her that her happiness is being threatened. She can't tell him to stay away from Belle because she knows Belle does not, cannot, love him as she does. All she can do is look into his eyes and reassure him that he is doing the right thing for his daughter, because he is.

She leans down, cups his cheek with her hand and kisses his lips, his warm and garlicky lips.

'Leave the dishes,' says Sean. 'Leave them.'

They go upstairs, into her bedroom, and he draws the curtains and takes her hands to pull her to him. She steps forward and their bodies meet. They kiss and he strokes her hair, smoothing it down her back; she puts her hand on his neck to bring his head down so that she can reach his lips. He presses against her.

She knows that her desire for him turns him on,

she knows this and she wants him to make love to her, she wants it very badly. She wants him to prove to her how he feels. She wants him to commit his body to hers.

She finds his belt buckle, unfastens it, sits on the edge of the bed and one by one undoes the buttons on his jeans. They are straining. She finds him with her fingers, strokes him, then leans forward.

'Fen,' he says, 'you don't have to do that.'

She looks up. 'I want to. I like it.'

'No. No, wait.'

He sits beside her on the bed. He puts his arm around her and pulls her close to him. She puts her face into his chest and breathes in the warmth of him.

'Listen,' he says, taking her head in both hands, and holding her so that she has to look at him. 'Listen, I've told you a hundred times and I'm telling you again. I don't want Belle, not any more, not at all. I don't want to be with her, I don't want to sleep with her. I don't much like her. And it's reciprocal. Belle doesn't want me. She hasn't wanted me for a long time.'

Fen nods.

'Is that clear?'

She smiles. 'Yes.'

He leans down then and kisses her and they make a pact with their bodies. And although she is not convinced by what Sean said, Fen thinks that's the best that either of them can do for now.

★   ★   ★

She lies beside him with her head on his chest and she feels and hears the beating of his heart beneath her ear. She runs her fingers up and down his chest just for the pleasure of her skin being so close to his. He is twining his fingers in her hair. She is naked, but she doesn't feel vulnerable. There's a sexy, musty smell to Sean's skin.

'Tell me,' he says. 'Tell me what happened with Tomas and Joe. Tell me why you feel so responsible.'

'I can't.'

'You can.'

'It would make things worse,' she says.

'How do you know? You never talk about it. You just think about it and you've probably got it all out of perspective. If you told somebody, if you told me, maybe it wouldn't seem so bad.'

Fen sighs.

'Listen,' he says, 'that night when I lay here, on your bed, and talked about me and Belle, well, it changed everything. It turned me round. Once it was out of my system, I could move on. And I have.'

'But you hadn't done anything wrong.'

'Fen,' says Sean, 'whatever happened, whatever it was, you were just a kid, you weren't responsible for your brother. Nobody is responsible for any other person's life.'

'No, you're wrong. We *are* responsible for the people we love,' Fen whispers. 'That's the whole point of everything.'

'Then just tell me the beginning of it. Tell me when it started to go wrong.'

'I don't know when it started.'

'What about the drugs? When did you first know your brother was into drugs?'

Fen remembers. She was fifteen. It was the summer holidays, night-time, and she was asleep in her bedroom in her father's house in Merron. She was woken by a noise, like gunshot, just above her head, and then another noise. She was frightened and she almost screamed for her father, but she heard a familiar whistle and realized that the noises were pebbles bouncing off the panes of her bedroom window.

She slipped out of bed, drew back the curtain, looked out and saw Tomas, standing in the middle of the road, swaying like seaweed in the tide.

She crept downstairs. The stairs were old, creaky, taletelling stairs that threatened to give her away. She didn't dare turn on the hall light. She opened the front door carefully and Tomas stepped through.

He embraced her. 'Fen,' he whispered.

He held on to her. His breathing was strange.

'Tom, what is it? Are you all right?'

'Oh,' he sighed, 'I've never been so good.'

'What is it?' she asked, suspicious. 'What's wrong with your eyes? Tom, what have you done?'

He held a finger to his lips.

'Tom!'

'Fen, it is so amazing. It is such a beautiful feeling.'

It was as if he had undergone a religious transformation. He was evangelical. Fen had never seen him like this before. And he smelled strange. Everything about him was weird.

'You have to get to your room,' she whispered. 'Come on.'

'You don't understand. It's beautiful and for the first time in my whole life I feel like I—'

'Come on, you're scaring me,' she said, more firmly. She put her arm around his waist and pushed him, and slowly they went upstairs together.

'Do you need the bathroom?' she asked.

'Yes, no, dunno.'

Fen pushed him through the door, leaned against it, slid the bolt and pulled the cord to turn on the light. She knew Tomas had taken or smoked something he shouldn't have, but she was afraid to ask the question outright. And she was even more afraid of her father, or Deborah, coming along to investigate.

'Hurry up, Tom,' she whispered. 'Brush your teeth. You probably ought to lie down.'

She turned her back so he could use the lavatory, and chewed at her fingernail.

'Tom . . .'

'Sorry, Fen, I don't feel too good.'

He was sick. Horribly sick. Their father must have heard for moments later there were footsteps on the landing and knocking on the door.

'What's going on in there?' he called. 'Is everything all right?'

'Tom's poorly,' Fen called back. 'It's probably something he ate. He'll be OK in a minute.'

'Should I ask Deborah to come?'

'No,' said Fen. 'No, don't worry. I'll look after him.'

Sean sighs. He plays with Fen's hair.

'So you looked after Tomas. That time and all the other times?'

'I tried to.'

'Was it heroin?'

'Later it was. I don't know about then. It wasn't something we ever actually talked about. Tom using drugs was always there between us, but we used to do our best to ignore it.'

'I know that feeling,' Sean says quietly. 'Go on,' he whispers. 'Tell me what happened to Tom after that.'

For a long time, more than three years, Tomas was a functioning addict. He managed to keep his life going; he went to university and completed his degree. He did it for Gordon. He made his father proud. Lucy still has the photo of Gordon and Deborah standing on either side of Tomas in his robes and mortarboard on the day he graduated, and everything looks absolutely perfect. Nobody who did not know would ever guess that anything was wrong.

After that, Tomas found a flat in Manchester and Joe went to join him. Joe was bright and clever and he could have done anything, but what he wanted to do, what he believed he had been put on the planet to do, was to be with Tomas.

★   ★   ★

'Were they lovers?' asks Sean.

Fen shifts herself up onto her elbow and gazes down at him.

'How did you guess?'

'Just the way you talk about them. It's kind of obvious.'

'It was a secret,' she says quietly.

Sean snorts. 'Why?'

'Oh, Sean, Merron isn't like Bath. It's isolated. It's set in its ways.'

'Surely it's not *that* medieval.'

'You'd be surprised. And at the college, it being a boys' school, anyone who was the slightest bit different used to get bullied. You couldn't show any sign of weakness, any vulnerability . . .'

'Too much protesting?'

'It was a very macho place. And our father – he was the headmaster – was forever writing assembly speeches subtly condemning . . . you know, *that* sort of thing. He didn't want any sodomy going on in his school. Not on his watch, that's what he meant.'

'But it must have gone on.'

'It did. And it wasn't that Tomas was ashamed or anything, but he was just worried there'd be a scandal if people knew the truth.'

Tom had read cruel things in the papers; he knew how people would talk, and point fingers. He wouldn't have minded what people thought of him, but he was worried about his father's reputation, and Joe. He was afraid of the damage the truth

284

might do to him and his mother. Mrs Rees worked in the college kitchens. She was very upright and God-fearing, very proud. Both families were vulnerable.

'Who else knew about their relationship?'

'They had friends in Manchester. But in Merron nobody knew. Only me.'

'Were they very close?'

'Oh yes. They were soulmates.'

Sean reaches up and strokes the side of her cheek with his knuckles.

Fen's hand rests still on Sean's chest. She can feel the vibrations of his heartbeat beneath her fingertips.

'Did Joe take drugs?'

'No, never. He hated them. When they started living together he helped Tomas get clean. I always thought Joe would be the making of Tom. He loved him so much. And once they were in Manchester, when Tom was normal again, they were so happy.'

'So what went wrong?'

Fen sighs and lies back down on the bed. Her head sinks into the pillow. 'My father became ill,' she says. 'It was cancer. Tomas had to come home.'

CHAPTER 37

Connor has a physiotherapy session in the pool. Fen is in the water, warm as a bath, watching what the therapist does so that she can replicate the exercises. Connor loves the water, and he is noisy and physical. Fen likes seeing him in this environment; he's such a boy, naughty, splashing the therapist and then behaving as if the splash movement was involuntary.

'I'm on to you, Connor Weller,' says the therapist, pulling a mock-cross face and wagging her finger.

Connor laughs again. Fen leans back into the pool. The ends of her hair float around her. She fingers the golden M and looks down at her legs which are distorted, white, rippling in the water. She thinks of Sean and she twists the chain round and round her fingers and she drifts.

She thinks of the things she can't say aloud to anyone, and she wonders if Sean is right. She wonders if it is time to let go of her secret. She could tell Sean what happened the night Joe died. He would understand. But there is somebody else she should tell first.

Connor squeals and splashes and the noise echoes

in the chlorinated, hot atmosphere of the hospital pool and yet Fen hears nothing. She thinks of her brother, falling. She wonders what was in his mind. The room, the pool chamber, revolves around her in slow motion as she bends her legs and immerses herself, then drops right down so that the water covers her face. She keeps her eyes open. Chemicals sting her eyes and she sees colours and movement, distorted, beautiful and unshaped, like underwater kaleidoscope patterns; in the bubbles and waves and currents she hears the underwater winds and the strange sounds that remind her of whale-song.

Her body wants to rise. The air in her lungs pulls her to the surface. Her feet won't balance on the tiled bottom of the pool. She straightens her legs and emerges from the water. She pushes the hair out of her face with her two hands.

'Watch this, Mum!' says the therapist, and she lets go of Connor, who gamely doggy-paddles to the side of the pool, holding his chin high out of the water, laughing and gasping for breath all at the same time.

'Hooray!' Fen calls, clapping her hands together. 'Hooray for Connor, the best boy in the whole wide world!'

CHAPTER 38

A my has her nose pressed up against the window. She's watching the sea lions dive and swim. Her hands are flattened against the glass on either side of her face. Each time she exhales she clouds up the window in front of her mouth. She is transfixed by the movement of the creatures, by their sleek, muscular ballet, by their eyelashes and their snouts. Sea lions are her favourite animals. She loves them in the water, and out. It is her ambition, one day, to be the keeper of the sea lions at the zoo.

Belle takes her camera out of her handbag.

'Go and stand beside her,' she says to Sean.

He obliges, feeling awkward, like a boy in a new school uniform.

'Amy, Mum wants to take a picture. Turn round for a moment,' he says, nudging his daughter.

She doesn't hear him. Or else she ignores him.

Belle takes a picture anyway. Then one of the wardens offers to take a picture of the three of them together, and Belle comes to stand on the other side of Amy. The resulting shot, when they look at it on the little screen at the back of the camera, shows the two adults smiling self-consciously, leaning their heads towards one another above the child, who stands oblivious, with her back to the camera and her fingers star-fished against the window.

'That one's my favourite,' she says. They all look exactly the same to Sean. 'That one's called Ariel. The big one is Nancy and the one with the cut on her tail is called Keisha.'

'They're all girls?'

'Mmm.'

Sean watches for a moment. He can see why Amy likes the sea lions. They seem to be enjoying themselves in the water.

'When I'm looking after the sea lions, I'm going to wear a wetsuit and swim with them,' Amy says. 'I'm going to be one of their family.'

'What? You're going to eat *raw fish*!' Sean exclaims, raising his eyebrows. 'You're going to swallow them whole?'

Amy shoots him a withering look.

'Just because you're in the same family doesn't mean you have to eat the same things.'

'No,' Sean agrees, 'it doesn't.'

He looks behind him. Belle is sitting on a bench, holding her bag on her lap. She is gazing into the middle distance.

Sean feels not quite right, as if he's drunk or dreaming. He and Belle are behaving with artificial politeness and courtesy. Conversation between them is stilted, every question seems loaded, every answer evasive. They have to be careful not to touch on subjects that could accidentally hurt the other, or prompt the memory of some lie or argument or even some good time that they shared. Belle seems to be finding the situation as awkward as he is.

Sean wanders over to the bench, sits down and offers Belle a piece of chewing gum. She shakes her head. Sean thinks they are behaving like a Victorian couple who have just been introduced and who know nothing about one another, not two adults who shared the same bed for eleven years. He rests his elbows on his knees and folds the gum wrapper into a tiny square.

'You're looking really good,' she says eventually, with a tentative smile. 'The bachelor life obviously suits you.'

'I'm doing OK.'

'Your shirt is ironed.'

Sean looks down. He hadn't noticed. 'That must have been Fen,' he says.

'You've got her well trained.'

A shiver of irritation Mexican-waves through his body, from one set of fingertips, via his brain, to the other.

'It's not like that,' he says.

'No. Of course not.'

She pauses then asks: 'So is it serious? You and her?'

It feels entirely inappropriate to Sean to discuss Fen with Belle.

'I don't know,' he says, to buy time, but even as

the words come out he recognizes their ambivalence. 'Yes,' he says quickly, 'yes, it is. I mean I'm serious about her. She's been very good to me. She's all that's got me through these last months.'

Belle nods. 'Thanks for rubbing it in,' she says. 'Actually, I know what I did to you.'

'Look, I'm not trying to be difficult, but you asked and—'

Amy is beside him, patting his shoulder.

'Daddy, the man said they're going to feed the sea lions at three o'clock and I told him I wanted to be the person who looks after them when I grow up and he said I can give them a fish so I can practise!'

'He never did!'

'He did! And I said it was my birthday and he said I can give them two fishes! And I said I wanted to give Ariel the fish because she's my favourite and he said . . .'

Belle stands; she walks away.

'That's fantastic, Ames!'

Sean watches Belle's back, her defeated air. She walks away, out of earshot. Then she looks up, towards the sky, as if she is taking a couple of deep breaths. God, that woman knows how to wind him up. He puts his hand on Amy's shoulder, then rubs her arm affectionately.

'Amy, is Mummy all right?'

'Mmm . . . only she cries sometimes when I'm in bed.'

'She cries?'

'Yes, she's sad because Lewis has moved out.'

'Oh.'

'At first she cried all the time and then Nanna Amanda came to stay and she took Mummy to the doctor and he gave her some pills to make her better.'

Sean swallows. 'Oh dear.'

He looks again at Belle, standing some way away. Then he takes Amy's hand. 'Come on, you,' he says. 'We ought to feed you before you feed those sea lions.'

They run to catch up with Belle, then they walk through the zoo gardens together.

'So how is everything with you?' he asks his wife.

'Fine. Everything's fine.'

'I haven't had any letters from your solicitor,' he says, keeping his voice low so Amy can't hear.

'No.'

Sean waits, but Belle does not expand on this.

'Amy told me Lewis has left,' he says gently.

'Yes.'

'Was there somebody else?'

Belle bites her lip. She says to Amy, 'See that giant tortoise over there? You run ahead and we'll catch you up.'

When Amy is out of earshot she sighs. 'No, there was no one else. It would have been easier if there had been. I asked him to leave. I couldn't stand living with him.' She laughs in an ironic and knowing way. 'He turned out to be an arrogant pig,' she says.

'He never stopped talking about himself and his work. It was so . . . wearing.'

'Oh.'

'I don't think he really cared for me. I was something of a trophy, that's all.'

'I'm sorry,' says Sean. 'I'm sorry it didn't work out.'

Belle glances at him sideways. 'Thank you,' she says. 'It means a lot to me that you still care.'

They walk over to the tortoise pen where Amy is watching a giant tortoise eat a tomato, masticating with regal solemnity.

'How're your . . .' Belle and Sean say together, at the same time, and they both laugh.

'My parents are good. They went on their first cruise,' says Belle, 'in the Med. Spending my inheritance. How's Rosie's fashion business doing?'

'It's just a cover for her unhealthy obsession with the early 1970s. I don't think she makes any money but she gets to email David Essex fetishists worldwide.'

Belle laughs. She clutches her handbag.

'Darragh puts up with it,' says Sean. 'It leaves him free to play unimpeded golf.'

Belle laughs again. It's a false, brittle laugh.

Sean does not like to see her like this. Oh, it's true that she drove him mad with her superior, supercilious, patronizing act when she was with the Other, but he prefers that to this nervy unhappiness.

As they walk through the gardens Belle wants to stop and look at the flowers and read the labels, but Amy is impatient and neither parent can refuse her any whim today. Their joy in their daughter is the only thing they have left that is mutual and pure. Amy bobs between the two of them, insisting on walking in the middle and holding their hands; she is the link between her disconnected mother and father.

They walk among similar families, men, women, children. They are part of the pattern. Sean finds the conformity intensely relaxing. He fits. He belongs. He knows how to act this role.

Amy looks sweet today, in yellow shorts and a yellow T-shirt appliquéd with daisies. Her hair has been cut into a shorter bob. Her eyes and her eyelashes are so pretty, so dark, her little features so neat. Sean squeezes Amy's hand and feels a swell of pride in his heart. She won't be a child forever. He determines not to waste a moment of his time with his daughter, no matter what the circumstances.

'It's nice to be together again, as a family, isn't it?' says Belle.

'Yes.'

'We should do this more often,' says Belle, smiling down at Amy. Amy is skipping, swinging on their arms.

'I would like pesto for my lunch,' she says. 'Pesto and pasta and tiramisu.'

'It's her Italian phase,' says Belle.

'*Per favore*,' says Amy. '*Ciao. Mi chiamo* Amy Scott. *Ho sette anni.* Yesterday I only *ho sei anni.*'

'Very good!' says Sean. 'Where did you learn all that?'

'Lewis taught her.'

'Oh.'

'And,' says Amy, 'I've got my first wobbly tooth. Look, Daddy!' She stands in front of him and opens her mouth wide, using her forefinger to press one of her front teeth. Sean detects no movement but pretends that he does, and praises her to the ends of the earth.

They eat a pleasant lunch in the zoo's delightfully old-fashioned restaurant and then Amy badgers to go on the play equipment until the adults give in.

'Amy, the whole point of a zoo is the animals, not the slide,' Sean says. 'We might just as well have gone to the park if all you want to do is play.'

'I don't want to be in Bath today,' says Amy.

Sean nods. He strokes his chin. He watches as she climbs the ladder, agile in her yellow sandals. She is growing. Her legs are long and slim, tanned. She's going to be a beauty, like her mother.

As the day wears on, Sean relaxes into it. The sun warms the air; even the animals seem sleepy, content. The flamingos, with their exaggerated, salmon-pink, question-mark necks, pose as if enchanted by their own reflections, and the inscrutable but friendly-faced okapi stands dreaming of open spaces it will never know.

Amy puts on an apron and a pair of comically large, heavy-duty rubber gloves and helps a thin young man with a bucket and a microphone feed

295

the sea lions. She holds a decapitated fish by the tail and one of the sea lions, perhaps Ariel, claps its flippers to beg for the fish. Amy drops it, the sea lion catches and swallows it and the assembled audience applauds. Afterwards, Amy tells her parents that it was the best moment of her whole entire life.

Sean and Belle slip back into how they used to be, together, sharing the same space comfortably, predicting each other's movements because they know one another so well, and have done for so many years. More than once, Sean has to stop himself from reaching out and taking Belle's hand. It's the way his brain and body have been wired. It's a difficult habit to break, but habit is all it is.

They stop beside the meerkat park. Amy gazes over the wall. Belle takes a compact from her handbag and touches up her lipstick. She raises her chin and purses her lips and peers into the little mirror. There are only a few years between them, yet she seems infinitely more adult than Fen. She's confident and graceful and elegant in her movements. She feels Sean's gaze on her face and turns to smile at him. She gives him one of her best smiles, one of her all-encompassing, beautiful smiles.

'I've missed you,' she says very quietly.

'Don't,' says Sean.

'I'm so sorry for everything. I wondered if we—'

Sean shakes his head. 'No, don't,' he says. 'Don't say any more.'

'You don't know what I was going to say.'

'Whatever it was, there's no point. It's too late.'

She nods, and then turns away again. Her eyes are glassy. Sean feels helpless. He does not want Belle to be unhappy, but how can he help her? Frustration digs its claws into his back. After all she's put the family through, after so much heartache and grief, why can't Belle be satisfied with what she has? If he had let her continue, would she have asked him to come back to her? Is that where this whole day has been leading? Was Belle's intention to entice him with a snapshot of his old, perfect family life and then seduce him with her remorse and vulnerability?

She's walking away again, on her own, with an air of abject resignation.

Amy looks up at Sean over her shoulder.

'What's wrong with Mummy?'

Sean does his best to give his daughter a reassuring smile. 'Nothing,' he says. 'Nothing's wrong.'

But Amy's buoyant mood disappears. She deflates in front of him.

'Then why is she crying?'

Sean sighs. He doesn't know what to say. He holds his daughter's gaze; he can't lie to her but he can't tell her the truth either because the truth is far too complicated.

The zoo is starting to empty, there are strange animal calls in the air and Sean's sense of being in a dream mutates slightly. Now he feels uneasy. He feels as if he's in some kind of nightmare. He feels responsible for his daughter. He has to do something to make things all right again.

He squeezes her shoulder.

'Come on,' he says, 'it's time we were off.'

'We can't go yet. We have to go to the reptile house.'

'We've been to the reptile house.'

Amy shrugs off his hand. Now her voice is high and whiney. 'Yes, but we didn't see the . . . thing . . . you know the thing we didn't see because they were cleaning its cage.'

'The iguana.'

'Yes.'

'I think the reptile house is probably closed by now.'

'And we didn't see the gorillas.'

'We did.'

'No, we only saw one, and there's a whole family, you said. You said there's a baby gorilla, Daddy. You *promised*!'

Sean looks across the gardens. Belle is some way away now, standing on her own again. He crouches down so that his eyes are level with Amy's. From this perspective it hurts him to see the anxiety in her face.

'Come on,' he says again.

He stands, picks her up and puts her on his shoulders as he used to when she was a toddler. Her legs come down almost to his waist. She squeals and holds on tightly to his hair.

'The plan,' he says, 'is to find Mummy and then we'll go to the shop and see if we can buy you a toy sea lion, and after that we'll go somewhere nice for dinner.'

CHAPTER 39

The lights are off and Fen is curled up in the armchair watching an old Hitchcock film on television when he comes in. Her sewing box is on the carpet beside her, its lid open, different fabrics and threads spilling out. She enjoyed a thrill of anticipation when she heard his car pull up on the road outside – she recognizes the sound of the engine – and her heart skipped when she heard the clanging of the gate, his feet on the steps and his key in the door. Now she smiles at him sleepily, her chin in her hand.

'Hi,' he says, leaning down to kiss her. He smells of baby powder, of Amy.

'Did you get my message?' he asks.

She nods. Her eyes flick back to the television screen.

'Amy asked me to go back and read her a story and . . .'

Fen looks back at him. 'I know. I'm glad you were there to tuck her in on her birthday.'

'Yeah.'

'Are you all right?'

'Is there any beer?'

299

'I think so.'

'Are you having one?'

Fen glances at the television. Cary Grant has just found out that Eva Marie Saint is in mortal danger. He's hiding upstairs in the house she shares with evil-but-charming James Mason, who is moments away from killing her.

Fen looks back at Sean. He stands in the doorway. He looks . . . defeated.

'OK.'

Fen switches off the television and follows him barefoot into the kitchen. She chews at the side of her thumbnail. He does not turn on the light. He opens the fridge door and the front of him is illuminated. He takes two beers out of the fridge, shuts the door, flips the lids and passes one to Fen.

Fen does not touch him. She holds the cold beer bottle in her hand and says nothing, although her heart is thumping. Something is wrong.

Sean drinks his drink. He doesn't say anything either. Somehow, though, it's important that Fen stands with him. She picks at the label on her bottle. She peels it from the glass and rolls it into a narrow pipe.

After a long time, Sean puts his empty bottle down and leans on the counter. He looks dog-tired.

'Do you want to tell me what happened?' she asks, softly.

'Nothing happened,' he says. 'We went to the zoo.

Amy fed the sea lions. We had dinner in a Harvester. She went to bed and I read her five chapters from *Heidi*.'

Fen bites her lip. She does not touch Sean or move closer towards him. She doesn't speak. He takes the vodka bottle from the freezer and pours himself a large glass. He doesn't ask if Fen would like another drink, he doesn't apologize or explain.

'Lewis and Belle have broken up,' he says quietly.

'Oh.'

'It's hard for Belle,' he says. 'Usually she knows what she wants, and she gets it. This time it turned out that Lewis wasn't what she wanted after all.'

Fen fiddles with the rolled paper in her fingers.

'Does she want you back?' she asks.

He does not answer this directly. He says: 'She'll be OK. Things will sort themselves out. They always do.'

Fen doesn't ask again. She doesn't need to. She knows.

Sean drinks his vodka. She stands beside him. She watches his Adam's apple move up and down his throat; she watches the light on the rim of the glass.

Then he says: 'I'm going to bed now.'

Fen nods.

She waits downstairs until she hears the toilet flush, the rattling of the never-mended pipes, then she goes up. Sean is standing on the landing in his boxers. Connor has made a traffic jam of toy cars along the middle of the carpet and Sean has a leg on either side of the cars, making a bridge. His knees are bony. She wonders if he wants to sleep alone tonight.

Sean reaches out to her. She takes his hand. It's warm. It's strong. 'Fen . . .'

'Yes.'

'What was it you said, about having a duty to look after the people we love?'

'Not a duty,' she says. 'A responsibility.'

'Oh yes.'

'Is it Belle? Are you worried about how she'll cope on her own? Is she really unhappy?'

He shakes his head.

'Not Belle,' he says. 'She's made her choices. It's Amy. I can't bear what all this is doing to Amy.'

CHAPTER 40

They see the rain coming from a long way off. The Lady Chapel is situated high up the hill and the workmen have a perfect view of the threatening clouds that move slowly and inevitably over the city towards them. They are preparing to replace the cupola. The stones have been restored and repaired and the original bell has been brought out of storage. The scaffolders have already set up a frame, but the first spots of rain spat onto the tarmac path before they had the chance to protect the chapel roof with plastic. Thunder rumbles in the throat of the cloud.

'What do you think?' asks the foreman.

Sean checks his watch. He looks up at the sky.

'Let's call it a day,' he says.

The foreman nods.

Sean helps tidy the site and checks that all the relevant safety signs and barriers are in place. He swaps his work boots for his trainers, gets into the car and drives back to Lilyvale.

The house is empty. Fen is still at work. He goes into the living room and switches the TV on for company, then he washes his hands in the kitchen sink and opens the fridge door.

There's not much in it, but there's enough to make a bacon and egg sandwich.

So he turns on the grill and lays some strips of bacon on the tray; he takes a small pan off the drainer beside the sink, rinses it, fills it with water and sets it to boil on the hob. There are no mushrooms, but there are a couple of tomatoes in the salad drawer. He slices them in half and puts them under the grill too. He opens the back door to let out the fat smoke. The thunder is still grumbling on the other side of the valley and the air is steamy with the smell of rain.

The water is boiling so he puts in some salt and breaks an egg against the handle of the pan, then carefully slides the unformed substances into the steam. The egg white congeals as soon as it touches the water; it whitens protectively around the yolk and a lacy frill forms around it. Sean watches. He butters some bread then turns the bacon.

He eats from a plate on his knees in front of the television.

When he has eaten, he checks the time. He could let Fen know he is here to meet Connor off the bus. She may want to stay in the city and do some shopping. He tries her phone, but it's switched off. He does not leave a message. He wanders into the kitchen. There's a Bath Rugby calendar hooked under the cabinets. Amy gave it to him for Christmas. He checks the date and beside it Fen has scrawled: 4 p.m. Speech Therapist.

She must have gone directly to the school.

Sean yawns. He wanders into the living room. He turns down the volume on the television and picks up his guitar. He plays some chords, a blues riff.

He left his phone on the kitchen counter and he doesn't hear it ring the first time. The second time he goes into the kitchen and sees who it is, and he almost does not pick it up.

It's Belle's number.

She keeps calling. She keeps talking to Sean, not telling him directly what's wrong, but complaining about trivial things that it's in Sean's power to resolve: squirrels in the roof, a knocking noise from her car's exhaust, whether or not Amy should start piano lessons. Sean knows she's lonely, he knows she needs someone to lean on but these calls drag him down. They exhaust him. So he almost doesn't answer and when he does he says, 'Hi' with a sharp edge to his voice as if he is in the middle of something important and has been inconveniently interrupted.

'Daddy?'

'Amy, honey, hi! How are you?'

'Daddy,' she replies and her voice is small and terrified. 'I came home from school and Mummy's lying on her bed and I can't make her wake up.'

CHAPTER 41

Fen checks the clock. It's nearly midnight. She feels empty inside, hollowed out and dry like an old tree. She pours herself a glass of water from the tap, wonders if it's too late to call Lina and decides it probably is.

On his way out, Sean left a message on her phone telling her everything he knew. He sounded out of breath. In the background Fen heard him closing the door, running up the front garden steps, opening his car door, starting the engine. He said he'd call and let her know what's happening but he hasn't.

Fen does not know how bad it is. She does not know if Belle is perfectly all right or critically ill or even . . . She wishes her mind would not keep thinking the worst, but she can't help herself.

She can't help thinking . . .

What if Belle has been so lonely, so desperate, that she's swallowed a bottle of vodka with her antidepressants? What if she doesn't regain consciousness? It would be Fen's fault, wouldn't it? It would be because Fen is with Sean.

She goes upstairs and into Connor's room. He's

fast asleep, his head a little sweaty on the pillow. Fen blows on his forehead to cool him down. He pulls an exaggerated face in his sleep. She sits on the window ledge and peers through the curtains out onto the street, but there's nobody about. She can see the blue-grey screens of televisions flickering in the living rooms of the houses opposite, the ones whose occupants haven't drawn their downstairs curtains. A cat creeps along the kerb and somewhere an urban owl hoots.

Connor grinds his teeth. Fen moves back to the bed and strokes his face gently with the back of her hand.

She's never met Belle. She only knows her through things that Sean has said and stories Amy has recounted. She's seen Belle's photograph. She feels a vague sense of pity towards her because she genuinely believes that any woman who had Sean, who had his love, who had his child, and did not love him as he deserved to be loved, must be blinkered, or a fool. Much stronger than the pity is Fen's fear of Belle. She knows that Belle has the power to change everything. Fen knows that if Belle is going to use that power, there is nothing she can do about it. And now there's another, worse fear: the fear that something terrible has happened to Belle. Fen could not bear to see the pain on Sean's face, or Amy's, if Belle were to die. She does not know how she would begin to comfort Sean if he were to even taste the guilt she has experienced. She would do anything to protect him from that.

She sits with her son until her glass is empty. She breathes from her diaphragm – in on four counts, out on six – to make the panicky feelings stop, and she turns her thoughts over and over in her mind.

It's very late. The lights of the televisions up and down the street have mostly been extinguished. Most of the windows, even the upstairs ones, are in darkness now.

Fen goes back downstairs to switch off the lights, and she's in the kitchen, locking the back door, when her phone rings.

'Sean?'

At the other end of the connection, through all the miles that separate them, she hears him sigh.

'Sean.'

'It's good to hear your voice,' he whispers.

'Where are you?'

'At home. I've only just got Amy off to sleep. Poor little sod.'

Fen tries to ignore the 'at home' but her confidence unravels a little further.

'Are you all right?' she asks.

She imagines him. He'll be sitting on the stairs with his knees wide apart. His elbows will be perched on his knees. His shirt sleeves will be rolled up. He'll be holding the phone to his right ear with his right hand and he'll be scratching the scab on his cheek with the fingers of his left hand, picking at its perimeters. His wrists are strong and hairy.

He will need a shave. There's a hole in the toe of one of the blue socks he's wearing. Fen meant to repair it but there were no other clean socks for him this morning so he took the blue ones from her mending basket. She thinks of him and she is afraid she is losing him.

'Yeah,' he says, 'I'm fine.'

'Where's Belle?'

'She's in hospital.'

'What happened?'

'It was an accident,' he says slowly. 'She says it was an accident. She was worn out and she took a mild overdose, not enough to do any damage. It was carelessness, nothing more than that. She's going to be fine.'

There's a pause and she hears him swallow. Her heart contracts with love.

'Oh God,' she whispers, 'I'm so sorry.'

'No, no, it's all right,' says Sean with the kind of emphasis she has heard him use when he is trying to convince himself of something, rather than anyone else.

'You have talked to her, then?' Fen asks.

'Yeah, I took Amy in to see her, to show Amy she's all right. Belle's upset, embarrassed, a bit confused, but she's OK. They're keeping her in hospital so she can have a proper rest tonight. Apparently she hasn't been sleeping, that's why she took an extra tablet. She only meant to knock herself out for a couple of hours until Amy came home. That's what she says; she just wanted to sleep for a while.'

'And you believe her?'

'Why shouldn't I?'

'Maybe . . .'

'No, don't. Don't even think that. I can't go down that route, OK? I cannot doubt her story. Nothing like this has ever happened before; she's generally a together sort of person. And she's seeing some shrink or something in the morning. They won't let her out of hospital if they don't think she's up to it.'

'Oh,' says Fen, 'OK. What about Amy?'

'She's scared. She'd walked home with her friend from down the road, and she let herself in the back door. When Belle didn't come down she went upstairs and found her. It was only luck that I'd finished work early and my phone was switched on. That's what keeps bugging me. What if it hadn't been? What would she have done then? What's this going to do to her mind? How's she going to feel every time she comes into the house on her own now?'

Fen knows exactly how Amy is going to feel. She knows that Amy will never again have the luxury of assuming that the people she loves are invulnerable. She knows that Amy will always, now, worry about her mother. That worry will taint her every moment.

'Oh, Sean,' Fen whispers. She looks up at the ceiling.

'What am I going to do?' he asks.

'Stay there,' Fen says. 'Stay there for as long as they need you.'

'It may be some time.'

'I know.'

Fen turns off the lights and she goes back upstairs. Sean's bedroom door is ajar, the curtains are still open and the room is dark and empty. She goes into the room and draws the curtains. She finds the Beck CD and she slots it into the machine, then she lies awake in Sean's bed, listening to the words.

Fen and her brother and sister were brought up to believe in God, not karma, although Fen thinks that really it's all the same story, the same message, just told in a different way. After the accident that killed Joe, she could not believe in anything. Now she wonders if these bad things are happening to the people she loves because of the lies she once told, and the secret she harbours. She wonders whether she has the power to change things, whether she might ever put things right and restore the balance.

Ever since Lina told her about the newspaper article, ever since she said that Emma Rees would find no peace until she knew the truth about the accident, Fen has known, in her heart, what she should do. Whatever the outcome, whether or not it makes any difference to what's going on between Sean and Belle and Amy, she must go and see Mrs Rees and tell her what happened the night her son died.

CHAPTER 42

The first part is easy. On Friday night she packs a bag for herself and one for Connor and on Saturday morning she locks up the house and they catch a taxi to the station, then at the station they take the train to Merron. During the journey, they play word games. Connor never tires of I Spy but when it's his turn the word always begins with 'c' and the answer is always 'cow'. Fen tries to find ways to distract him. The other passengers give her kind, amused looks. He takes his crayons out of his rucksack and together they colour in pictures of dinosaurs.

Alan and Lucy meet them at the other end. Alan is carrying William in a sling around his neck. Connor enjoys the fuss made of him by his uncle and aunt, and he is fascinated by the sling, and by the baby.

'Can I carry Baby William?' he asks Alan, and Alan ruffles Connor's hair and says he can help push the buggy later.

They drive back to Alan and Lucy's house, and Fen waits until Connor is comfortable with his aunt and uncle, lying on his tummy on the floor doing a jigsaw with Alan, before she leaves.

'I don't know how long I'll be,' she tells Lucy.

Fen has tried to tell her sister where she is going, and what she is about to do, but Lucy does not want to talk about it, she doesn't want to know. She says she doesn't mind looking after Connor for a couple of hours, and tells Fen not to rush back.

Fen does not have to think which route to take; her feet lead her, one after the other, along roads which gradually fade from Victorian grandeur to 1970s pragmatism. The size of the houses, and the distance between them, gradually reduce until Fen is on the pavement of a neat road lined with terraced, brick-built former council houses. Their gardens are tidy, bedded with brightly coloured flowers and decorated with garden-centre ornaments. Fen did not have to check the address. She knows which house belongs to Emma Rees. She has been there a hundred times before.

She telephoned last night. She got the number from directory enquiries, and when she heard the number she recognized it. It's the same number she used to dial all those years ago when she wanted to speak to Joe, to pass on some message from Tomas. The same order of digits. People come and go, but phone numbers remain the same.

She dialled the number and spoke, briefly, to Mrs Rees. She said: 'You won't remember me but . . .'

And Mrs Rees said: 'Hello, Fen, of course I remember you.'

She said: 'You can come and see me whenever you want. I've been hoping you'd get in touch.'

She said: 'You have never been far from my thoughts, Fen. I know how hard it must have been for you.'

She said: 'I'll be at home tomorrow. I'll have the kettle on.'

And now Fen stands at the end of the short path that leads to the door of 90 Cartref Close and, before she has time to think, the door opens and a small black cat streams out, bringing the smell of warm air and washing powder with it, and there is Emma Rees in slippers and a housecoat looking even more frail and haunted than she did at Gordon's funeral. Fen is caught off guard by a wave of pity for this broken woman. She steps forward and, awkwardly, the two embrace.

'Come in, Fen,' says Mrs Rees. 'I was watching out for you. Come on in.'

They sit in the conservatory, which takes up most of the tiny back garden, and talk for a while about the birds that congregate around the feeders dotted all over the lawn. Mrs Rees loves the birds. She especially likes the blue and great tits, which are sociable and feed in family groups, but also has a soft spot for the bumptious little robin, who is the self-appointed king of the garden.

Fen sips her coffee – it is decaffeinated and too milky for her taste – and takes a biscuit, even though her mouth is as dry as sand, and when

Emma Rees asks: 'What really brought you back here after all these years?' she is honest.

She clasps her fingers tightly, holds her breath, then says: 'I came to talk to you about the accident.'

Mrs Rees's face clouds. She says: 'Fen, please, I'm sure you mean well, but whatever your brother told you—'

'No,' says Fen very quietly. 'Tomas didn't have to tell me anything.' She continues: 'I was there.'

Emma Rees sinks back into her chair. She pales.

'You can't have been,' she says. 'You were with Deborah. Deborah told me you were with her that night. You went to the hospital to see your father, you . . .'

Fen shakes her head. She wonders if she should carry on. She wonders if she is, in fact, doing the right thing, or something terribly cruel.

'You told the *Gazette* that you wanted to know the truth,' she says carefully. 'I didn't read the article, Mrs Rees, so tell me if I misunderstood. But I think you said you couldn't rest until you knew what really happened that night. That's why I'm here. I can tell you . . .'

'You were really there?'

Fen nods.

'You were with Joe?'

'Yes.'

'Oh!'

Emma Rees puts her fingers over her mouth and stares at Fen.

315

'I'm sorry . . .' Fen whispers.

'Go on,' says Mrs Rees in a very small, shaky voice. 'Tell me.'

It was the autumn term, the start of Fen's last year. Tomas was waiting for Fen when she came out of school. He was leaning on the fence on the other side of the road, looking like a film star, so tall and handsome. Cigarette smoke blew away from the roll-up between his fingers and she was especially glad to see him because he'd been away in Manchester for a couple of days with Joe, working for a friend who owned a stage lighting company. Their father was fading like old silk left out in the sun, and he was missing Tomas, he kept asking when he'd be back. The house was emptier and lonelier and bleaker without Tom. The whole situation was less bearable. Tomas being back took the pressure off Fen. He was her ally.

Now Fen's handsome brother waved to her, and she smiled and broke away from the group of girls she was with. She ran across the road, swinging her bag, and slipped her arm through his. She could tell from his face and from his demeanour that he hadn't come with bad news. In fact, he looked cheerful. He looked happy.

'Hey, you,' he said, turning immediately, leading her away from the school.

'Hey,' she said, trotting to keep up. 'How was Manchester?'

'It was magic.'

She swung on his arm. 'Is everything OK?'

'Yep,' he said, throwing the cigarette end onto the road. 'Everything's fucking wonderful!'

They went into the Star, which was a pub for older people; it did two-for-one meal deals for pensioners and was carpeted and fussy with dusty and faded fake potted plants on the window ledges. Fen had never been inside before. It smelled of toilet-rim air freshener. It was the pub where they were least likely to meet anyone they knew but it was also the closest to the school. Tomas bought two pints and a bottle of Becks for Fen and they sat in the window seat. Outside people held on to their coats and hats.

Tom was animated, happy.

'Who's that for?' Fen asked, nodding at the extra pint.

'My man Joe.'

Fen felt a squeeze of pleasure in her belly. She loved being with both boys. She loved being the only one who shared their secret, and she loved acting as a go-between for them, running errands, taking messages. When they were together, the three of them, those were the happiest times for her. It was as if they were a secret society from which the rest of Merron's population was excluded.

'He should be here any minute,' said Tom. 'He's just gone to fetch his mum's car.'

'Why? Are we going somewhere?' Fen asked. 'Am I going with you?'

Tomas grinned and tapped the side of his nose. 'Wait and see,' he said happily, 'wait and see.'

Then he said: 'Oh fuck "wait and see" – look what I've got!' And he put his hand into his jacket pocket and pulled out tickets to see James in concert in Manchester that night. 'Freebies,' he said, 'for the backstage staff. And I've checked with Deborah and Dad's in hospital overnight so she doesn't need us at home. She said we deserved a night off away from the sickbed.'

'Oh my God, Tom!' cried Fen, clasping her hands together. 'What, I'm going with you? Really? I'm really going with you? Thank you, thank you, thank you!'

'Who's the best brother in the known universe?'

'You are,' said Fen. 'You're definitely the best.'

'Were you going out with my son?' asks Emma Rees. 'Were you his girlfriend?'

Fen shakes her head.

'Then what was that about you sharing a secret? There was something Joe wasn't telling me, wasn't there?' says Mrs Rees. 'Was he on drugs? Had your brother got him onto drugs?'

Her voice is cold and terrified.

'No,' says Fen. She is so afraid of the rest of the story that she can hardly concentrate. She can't think. She doesn't know what the right thing to say is any more. Also, she is terrified, afraid of inflicting more damage than is necessary.

'I used to hear Joe on the phone, speaking to

Tomas,' says Mrs Rees. 'He'd be whispering. He'd change the subject when he heard me coming. It was drugs, wasn't it?'

'No,' Fen says, more convincingly.

'Then what was it? What was going on?'

'I promised I wouldn't . . .'

'Fen, for goodness sake, my boy is dead! My son is dead. Nothing you tell me can make that any worse than it already is. I don't *care* how bad it is . . .'

'It's not a bad thing,' says Fen. 'They were in love.'

'Who were?'

'Joe and Tomas.'

Mrs Rees makes a little squeak of shock. Fen looks up at her and holds her eye.

'No,' the older woman whispers.

Fen nods. 'Yes.'

Mrs Rees is silent for a very long time.

Then she says: 'Was it some phase they were going through?'

'No, it wasn't like that. They really loved one another,' Fen says as calmly as she can.

'In that case, why didn't Joe tell me?' Mrs Rees asks. 'Did he think I'd be angry? Did he think I'd stop loving him? Did he think I'd be ashamed?'

'I don't know. It was difficult for them, in a place like Merron. They didn't want to hurt you.'

'No,' says Mrs Rees. 'No, you're wrong. It can't have meant anything to Joe. Maybe he was confused. If it had been important, he would have told me. He always told me everything.'

Fen thinks maybe she should leave. Emma Rees said she wanted the truth, but now she's had a part of it, she's denying it. If she can't accept this much, how will she deal with the rest of it?

She puts her hands on the chair arms to push herself up. 'Perhaps I should go,' she says.

'No.' Mrs Rees shakes her head. She pushes Fen's shoulder; she pushes her back down into the chair quite roughly. 'Oh no, you're not going yet. Not until you've told me everything.'

'Then you have to believe me when I tell you they loved one another. Otherwise none of it makes sense.'

Mrs Rees laughs, a horrid, bitter laugh. 'Oh, they loved one another, did they? They loved one another, my Joe and your Tomas? That's why your brother left my son on his own, dying in the rain, in the dark, at the side of the road? Because he *loved* him? Yes, yes, that really makes sense.'

'It wasn't like that. He didn't leave Joe.'

'No? So how was it, then, Fen? You tell me how it was.'

Joe arrived at the pub a short time later, shrugging his shoulders apologetically because he hadn't brought the car. His mother had already taken it. It didn't matter because Tomas had an alternative plan. They drank their drinks and then the three of them went back to the Wellers' house. It was empty of course. Lucy was married by then and Deborah and Gordon were at the hospital.

Fen knew where the keys to her father's car were kept. He didn't use it any more; he was too ill to drive. It wasn't taxed or insured and probably hadn't been serviced for ages. It wasn't in the best condition and one of the headlights wasn't working, but none of them worried about that. It was a car, there was petrol in the tank, they had the keys and they were going to Manchester. That was all that mattered to them.

The boys sat in the front and Fen sat in the back, behind her brother. It was a big, powerful German car. It ate up the miles. On the way into the city, it was still light and although the wind was strong it hadn't yet started to rain. They stopped to buy chips and maybe the boys were drinking beer, Fen can't remember exactly. They were all happy and talkative. For weeks, months, Fen had been creeping around her father's house, being quiet, feeling sad and frightened, hearing his groans, learning new words like 'thoracotomy', 'pleura' and, most recently, 'palliative'. She hadn't laughed or gone wild for months. That night she felt like a can of Coke that's been shaken and is about to have its ring peeled back. She felt effervescent, full of energy and excitement and joy.

'Joy?' asks Mrs Rees.

Joy, yes, that's what Fen felt, at the start of that evening.

When they reached the city they left the car parked

in a residential side street and followed the crowds milling along the pavements. There was the usual pandemonium, the jostling and shouting and anticipation outside the venue, and after all that, the concert was great, it was brilliant. Fen hung on to Tom's arm and watched his face change colour in the lights and admired him for knowing all the words to all the songs, and Tom's other arm was around Joe's shoulders and nobody minded, nobody stared, nobody even noticed that Joe's hand was in the back pocket of Tom's jeans, that the two of them were so close they were almost the same person.

Everything was fine, perfect, happy, hot, steamy, cheerful. Fen's eardrums were ringing, her throat was hoarse and her feet ached with dancing, but she wanted to dance forever; she never wanted the evening to end.

Towards the end of the concert Tomas wandered away. He just faded into the crowd and Fen thought he must have gone to the toilet. It was only when he came back that she could tell by his eyes that he had taken something. But it didn't really seem to matter, because all three of them were as high as kites on the music and the energy and the atmosphere. They were singing as they walked back to the car. They'd get home somehow.

'You let your brother drive, even though he had taken drugs?' asks Mrs Rees, incredulous. 'You let him get behind the wheel of that car *knowing* he was off his head?'

'No,' says Fen, 'no, we didn't.'

'What happened, then? Was Joe driving?'

Fen shakes her head.

'No, he'd had too much to drink.'

'Who, then?'

'It was me,' says Fen.

Mrs Rees holds one hand to her mouth, the other rests on her hip, and all her fingers are trembling.

'Did you know how to drive?'

'I'd had a few lessons.'

'A few lessons?'

Fen nods.

She feels slightly dizzy, faint. The truth hangs exposed in the small, hot room and it is crushing, blinding, awful.

'Go on,' says Mrs Rees, 'go on. Tell me. Don't stop now.'

Fen continues although her voice fractures and fades, eroded with emotion.

She knew what she was doing when she slipped into the driver's seat of her father's car and took off her shoes, then reached between her knees to find the bar that would pull the seat forward so her bare feet could reach the pedals. She knew it was a reckless and dangerous plan and that she had neither the experience nor the skill to make such a long journey in the dark, and the weather was worsening, yet as soon as Tomas suggested it she agreed to drive without a murmur of dissent.

She agreed because she wanted Joe and Tomas to love her, not because she was coerced. She wanted to be one of them. She craved their attention and their admiration. She wanted to be a hero too.

She could have said: 'No.' She could have suggested they stay in Manchester overnight; they could have slept in the car. It would have been OK. The boys would never have forced her to do anything she did not want to do. She was the one who insisted she was competent.

It was a long journey home, longer than the outward drive had seemed a few hours ago, in daylight. They were taking what Tomas called the Scenic Route along the country roads, to avoid running into police patrols. The broken headlight made them conspicuous and vulnerable to being stopped, and none of them wanted to be caught in an illegal car, with no L plates and a learner driver in control. It was dark, gone midnight and by now it was raining. Fen had never driven in the dark before. She sat forward, holding tightly to the steering wheel. The wipers went backwards and forwards, and in between their strokes the screen spattered with water that shattered the view of the narrow road, always disappearing around another bend. From time to time a wheel hit a pothole and the car would lurch. Fen stared into the darkness ahead.

The boys were noisy at first, but then their banter, their relentless mickey-taking, eased off and they too went quiet. Joe, in the passenger seat beside Fen, fiddled with the radio; Tomas wound down his window in the back and smoked. And then, because he'd let the rain in, all the windows steamed up. Fen leaned forward to wipe the windscreen with the elbow of her jumper, to clear a space through which she could see. They travelled along the unlit, winding country roads, the wet, potholed tarmac shiny in the greasy, yellow gleam of the single functioning headlight. Fen felt the car slipping on the bends, she felt the pressure of the pedals beneath the soles of her feet, but she'd come this far, she was doing fine. The boys kept telling her she was doing fine.

They were driving along the bottom of a wooded gorge and the rain was coming down in sheets. Tomas yawned. He sat forward between the two front seats so that the point of his right elbow nudged Fen's shoulder, and he said: 'I'm going to close my eyes for five minutes.'

Joe turned his head. He cupped Tom's face gently in his hand and pulled it towards his, and they kissed. And Fen took her eyes off the road for a second, just a second, as she turned to watch them, more than a second, maybe, a few seconds, and it was the most beautiful, gentle, tender kiss and then . . .

'What?' asks Mrs Rees.

. . . then . . .

'Then what?'

. . . there was a jolt and the car was going sideways. It was at right angles to the road and . . .

'It rolled over?'

Fen heard Joe say: 'Oh shit!' in a voice so calm
that she was not afraid.

'At the inquest they said it must have aquaplaned,'
said Mrs Rees.

Fen felt the car roll and lurch, and the steering
wheel tore itself from her hands and spun as if
possessed.

They were in the air, flying.

A blast of cold air smacked Fen hard in the face,
then something more solid hit her, but she was
so disorientated she didn't know what was
happening and there was no time to think.

She was thrown forwards and backwards, she
banged her head and her elbow and then she slipped
and became wedged between the steering column
and the front seat. And when she pulled herself up,
half-choked by the seatbelt, her fingers hooked
under the dashboard, the car was stationary, the
right way up, rocking violently and then more gently
on its wheels. Through the crazed glass of the
buckled windscreen, in the alarming on–off glare of
the hazard-warning lights, she saw distorted trees

326

bending broken limbs towards the car and a vicious swathe carved into the verge behind her, the grass turned over and churned to mud, and, way back, appearing and disappearing in the flashing lights, an incongruous bundle of leather and denim lying almost flat to the ground.

And it was strange, but the engine was still running and the radio was still playing, still playing the same song it had been playing a few seconds earlier, as if everything was still the same and all right. Elvis Presley was singing 'Suspicious Minds'.

Mrs Rees hardly seems to breathe. She gazes at Fen. Fen licks her lips. She is finding it more and more difficult to speak.

She listened to the music for a moment or two. Then she heard Tom's voice behind her shoulder. He was asking: 'Fen? Fen? Are you OK?'

'I think so,' Fen said. 'What happened?'

'We must have hit something in the road. We rolled over.'

Gingerly, Tom leaned forward and wiped blood from Fen's chin. She saw the black smear glistening on his palm. Her lip was stinging where she had bitten through it.

'Where's Joe?' she asked.

'Where was he?' asks Emma Rees.

Fen's breath comes shakily. Now Mrs Rees

seems very calm. Her eyes are cold; her lips are set in a line.

'He had fallen from the car,' says Fen. 'He must have fallen when it rolled. He was a little further up the slope.'

'What did he look like? Did he look badly hurt?'

'He looked . . .'

'What?'

'He looked . . . normal. He was lying on his front with his arms bent, his hands on either side of his face, like he was lying out in the sun . . . He looked relaxed.'

'Relaxed?'

'Yes.'

'Did he say anything?'

Fen shakes her head.

'Was he conscious?'

'No, but he was alive. He was breathing.'

'And you left him?'

'No . . . No . . .'

Suddenly Fen feels muddled. So many times she has tried not to think about this, so many times she's put it from her mind, that she's not one hundred per cent sure what did happen. When she described the events to Deborah in the early hours of the morning after the accident, when she told her stepmother about her shaking, the giddiness, the feeling that she was spinning so fast she would shatter or spin off the face of the earth and disappear into space, Deborah said she was describing the symptoms of shock.

She thinks she screamed – she remembers her screams rising up into the forest, echoing off the gorge walls so sharp and bright and cold – and she thinks Tom was holding her, trying to contain the shaking, telling her to be calm, telling her that everything would be OK, but she can't be sure.

Still there are some things she definitely remembers, things she cannot forget.

She tells Mrs Rees what she knows to be true. She says: 'Tom said we shouldn't move Joe in case his back was hurt. He fetched our coats out of the car to put over Joe, to keep him warm.' She is sure of this much. She remembers how gentle Tomas was with Joe, how he took off his own hoodie to make a pillow for Joe's face and how, when he lifted Joe's head, just a fraction, to slide the pillow beneath, the blood was terrible. Fen recoiled but, while he was within earshot of Joe, Tomas was calm. He spoke to Joe in a low, private, reassuring voice.

'Then he said he would take the car and find a phone box, and he'd call an ambulance. He told me to stay with Joe until the ambulance came, then go back to the road and keep walking. He said it wasn't that far. He gave me his money. He said not to tell anyone I was ever there. He said he should have been driving. He said he was responsible. He was panicking. I don't think he knew what he was saying. He gabbled something about taking the car and dumping it somewhere, that he'd disappear for a while, so everyone would assume he was driving the car, and that way my life wouldn't be ruined . . . and . . .'

'And?'

'He knelt in the mud and he leaned down and whispered something to Joe. He whispered in his ear. And then he kissed him on the forehead, and he stayed there for a moment, bent over him, and it looked like he was praying . . . and then he stood up and said, "Goodbye" and he got in the car and drove away . . .'

Fen trails off. She feels herself there again, in the woods, the rain coming down and the sound of the car engine fading and the wind in the trees, and how noisy that was, the trees groaning with the weight of the wind in the branches. She wrapped her arms around herself and she spun round, hearing noises, afraid of the kind of things that used to terrify her as a child – ghosts and wolves and madmen with axes – and the rain was in her eyes, on her face, making her jumper stick to her back, and when clouds covered the moon it was as dark as her worst nightmare and she was shaking, shaking like a shutter in the wind.

She swallows and she says: 'I went back to Joe and I rearranged the coats to keep him as dry as possible and to keep the rain off his face, and that's when I found his phone, in his jacket pocket. We didn't know he had it with him. So I called the ambulance. I called it in case it took Tomas a while to find a phone, and they said they'd be quick, they said they'd come as quickly as they could. Then I stayed with Joe until they came. I talked to him; I thought that was what you're supposed to do. I talked to him about Tom and about you and, oh, other things, things him and Tom did when they were younger, and television programmes and . . . He was quiet . . . He was just breathing slowly like he was sleeping. I lay down next to him and put my arms over him to keep him warm and I could feel him breathing, only . . .'

'What?'

'After a while I couldn't feel it any more. I couldn't feel him breathing.'

'He died in your arms?'

'I don't know. I'm not sure.'

'Didn't you check?'

'I was too scared. I thought maybe I was just imagining he wasn't breathing. I . . .'

'You what?'

'I didn't want to know that Joe had died.'

Fen breathes out. She pauses for a moment.

Then: 'I don't know how long it was, but I saw the lights coming along the road. I could see the emergency lights through the trees. There weren't any sirens. I'd been listening out for the sirens but I suppose they didn't need them: there was no other traffic about. It can't have been hard to find the place because of the tracks. The ambulance stopped and there was a police car too. Then I

331

moved away, just a bit; I hid in the woods. They had torches. I waited until they were all leaning over Joe and I watched them taking care of him. I was only a few feet away. He wasn't on his own for more than a moment.'

Fen glances up. Mrs Rees holds her eye.

For a few seconds nothing happens.

Fen can hear the ticking of the clock on the window ledge.

Mrs Rees looks at Fen. She says quietly: 'For ten years the worst thing for me has been imagining my son lying in the dark among the broken glass and mud, terribly injured, abandoned by his best friend, on his own, waiting to die. That has been my worst nightmare. And all this time you had it in your power to take that nightmare away from me and you didn't.'

Fen looks away. She stares down into her lap.

The older woman shakes her head. She turns again and gazes out of the conservatory, at the birds in the garden going about their business, their pecking and hopping and chirping.

'All these years . . .' she says. 'It's as if he's been out there, on his own, all these years.'

'No,' whispers Fen. 'He wasn't on his own.'

There is a terrible silence. Fen can smell the sadness on Emma Rees's breath. She can taste the emptiness of the older woman's life. She can feel her nightmares.

'Deborah knew you were there,' says Emma Rees. 'She must have known. She told the police you were with her that night. She told me too. She must have been lying.'

'She lied for my father's sake.'

'And what about my son? What about me? Did neither of you think of us?'

Mrs Rees is calm. She speaks with dignity. Fen twists her fingers on her lap. She cannot answer this, for the truth would be too hurtful. She simply finishes telling what she knows.

When Fen arrived home in the early hours, Deborah was waiting up. She knew the car was missing, she knew Fen and Tomas were missing, and she was going out of her mind with worry. She took one look at Fen, who was covered in mud and blood, soaking wet and cold, without shoes and without a coat, and it was as if she read in Fen's eyes everything that had happened. She didn't ask any questions. She took Fen upstairs and undressed her while she ran a bath. She helped Fen into the bath and sat beside her, feeding her sips of tea liberally laced with whisky, which stung Fen's lip, topping up the water every time it cooled and pouring warm water over Fen's shampooed hair.

'Where is Tomas?' was the only question she asked.

Fen told Deborah everything. Deborah was very calm and did not appear shocked. All she said was: 'Fen, we have to keep this from your father or it will be the end of him.'

She stroked Fen's wet head and said: 'This is what we will do. We'll tell everyone that you and I went to the hospital together to visit your father, and that after that we spent the evening here, watching television. Gordon can't remember which day is which and Tomas was right: there's no point getting you into any kind of trouble. It won't change anything, it won't help anyone and it would kill your father.'

'But he'll wonder where Tom is . . . He'll wonder where he's gone . . .'

'He doesn't have to know,' Deborah said, and her fingers were very gentle but also very strong and firm on Fen's scalp. They went round and round and they soothed Fen, they made her feel as if Deborah was in control and all she had to do was acquiesce. 'We can keep this from him. We'll tell him Tom's still working in Manchester. Don't you think that's for the best? He hasn't got long, Fen. Just a few weeks. Don't you think you owe it to him to make those last few weeks peaceful?'

She said: 'You can't turn back the clock. You can't change what happened tonight. You can't change what's happened to Joe, and you can't bring Tomas back from wherever he's hiding. But you can choose either to give your father a few last weeks of contentment and peace, or to make his last days a living hell.'

Fen knows Deborah loved her father. She did what she thought was the right thing to do. Certainly

Deborah felt sorry for Emma Rees. She felt, and still feels, a duty towards her, but she never really cared for the woman.

Fen does not say this last part out loud, but in her heart she knows it is the truth.

'I thought she was my friend,' says Mrs Rees.

'I'm sorry,' says Fen. 'I'm so terribly sorry, for everything.'

'What's wrong with your family?' asks Emma Rees. 'Why is everything so secretive and twisted? Why did it take you so long to bring me the truth? Why didn't Lucy tell me?'

'Lucy doesn't know. And I was afraid.'

'Of what? That I might call the police? Have you done for manslaughter? Drag you through the papers? Tell the truth about your poisonous family? Ruin your life, like you ruined mine?'

'It wasn't that,' says Fen. 'I know that's what I deserve, but it wasn't that. It was because I was so ashamed.'

Mrs Rees nods.

'You have a child now, don't you?'

'Yes.'

'A son?'

'Yes. I have thought about what I would do if I were in your shoes,' Fen says very quietly. 'I have thought of how I would feel if anyone were to hurt him.'

'You keep thinking about that,' says Mrs Rees without looking at Fen. 'I'm not going to report you now – that won't do me any good. It won't help Joe. But I want you to think about that every moment of every day for the rest of your life.' She pauses then continues, 'I'd like you to go now. Please don't ever come back.'

Fen stands up. She does not look at the other woman. She says: 'I'm sorry. It would have been better if I hadn't come.'

'It would have been better if you'd come ten and a half years ago,' says Mrs Rees.

CHAPTER 43

Fen is so glad to be back at Lilyvale. Her heart lifts and lightens. The delicate, swirling-petal pattern of the yellow roses on the bush in the front garden makes her feel better, the sunlight on the windows soothes her, even the shadows on the roof tiles are like a salve. She wants to be inside, safe, back where she belongs. She holds Connor's hand and trots down the steps, and before she can put her key in the door it opens and there's Sean.

Fen is grateful. She steps into his arms and it's like coming home. She presses herself into his chest and she thinks: Thank God, thank God, thank God you're back.

'Where have you been?' he asks.

'I went to Merron.'

'Why?'

'To see Joe's mother. I told her about the accident. She knows it was my fault. She knows everything now.'

'Oh, Fen,' he says, his hands in her hair.

Over his shoulder, Fen sees Amy's pale little face beside the kitchen door. Her hair is messy and her eyes are very dark. She is leaning against the frame, standing on one leg and holding the bare foot of the other in her hand. Fen pulls away from Sean and smiles at the child.

'Hello, you,' she says, 'how lovely that you're here.'

'We bought you a present,' Connor tells Amy, pushing past the adults. 'Where is it, Mum?'

'On the shelf beneath the TV.'

Connor takes Amy's hand and leads her into the living room. He and Fen have bought her a dance DVD as a surprise. Fen knows it won't entirely take her mind off things, but hopes it will help.

Sean stands up straight again, stretches the pain out of his back and smiles. 'Are you all right?'

She nods. 'I think so.'

He follows her into the kitchen,

'Coffee?'

'I thought you'd never ask.'

They take their mugs outside into the garden, where they can talk without the children hearing them. Little insects drift lazily in shafts of sunlight. An upturned watering can has stained a patch of soil dark and Connor's bicycle sprawls on the grass. Plastic windmills spin in the breeze and music drifts down the hill. The back doors of the houses are open. Somebody close by is cooking curry.

Fen does not know if this is the real beginning of her and Sean, or if it is the end. It feels like a turning point.

'You didn't pick the beans,' says Sean, wandering over to his vegetable patch. 'They're too big. They'll be stringy now.'

'I'm sorry,' says Fen. 'I didn't notice.'

He shrugs. He picks a bean and prises the green pocket open with a fingernail.

'I cut the last lettuce the other day,' she says. 'I made a salad.'

'Was it nice?'

'It was lovely.'

The silence between them is like a blanket of gentleness. The not mentioning Belle means she cannot hurt them; she can't change them, not for a few moments at least.

'Do you feel better now you've seen Mrs Rees?' Sean asks, sitting down on the grass. He frees a dandelion fairy that has caught in Fen's sleeve, lets it loose into the warm air and watches it dance.

'I feel . . . relieved.'

'Do you want to talk about it?'

Fen shakes her head. 'No. It's over now. There's nothing else I can do.' She changes the subject: 'Is Amy all right? She looks exhausted.'

He shrugs. 'I don't know. She wants us all to go out this evening, to that restaurant – you know, the first one we ever went to, where we had pizza after we'd been to the park.'

'That'll be nice.'

'I think it reminds her of a happier time.'

Sean looks down. Fen knows what he's thinking and doesn't know what she can say to make him feel better. She sips her coffee. It's too hot. It burns the top of her mouth.

'Is she going to be here for a while?'

'Until the end of the holidays. Belle's gone to stay with her parents until she feels a bit better.'

'Oh. Good.'

'We haven't talked about after that,' says Sean.

'No. But . . .'

'What?'

'Oh, Sean, you know.' Fen bites her lower lip and stares out over the valley. 'It's not like you really have a choice.'

'There is always a choice.'

Sean is worn out with emotion. Fen can see it in his face. He's done too much thinking, too much hurting.

And so has she.

She tries to muster a smile. She says calmly, 'This is what you wanted, a few months ago: Lewis out of the picture and the chance for you to go back, to have the family reunited, a stable home for Amy, your life back how you wanted it.'

'I should be more careful what I wish for.'

Fen picks at a daisy in the lawn.

She says: 'You know, I never thought we'd be together forever. I didn't think I deserved you, I—'

Sean snorts. 'Don't talk crap,' he says. Fen looks up at him. He stands, throws the remnants of his coffee onto the lawn and strides the short distance to the gate at the end of the garden, and then he turns and comes back.

'You've spent too long feeling sorry for yourself, Fen Weller,' he says. 'You've spent too long beating yourself up over some stupid mistake you made when you were a kid. And yes, I *know* the repercussions were awful, terrible, but it happened, it's over, you've done the right thing now, you've told the truth to the only person who still cares, so leave it behind you, move on.'

Down the alleyway children's voices hush, dogs stop barking.

'Christ,' he says, 'you're entitled to some happiness. We all are.'

And he leans down and takes hold of Fen, one hand on either side of her face, his fingers pressing hard into her cheeks, and he kisses her and she knows the kiss is meant to be a commitment, but something about it tastes of desperation. He says: 'We'll think of something. We'll sort something out. We'll be all right.'

Fen nods.

'Daddy?'

They turn together.

Amy, flushed and sweaty in her shorts and vest, is standing at the top of the steps, in the kitchen doorway. She has Sean's phone in her hand. She's holding it out to him.

'Who is it, Ames?'

'It's Mummy. She's crying.'

341

CHAPTER 44

Fen showers, and while her hair dries she sits in front of the mirror in her bedroom, wrapped in a towel, and makes up her face. She is careful to do it properly: she highlights her cheeks, glosses her lips and curls her lashes. Warm air and summer noises come through the open window beyond the dressing table. The edges of the curtains billow in the breeze. She puts on her new dress and her flip-flops, perfumes her wrists and her throat, fastens the chain around her ankle and tilts her chin as she struggles to put silver hoops in her ears. Amy lies on the bed, watching and scratching at the eczema that's bloomed on the backs of her hands and around her eyes.

'You look nice,' she says.

'Thank you, Amy. What are you going to wear?'

'I don't know. Daddy didn't pack any of my best things.'

Fen turns and pulls a sympathetic face.

'Shall we have a look together?'

Amy fetches her rucksack and they go through its contents, and she's right. Sean has just packed T-shirts and shorts and underwear, a mishmash of wrinkled clothes all tangled together, still damp and smelling musty because they've been bundled straight from the washing machine and not taken out to air.

'OK,' says Fen, 'laundry really isn't one of your dad's strong points. Come with me.'

She opens her wardrobe door, flicks through the clothes on their hangers and pulls out a long, cherry-red, silk T-shirt. She holds it up against Amy. It's about the right length for a dress for the child.

'Do you like it?' she asks. Amy nods.

'You can wear it over your trousers and we'll accessorize,' says Fen. 'I'll find you a belt and you can go through my stuff and choose whatever else you want.'

'Anything?'

'Yes, tonight absolutely anything.'

Amy's sore eyes widen with pleasure. Fen leaves her to rummage through her jewellery box and calls Connor upstairs to get changed.

Later, they sit in the restaurant, at the same table as before, eating the same food. They look smarter than they did last time; they have all dressed up as if, by unspoken agreement, they acknowledge this is a formal occasion. Amy is wearing so many beads and bangles and brooches, she twinkles in the candlelight. Her hair is done up with a butterfly clip. The T-shirt is already smeared with tomato paste and Fen notices the stain fondly and thinks it will be a permanent reminder of this evening. Sean leans across the table and fills Fen's wine glass. The neck of the bottle clinks against the rim of the glass.

'Thanks.' She smiles, raising the glass then taking a sip. Her lips are still sore where he kissed her earlier.

When they have finished their pizzas the waitress comes round and asks if anyone wants dessert. The children ask for ice cream, Sean asks for coffee.

'And what about your mummy?' the waitress asks Amy. 'What would she like?'

'Oh, I'm not—' Fen begins.

'She'd like ice cream too,' says Amy.

They walk back through the city. The air is already cooling. Connor rides on Sean's shoulders. Fen wraps her cardigan around Amy's shoulders and holds her close. They look at the lights, at the buildings, and swerve to avoid the bundling, lairy young people, but they're all very quiet.

When the children are in bed, Fen asks: 'Why was Belle crying?'

Sean sighs. 'Same old same old.'

'Do you think she's well enough to look after Amy?'

'I don't know. Not on her own. Not as she is now.'

'What are you going to do?'

Sean runs his fingers through his hair and scratches his head.

'I don't know,' he says again.

He thinks for a while then says: 'Well, Amy's staying here until the end of the school holidays. I guess I'll have to go back for a couple of weeks when term starts, just to keep an eye on things and make sure they're all right. I don't see any way round that. But I'll come back as soon as everything has settled down. And we can still see one another. I'll still be working in Bath. We can go out for lunch and—'

'No.'

Fen moves away, she walks into the dark dining room and looks out through the window with her back to him, so that Sean won't see her face.

'I can't do that, Sean. I won't be your Other.'

He says: 'But I won't be *with* Belle, not like that, I—'

'No,' says Fen. 'No. Amy needs you. She needs to know how things are and where she stands. She can't be sitting at home wondering who you're with and where you live and whether or not you're coming back, and whether she's responsible for her mother – not in the state she's in now. I won't let you do that to her.'

Sean steps forward to touch her; she sidesteps away.

He says: 'Fen . . .'

'No,' she says again.

In the silence she hears Sean breathing. She hears him scratch the back of his head in frustration.

'Fen . . .'

'Please don't say anything else.'

'But I—'

'I've got a terrible headache,' she says. 'I'm going to bed.'

And she pushes past him and runs up the stairs before he can say anything else. She goes into her room and closes the door and also her eyes, and she presses her back against the wall as she feels her world fall away.

CHAPTER 45

The next four weeks, the last month of the school holidays, are the most precious. It is because Fen knows her happiness is finite. She treasures every second of the month and tries not to think of the days going by, the dates following one another on the calendar, the time slipping through her fingers like sand.

August goes by – slowly at first, and then more quickly – in a succession of beautiful, hot days, days when waking up to the brightness of the morning is a pleasure that repeats itself, days that are spent together in the park, by the river, and, for one wonderful week, in a tent on a hillside overlooking the sea in Pembrokeshire.

Sean and Fen don't mention the future for the whole month. They don't talk about Belle. And when it comes to the last week, the week when they decide, on an impulse, to buy a tent and run away to the coast, they leave their phones at home so that they are unreachable.

For seven days, they exist only in the moment, with their children, in the sunshine. They are a unit of four. They spend their days on the beach

347

and in the evenings Sean and Connor gather driftwood and build fires and together they cook whatever food is to hand. Sean plays his guitar. It's magical: the music and the heat of the flames and their fingers sticky with smoky marshmallow. Most nights the children fall asleep beside the fire, their heads on the lap of one or other adult. Inside the tent, the four sleep in the same tiny space, bundled together like puppies. Their clothes are soon salty and sandy and smell of smoke but they all smell the same, like a pack of dogs, and nobody cares. They unzip the sleeping bags to make one big, communal bed. They eat in cheap, family restaurants by the little fishing harbour, the fresh air making them all wonderfully hungry, they are hungry all the time and food has never tasted so good. The children clamour for hot pasties and ice cream. Amy's eczema clears up like magic and the shadows disappear from her eyes. Connor becomes stronger and more confident every day. People no longer stare at him so much; Fen is less patronized. She feels as if this week is where she has been heading all her life.

And Fen and Sean, they are so easy together. There is no discord and everything fits. Fen sits between Sean's legs, on the beach, watching the children play ball with the children of a neighbouring family. Sean kisses Fen's sea-tangled hair as she warms herself in the towel wrapped around her shoulders, and she resists the temptation to wonder if she will ever be so happy again.

The last day, the day before they must pack up the car and travel back along the M4, crossing the bridge that spans the estuary, Fen and Sean hardly say a word to one another but they are full of little kindnesses and considerations.

As the sun sinks into the sky and the temperature falls, Sean rinses out their swimming things under the tap at the edge of the field, his bare feet cold in the muddy puddle he's making beneath the tap, and he watches the other campers packing up, because all the children have to be back home for the start of school in two days' time. Fen shakes out the sleeping bags outside the tent. The children are lying on their stomachs on the grass in the last of the sunlight, between the shadows of the trees. Amy is reading a story to Connor.

Sean takes the wet swimming clothes back to the tent and ties them to the guy line to dry.

'Shall I open the bar?' he asks Fen.

'Good idea,' she says.

He upturns two plastic beakers and fills them from the wine box. He passes one to Fen.

'Come and sit with me and watch the sun go down,' he says.

Fen smiles up at him.

'It's the working title for a new song,' he says and he means the words to be slightly self-deprecating and funny, but instead they sound forlorn, and rather sad.

She sits beside him on the hillside.

'Do you know how far it is to the horizon?' he asks.

She shakes her head. 'Fifty miles? A hundred?'

'Three miles,' he says. 'If we got in a rowing boat and kept going in a straight line, we'd only have to go three miles before we disappeared. That's all it would take. Three miles and nobody would know where we were.'

The sun turns the sky a violent apricot and the sea is alive where the light catches the rolling waves, and where it doesn't the sea is dark and deep and cold.

Fen leans against Sean and he puts his arm around her.

They both know what the other is thinking. They are both wondering how they will cope with the next day, and the inevitable separation, and all the days after that.

'We could always just not go back,' Sean says quietly. 'We could put the tent and the kids in the back of the car and fuck off to France. We could be refugees. I could busk and you could pick grapes. We'd get by.'

'Connor and I haven't got passports,' she reminds him.

'You could both hide in the car boot, just until we were safely on the ferry. Amy and I would talk our way through passport control. It'd be fine.'

She smiles. She rests her head on his shoulder.

'Ah, Fen.' He sighs.

He rests his head on her head. Then he shakes the wine box, and fills up their beakers again.

'Maybe the world will end tonight,' he says.

'If we're lucky,' says Fen.

But it doesn't.

CHAPTER 46

The day–night relationship has turned on its axis, the evenings begin earlier than they did last week, and Sean noticed condensation on the inside of the windows this morning. October is waiting in the wings of the year. Already the light is fading.

Sean has been back in the family home, with Belle and Amy, for two and a half weeks. He has not spoken to Fen in all that time. She doesn't answer the phone when he calls and each time he's called into the bookshop she hasn't been there. He has driven past Lilyvale several times hoping to catch sight of her. Once he saw her walking through the city centre, holding Connor's hand, her head inclined towards the child as if she were listening to what he was saying. She was wearing a purple hat, her hair billowing over the shoulders of her old green jacket, and her flat brown boots padded along the pavement. She looked smaller, younger, untidier and more tired than Sean remembered. He wanted to call after her, to take her for coffee, but he did not, because he could not imagine being with her and at the same time not being with her. He could not think what they would talk about, what he could say to her. The last thing she would want to hear would be the details of his revised life with Belle.

Lina has told him that Fen is all right. Lina is being a good friend to Fen, she's looking after her, but Lina's attitude to Sean has changed. She doesn't take the time to talk to him any more; she makes a point of not passing on messages. Sean assumes this is because Lina blames him for somehow hurting Fen.

She must be struggling with the separation.

As he is.

He misses her with every molecule of his being. He feels instinctively drawn to her, like a tide to the moon. He exists in his new-old life but he does not feel he is living it. He does not know what to do. He can't imagine a time when he won't have this longing for Fen inside him, unless he finds a way to deaden it.

He thinks it's so bloody ironic that it's doing the right thing that is keeping him and Fen apart when it was lies and dishonesty that threw them together in the first place.

Sean takes off his clothes, piles them on top of the linen basket and steps into the shower of the family bathroom. It's a proper, walk-in shower, not an over-the-bath affair like the one in Crofters Road. It smells of bleach.

Belle used to be meticulous in her domestic

routines, but since the summer things have slipped. Her mother has employed a cleaner to come in for a couple of hours, three times a week, to help Belle keep on top of the housework, and Amanda herself pops in regularly to lend a hand. She's doing everything she can to help, bringing round casseroles and cakes and offering to babysit; perversely her overwhelming desire to smooth the way forward for her daughter and son-in-law only serves to make them both feel more anxious and uncomfortable. Neither has much of an appetite. Neither feels like spending a night out.

The day he moved back, Sean realized the house had been comprehensively gone-over to ensure no atom of the Other remained and he appreciates Amanda's thoughtfulness but at the same time is embarrassed by it. His mother-in-law clearly put herself in his shoes, and went to the greatest lengths to remove all evidence; he has not found a single strand of Louis's grey hair, no overlooked sock or nail-clipping.

Steaming still, with a towel wrapped around his waist, he goes into the spare bedroom. It is a large, pleasant room overlooking the garden. A built-in wardrobe takes up one whole wall. Enlarged photographs of flowers hang above a Habitat chest of drawers.

Sean sits on the bed and dries his hair with the towel. Although it feels like a hotel room, he is more at home and less lonely here than he would be in the master bedroom. Belle has not objected

354

to the sleeping arrangements, nor questioned them. She seems relieved that Sean has made no physical move towards her. She's keeping her distance too. Sean can't tell what she's thinking. He keeps asking her, because he knows that is what he must do, and always she says she's all right, that she's glad the family is back together again. Her smile is bright but there's something artificial about it. Her fragility terrifies Sean. She breaks down at the slightest thing, a word misconstrued, or because she can't find a key or because Amy has not eaten her cereal, or spilled it, or made a mess in her room. Sean is acting as a buffer between Belle and the world. He can see no end to this situation. Because of this, he tries not to think ahead.

Sean dresses and searches for his comb. His bag, still only half unpacked, is on top of the chair beside the window. He puts his hand in the side pocket and his fingers close around a small object. He pulls it out and holds it in his palm. It's an oddly shaped thing wrapped in Christmas paper. Sean unpicks the Sellotape and finds a stone statuette of Ganesh. He holds it to his lips.

Before he goes downstairs, he pushes open the door to Amy's room. She is lying on her stomach, reading a book.

'Oughtn't you be in your pyjamas, Amy Scott?'

She looks up and smiles sleepily.

'I'm so happy you're here, Daddy.'

'Even so, you should be getting ready for bed.'

Amy rolls onto her back, holding the book to her chest.

'You won't go away again, will you? We'll all stay together now and you can look after Mummy and we can have a dog and I'll call her Polly.'

'Amy . . .'

'I like to know you're home. I don't like Mummy and me being here on our own.'

'Five minutes, OK? Then into the bathroom and brush your teeth.'

She nods.

'You didn't answer my question,' she says.

'Everything will be all right,' Sean says. 'I promise.' He blows her a kiss and she blows him one back, and he pulls the door to.

CHAPTER 47

Fen lies in Connor's bed, her arms around the child. If she lets go, she fears she will simply float away and disappear.

She feels insubstantial. She feels like a square of tissue paper that has been set alight and vanishes as it drifts towards the sky. She feels that her existence is no more real than that of an exhaled breath or a dream or the memory of a feeling.

Connor shifts in his sleep. He sighs. His breath is warm and damp, organic, sweet. Fen rests her lips against his forehead.

The world beyond the curtain is waking. She hears the milk float, the heels of dog-walkers and the rattle of leads, the odd car engine as it starts up.

She thinks: Oh, here we go, another day.

Another night without Sean has gone by.

Another day without Sean is about to start.

She is in the bookshop when the door opens and Emma Rees comes in. Fen does not recognize the woman at first, and when she does her heart starts to pound and her legs feel weak. The blood in her veins evaporates and is replaced by a mixture of adrenaline and fear.

Fen thinks, at first, that Mrs Rees has come to her by accident. She browses the local guide books, picking them off the shelves and reading the blurbs on their back covers, until the jolly American couple have bought their souvenirs and left the shop. Then she slips the guide book she had been holding back into its slot and crosses over to the counter where Fen stands. Fen wishes she could disappear into the floor, she wishes she could vanish, go away, not exist.

Mrs Rees is wearing dangly earrings. Her hair has been cut short and coloured chestnut brown, with dashing red highlights. She is wearing an orange coat with a rainbow scarf, trousers and boots, and she carries a hessian bag embroidered with flowers. She looks about twenty years younger than she looked the last time Fen saw her.

She looks less broken.

And Fen realizes that, although she has always thought of Mrs Rees as elderly, it was grief that was distorting her. In truth, the woman is in her prime.

'Hello, Fen,' she says.

'Hello, Mrs Rees,' says Fen. She glances at Vincent.

They have worked together for so long now that there is telepathy between them.

Vincent looks at his watch, coughs and says:

'Would you hold the fort for half an hour, Fen?' She nods and he disappears out of the shop, turning the OPEN sign to CLOSED on the way out.

There is a pause, then: 'I was coming to Bath on business,' says Mrs Rees. 'I thought, while I was here, I'd come and see you. Your sister told me where I'd find you.'

Fen doesn't know what to say. She thinks it would be impolite to comment on Mrs Rees's appearance; it would imply there was something wrong with it before. Instead she asks: 'Would you like a cup of coffee?'

'No, no. I didn't come to put you to any trouble.'

'It's no trouble. There's a secret kitchen behind that door.'

The older woman smiles and shakes her head.

'No, really, Fen. I'm all right. I have a meeting in half an hour and I'm sure I'll be plied with sandwiches, or paninis, or whatever.'

Fen bites her lip. She would like to ask about the meeting, but doesn't know if she should.

Mrs Rees, the new, more vibrant Mrs Rees, takes a breath and says: 'A lot of things have changed since you came to see me, Fen. I've been thinking about you every day. I have been praying. I asked God to show me the right thing to do and He told me to come and see you.'

Fen smiles as if she understands.

'I'm not saying this to hurt you but, for quite a while after you came, I struggled not to hate you for what you had done. Then I realized that you were the answer to my prayers.'

'Please . . .'

'It can't have been easy for you to come to my house and tell me what you did.'

'I should have come sooner,' says Fen. 'I should have told the truth straight away.'

'But I've been thinking about this,' says Mrs Rees. 'Deborah is a very strong woman; you and I both know that. When she's made her mind up about something, she is an unstoppable force. And you, Fen, you must have been so frightened. You'd made promises to Joe and Tomas too. It would have been difficult for anyone to know what was the right thing to do at the time. Your loyalty – your responsibility – was to your family. When I put myself in your shoes, with God's help I could understand.'

Fen holds her breath. She feels she does not deserve understanding.

'What He made me realize,' says Mrs Rees, 'is that you didn't have to come to me at all. Perhaps He spoke to you and told you what you should do, or maybe it was your own conscience. Either way, you came, and now that I know what happened that night, I feel able to say goodbye to Joe. I'm not waking up each morning imagining him out there, on his own, in the dark. So I am grateful to you, Fen. Things are better for me now.'

Fen swallows. Her mouth is dry.

'I'm so glad.'

'Do you feel better too?' asks Mrs Rees gently. 'Because I've been praying every night for you too, Fen. I've been praying for your burden to be lifted, as mine has been.'

Fen nods. She says: 'Thank you.'

Mrs Rees checks her watch. 'I've got to meet my supplier in half an hour,' she says. 'Did Lucy tell you I've left the college? I'm opening up my own cafe. It's going to be aimed at young people. I want it to be the kind of place where everyone can be themselves and where everyone can feel at home.'

'That sounds brilliant,' says Fen.

'Merron needs somewhere like that,' says Mrs Rees. 'It needs to stop pretending that everyone ought to be just like everyone else.'

'Yes,' Fen agrees. 'It does.'

They stand for a moment, separated by the counter, and then Mrs Rees leans forward and kisses Fen very gently on the cheek.

'It's over, Fen,' she says. 'You don't have to worry about this any more. Make your peace with your brother and then put the past behind you and start living your life again.'

CHAPTER 48

Fen has been waiting for the right day, and this is it.

While Connor sleeps, she slips out of bed and goes downstairs in the green T-shirt that Sean left screwed up on her bedroom floor, in need of a wash. She loves the smell of him. At least she still has that. And she won't wash the T-shirt until there's no trace of Sean left.

Fen goes into the kitchen and opens the back door, then she goes barefoot down the steps into the dewy garden and picks flowers. She picks lavender sprigs and cuts the stems of the last of the roses with a knife.

She wraps the flowers in newspaper, and then she makes herself a cup of tea and goes upstairs to wake Connor.

She feeds him his breakfast of Weetabix soaked in warm milk with sugared mashed banana. She gives him diluted orange juice to drink. As he eats she tidies around him and points to the birds in the gardens, to the grey cat licking its paws in the sunshine, to the people walking up the alleyway on their way to school or work. The radio is playing

362

happy, morning music and she hums along, she sings, she even dances a little, and Connor watches and smiles, a teardrop of sweetened milk crusting down his chin.

She wipes his face and brushes his teeth, then she tidies him and fastens his shoes, ready for the bus, and when they hear its friendly toot Connor rushes for the door, as he always does. Connor loves going to school on the bus. He likes the driver, who's called Jean and always says: 'Hello, me old mucker'; he likes the independence, and the grown-up feeling shows on his face; he likes seeing his friends and waving to people through the windows along the way.

'Hey, hang on a minute, you!' Fen calls. She leans down and puts her hands on his cheeks and she kisses his forehead. He wriggles.

'Don't I get one?' she asks.

'Mum!' Connor grumbles but he leans forward and kisses her hard, right on the lips.

'Thank you,' she murmurs.

He looks up at her.

'Go on,' she says, 'off you go.'

He climbs the garden steps as fast as he can, holding on to the railing. Fen watches from the doorstep. At the gate he turns and waves to her. She blows him a kiss and he pretends to catch it, and he blows one back and she does the same. Then he takes the hand of the helper and turns his back and forgets about Fen. Still she watches until the bus has gone down the hill.

It's eight-thirty.

She's already wearing her new dress over her jeans. She puts on some make-up in front of the little mirror by the back door. It's important that she looks her best. She pulls her hair back and holds it in one hand while she secures the ponytail with a clip with the other. Then she slips on her warm jacket and boots, picks up the flowers and leaves Lilyvale.

Fen walks uphill through the streets, the pretty back roads and residential rat-runs; she walks up to the lay-by at the side of the A46 where a boy sells flowers and cherries from a wooden trestle and a woman sells tea in china cups, and bacon sandwiches. She waits until a lorry stops and then asks if she can hitch a ride. She is specific: she has to get to the Severn on the M48, not the M4. The first lorry driver can't help but soon she meets a nice man, a family man, who is on his way back to Cardiff with a wagon full of electrical goods, and he says he doesn't mind using that route and that she's most welcome to travel with him.

The inside of his cab smells musty, manly, of a man not washed but wearing aftershave. It's very tidy. Everything is lined up. She sits up high on the squashy seat, so high that it's like riding a camel, and she watches the road roll by from her new perspective. Radio 2 is coming out of the speakers. They bump and roll past Bristol and then they go out onto the lonely stretch of countryside that separates the city from the bridge.

'You don't say much, do you?' the driver asks. His name is Ryan. He chews gum. He has high blood pressure, a baby daughter called Lottie and a strong Cardiff accent. There's a copy of the *Daily Mail* and a plastic packet of egg and cress sandwiches on the seat between them. His wife is a teacher in a primary school. In the evenings she goes to classes – Slimming World, line dancing, GCSE Spanish – and if Ryan's not home, his mum, who's called Sylvia, looks after the baby.

They reach the approach to the bridge.

'You're sure you want me to drop you here?'

'Yes, thank you.'

'This is no-man's-land. You can't go anywhere from here. Only back the way we came or over the bridge.'

'Here is perfect.'

Ryan looks uneasy. He's worried about her. The bridge has a reputation.

She finds a breezy smile.

'It's OK,' she says. 'I've just come to take some photographs.'

'Oh!' he says, relief chasing the fear from his face like sunlight following the shadow of a cloud. 'You had me worried for a moment. Thought I might be looking at your picture in the paper tomorrow, missing person and all that.'

'Thank you for the lift,' says Fen, 'and good luck

with your life, and everything,' and she slides across the seat and opens the door.

She climbs out of the cab and down the steps. Hundreds of vehicles are in the lines to pay the toll, cars and vans and lorries and coaches; holiday-makers and businesspeople, tradesmen and hauliers, men driving fuel tankers and cement mixers. The motorbikes don't have to pay. They buzz through.

She waves to Ryan's lorry as it accelerates towards the span of the bridge, but he probably can't see her in his wing mirror. The light reflecting off the surface of the estuary water hurts her eyes but the bridge is magnificent, spectacular as a lightning storm, imposing as a cathedral.

Fen turns away from the bridge and she walks on, finding a path which curls up to Severn View services.

She needs to see everything.

She needs to know how it felt to be Tomas as dawn broke that morning.

They found her father's smashed-up car in the car park. At first the attendant thought it had been vandalized and the police were called, but when they arrived and checked the number they discovered that their Welsh colleagues were searching for the car. They suspected it had been involved in a fatal accident the previous evening. The passenger-side door was missing and a hole had been punched through the shattered windscreen. The roof was buckled and twigs, leaves, mud and stone caked the bumpers and the wheel arches. The key was still in the ignition, the little red-leather fob dangling at the end of its chain.

This is the first time Fen has been here. She has tried never to think about this place, but now she's here, weirdly, she feels exhilarated. The anticipation of what she must do thrills her.

At the entrance is a sign saying you can only park for two hours but Fen doubts anyone ever checks. She walks around the car park. It's not a horrible place. It's not hectic and soulless like some motorway services, where people stop only to use the toilets or to buy coffee and sandwiches or to pass children from one separated parent to the other.

There are two bowls outside the electric doors at the entrance to the services. One contains dog food, the other, water. Fen is touched by the kindness of whoever puts out these animal refreshments.

She goes inside.

It's small, old-fashioned, poky. Fen has a quick look round.

People used to come here on day trips. They used to organize excursions, to eat a meal in the restaurant, to enjoy the views across the estuary. Then when they built the new bridge, further downstream, the powers that be thought people would stop coming here and they sold off some of the land. But people still come. They come for the views and to walk across the bridge.

★ ★ ★

367

Tomas was in the services in the early hours of the morning; the security cameras watched him come in and go out. He was inside only for a few minutes. Enough time to go into the toilets to swallow something, or sniff, smoke or inject something. Not long enough to drink a hot drink, or mingle in the cafeteria, looking for a lift.

Maybe he was lucky. Maybe he met somebody straight away who was prepared to drive him to the docks at Cardiff or Avonmouth, or to an airport. Or maybe he had already arranged to be picked up in the car park by a friend. Somebody with a false passport in his pocket for Tomas; a friend who would take him to meet his freight ship, or the plane that would take him to his new life on the beach. Maybe this is what happened.

But nobody believes this version of events any more. Not even Fen.

She retraces her footsteps back to the bridge. She notices everything. Beside the path that leads back to the motorway are pages torn from a magazine. Glossy cars photographed at arty angles. Glossy women in glossy shoes. Fen doesn't look at the detail.

She crosses the motorway at the tollbooths. The vehicles stream into the booth-queues like migrating animals navigating an obstacle, like sand rushing towards the nip at the centre of an egg timer.

Fen climbs down the steps and she finds the path that crosses the bridge.

It's such a long bridge that she can't see the

other side. Still, it's pleasant, walking with the noise of the motorway – all those people, all those wheels and engines – to her right, and to her left the quiet and the calm of the air, and the sky, and the water. The fabric of the bridge vibrates beneath her feet when lorries go by. The air is cool on her cheeks; it blows loose hair into her eyes. She can smell the water, the water and the ocean at the end of the estuary, and the mud and the sea creatures that live in the water in between.

Estuary birds, so far below they are little more than white commas, feed in the mud which is as glossy as fine silk at the foot of the cliffs, and curly brown streams swirl out through the gravel towards the body of the river. The tiptilted, blackened ribs of an old barge protrude sadly from the shallows and there's a long, bandy-legged pier supporting a giant pylon whose reflection in the water is softer and more beautiful than the silhouette of the original, which stands stark against a pale grey sky infused with the palest blue. Its cables trail a mile above the water, drifting towards the sister pylon on the Welsh side of the estuary.

If she looks, Fen can see for miles in three directions. To her left are the flatlands, spreading out like a painting towards the motorways and the factories, chimneys, plants and warehouses in the distance. To her right is the Welsh coast, and in front of her is the estuary, so wide, so still, so ancient and so wonderful it takes away her fear and makes her feel perfectly calm.

She puts on her jacket and pulls it tight then walks for ages with the traffic beside her. She walks to the middle of the bridge, where the metal moves quite dramatically beneath her feet. It's like being the only passenger on a boat. She holds on to the railings until she is accustomed to the movement. Then she leans on them and gazes out across the silver water and the silver-brown mud. The estuary looks entirely different from this perspective. It is immense and peaceful. Fen has forgotten the lorries and the cars hurtling along the road behind her; all she knows is the expanse of water, the air and the sea birds flying, white, below her. Land is irrelevant here. It's a lovely place to be, suspended above the river, between the land masses, with the huge tide rising and falling invisibly beneath.

The new bridge is a pencil sketch in the distance. Sunlight makes its way dreamily through clouds the colour of the water, and the grey-silver light and the colours and the slow, slow movement of the water are beautiful together.

Fen brushes the hair out of her eyes.

She stands there, just looking, for ages, for hours.

A couple of cyclists go past. They say: 'Are you all right, love?' and she says: 'Yes, I'm fine.'

Fen takes the flowers out of her bag. She throws them, one by one, over the railings. She does not see where they go. They are carried by the wind, and the water is too far below and she's not sure which direction the tide is moving. The lavender stems spin and the petals are torn from the rose-heads and float in the air by themselves.

Fen does not know where Tomas is.

But at least, she thinks, if he did come here, that morning.

If he leaned over the railings.

If he fell.

It was a beautiful place for him to fall.

The flowers fall into the water.

She hopes they find him.

CHAPTER 49

'More beef, Sean? Can I tempt you?'

Belle's father is holding a bloodied piece of meat on the prongs of a carving fork. He shakes it in Sean's direction.

'Really, John, I can't. I'm absolutely full.'

He turns to Belle's mother. 'That was a great meal, Amanda, thank you.'

Amanda primps. 'I hope you've room for some dessert,' she says. 'Gooseberry fool, your favourite. I made it specially.'

Sean thinks it is a peculiarly ironic choice of pudding. Belle sends him an apologetic little glance, which he accepts with good grace. This is just another one of those rituals to be gone through. Everyone is pretending that nothing has changed since the last time Sean and Belle spent a weekend with her parents. The atmosphere is so heavy with good intent it's given Sean a headache and the strain is telling on everyone's face.

'Belle was telling us,' says Amanda, 'that you're thinking of moving house. I think that's a very good idea.'

'You don't want to put your house up for sale

now,' says John briskly, 'not while the market's as it is.'

'It's all relative, Dad,' says Belle. 'And we haven't made up our minds yet.'

'It would be good for both of you, *all* of you,' says Amanda, touching Amy's shoulder, 'to get away from those . . . memories.'

Sean winces.

'Mum, please . . .' says Belle. It is the closest any of them has come, so far, to mentioning any of the events of the last fifteen months.

'I'd think you were insane if you tried to sell it now,' John says gruffly.

'It's their decision, darling,' says Amanda. 'They must do what they think is best.'

'I've never been happy in that house,' says Belle quietly to Sean as they stack the dishwasher together.

'Haven't you?' That's news to Sean. He thought she loved it there. He thought it was her dream house.

Belle shakes her head.

'It's always felt like a kind of prison to me.'

Sean passes her a rinsed plate. Belle takes it without looking at him.

He says, confused: 'You always said it was the perfect house for raising children and settling down. You used to tell everyone we'd found the perfect home.'

'It was. It is. But I don't think I was ready for

all that. I think I probably should have waited a few more years before I had a child. I was too young. I didn't want to settle down.'

Sean feels a pang of frustration. He feels somehow he's being blamed for something, but he's not sure what. He is certain he never railroaded Belle into marriage, or motherhood, or domesticity. It was the opposite, surely, wasn't it? He was always so eager to make Belle happy that generally he went along with whatever she suggested.

'I thought it was what was expected of me,' Belle says, as if that explains everything. 'I thought it was what I wanted.'

Sean rinses his hands under the cold tap.

'If that's how you feel, then I'm not sure that moving house is going to make everything right again,' he says.

'Never mind your father, I think it's a lovely idea,' says Amanda coming into the kitchen with the condiments. 'A fresh new start for the family. You have to do what's best for *you*, don't you, Sean? You have to be true to yourself. Any less than that and it just won't work.'

She hands a jar of mustard to Amy.

'Put that back in the fridge for me, would you?'

Amy takes the jar. 'Can we go and live with Fen and Connor?' she asks.

'Who are they, darling?' Amanda asks. 'Are they friends?'

'They're who Daddy lived with when Mummy

was with Lewis. They're really nice. Fen could look after me when Mummy needed a rest. She wouldn't mind. She said we're always welcome. She said . . .'

'That's nice,' says Amanda.

'Fen says—'

'That's enough Amy,' says Belle, sharply.

Later, Sean hears voices in the living room and he goes in to find Belle leaning over Amy with a hand on each of her daughter's shoulders.

Belle is leaning forward so her face is close to Amy's and she's whispering in a hissy, angry voice.

'Why do you do this to me? Why do you have to humiliate me like that? Don't you love me? Don't you think I'm a good mother? Would you prefer to be with your father's little friend? Would you?'

Amy is staring up at her mother. She shakes her head.

'No!' she says. 'No, Mummy. I love you the best I—'

'This is so hard for me,' Belle says. 'I'm doing my best and it's for your sake. I'm doing this all for you, I'm putting up with all this for *you*, Amy, and it's so hard just getting through each day and you have to keep hurting me—'

'Belle!' Sean steps forward, takes her right wrist gently and turns her away. 'What are you doing?'

Belle pulls her arm away. With her left hand she rubs the place where his fingers touched her.

'Mummy!' Amy reaches over and tries to take hold of Belle's arm. Belle shakes her off.

'I'm sick of you both!' she cries. 'I'm sick of this pretending. I've had enough of everything.' She runs out of the room. They hear her footsteps on the stairs beyond, and the slam of a door.

Amy looks up at her father, and then she looks towards the door. Her lower lip trembles and her face colours.

'I'm sorry,' she whispers. 'I want to tell Mummy I'm sorry. I never meant to make her cry.'

Sean takes her in his arms, smoothes her hair. She does not relax; she is stiff and rigid, brittle like her mother.

'It's all right, Ames, it's OK. You didn't do anything wrong,' he says, but it's not OK, it's not OK at all and they both know it isn't.

CHAPTER 50

F en takes Connor to pick blackberries from the bramble bushes at the lower, untidier end of the alleyway that runs downhill at the back of their garden. Connor has a red plastic colander and is wearing rubber gloves to protect his hands from the thorns and the little autumnal spider webs. Fen holds him up so he can reach the best fruit, and when they walk back up the hill, trailing spilled berries, she sees that his cheeks are smeared purple.

'Connor Weller, did you, by any chance, eat any blackberries even though I said we ought to wash them first?' she asks, pulling the sleeves of her jumper down around her fingers.

'No.'

'Are you *sure* about that?'

Connor narrows his eyes, passes her the colander, turns his back to her and wipes his mouth with the back of his sleeve.

Fen laughs.

'What?' asks Connor.

'Just you,' Fen says. 'Just you're the best five-year-old in the whole wide universe.'

'Mum, I'm *six*! You know I'm six now. You're just being *stupid*.'

He leans down to pull up a sock which has worked its way into the toe of his blue Wellington. Fen opens the gate to their garden and he runs on ahead awkwardly in his boots. She goes up the steps and through the open kitchen door, then puts the colander in the sink and runs the cold tap over the fruit, which is over-ripe and leaking juice, sticky with insect residue and sugar. Then she hears the knocking at the front door.

She can't help her heart racing; she can't help hoping every time somebody comes to the door that it's going to be Sean. Today is Sunday and who else would call on a Sunday? She checks her reflection quickly in the small mirror and hitches up her jeans, and then she goes to the door.

On the step is a dark-haired, slightly overweight woman wearing a duffel coat and a scarf, and behind her is a tall, thin young man with his hands in the pockets of his Green Day hoodie and hair all over his face.

'Hi,' says the woman. 'I'm Lola and this is Boo. I know it's rude to turn up unannounced but I've been calling Sean all day and he hasn't picked up his phone, so we thought we'd surprise him. Is he in? My degenerate brother?'

Fen makes tea and Lola props herself up against the kitchen counter while Fen explains what's been going on. In the living room, Boo and Connor watch

Top Gear and Boo explains the various automotive technical terms to Connor, who is sitting on the arm of his chair, bombarding him with questions.

Fen passes Lola a mug. Lola takes it and blows air up across her face so that her fringe lifts and then falls again.

'Bloody hell,' she says, 'it's all a bit of a mess, isn't it?'

Fen nods.

'So you haven't spoken to him?' asks Lola. 'You don't know how things are over there between him and Belle?'

Fen shakes her head.

'He used to call all the time,' she says, 'only I couldn't bear to speak to him . . .'

Lola puts down her tea, steps across the kitchen and takes Fen in her arms. Her gentle, sweet-scented kindness is so comforting, it's such a relief, that Fen almost faints with gratitude.

'You smell nice,' she says.

'Knock-off Chanel,' says Lola. 'Subliminally it makes people think I look like Nicole Kidman.'

Fen sniffs and laughs. Lola fishes a tissue from up her sleeve and passes it to Fen.

'No wonder he hasn't been in touch with us,' says Lola. 'Poor bastard. He really likes you, you know. He never stopped talking about you. We were all hoping things would work out.'

'So was I.'

'What we need to do,' says Lola, 'is think about this situation logically. Sean probably didn't tell you, but I'm training to be a counsellor, so I know a bit about relationships, and if Belle wasn't happy with Sean before all this, and frankly I *do* have some sympathy with her, he can be the most irritating sod and *I* certainly couldn't live with him, but if she wasn't happy before, well, why should things be any different now?'

Fen nods in agreement.

'He's trying to do the best for Amy,' she says. 'I think they both are. She was . . . damaged by everything that happened. Sean and Belle want to give her some stability.'

'Hmmm. I'm not sure the words "Belle" and "stability" belong in the same sentence. Listen, nobody, least of all Boo, knows that I smoke, but I'm dying for a fag,' says Lola. 'Can we go into the garden and you can tell me absolutely everything. Maybe we can think of a plan.'

'Thank you,' says Fen. 'You're very kind.'

'There's an element of self-interest. I need a decent case study for my coursework.'

Fen smiles.

'Don't worry,' says Lola. 'I'll protect your privacy. I won't refer to any of you by name.'

CHAPTER 51

S ean's in his office playing Battleships on his computer when Lina's number lights up on the internal phone. He picks up the handset and holds it between his head and shoulder.

'What?' he asks. He's playing expert level and is on course to beat his best-ever time. Concentrating on not blowing himself up is one of the few, sure-fire ways he's found to take his mind entirely away from its worries.

'"Thank you for contacting me, Lina,"' the voice at the other end replies in a heavily sarcastic voice. '"You obviously have some important and pertinent information to share with me so I will, in future, answer the phone in a polite and respectful tone of voice."'

Sean ignores this, clicks on a square and explodes the screen. 'Shit,' he says.

'Just because your life is shit doesn't mean you have to bring everyone else down too,' says the voice at the other end.

'Lola? Lo, is that you? You're here? In the office? Are you stalking me?'

'Well, what was I supposed to do? You won't

381

answer my calls and you didn't tell me you were living back in Swindon. Can I come up, or are you going to take me out to lunch somewhere nice where all your colleagues won't be able to hear us discussing your embarrassingly dysfunctional private life?'

'Lo, Christ, yes, of course we'll go out for lunch. Blimey,' says Sean, running his fingers through his hair and wondering how much Lola knows, and how he will explain everything to her.

They buy sandwiches and sit on a bench outside the Abbey. Most of the tourists have gone, and the pigeons peck and strut. Sean sees the city through Lola's eyes and realizes how extraordinarily beautiful it is. He thinks of Fen. The Gildas Bookshop is only a few hundred yards away. He wonders what she's doing, what she's having for lunch.

But there's not much time for thinking of Fen, because Lola demands his attention.

She asks Sean about himself and about Belle and Amy and he opens up, he tells her everything. He feels slightly ashamed of himself, regurgitating all these private facts and feelings, but he is so stuck in the situation he can't help himself. It all pours out in a verbal torrent, and once the words are out he feels empty and unburdened.

He looks sideways at Lola, who is patting her lips with a paper napkin and appears completely unfazed by what he has told her.

'Were you even listening?' he asks.

'Of course I was. Trust me, I've heard far, far more

complicated than that in our role-play situations at college.'

'It gets more complicated than that?'

Lola raises her eyebrows and tucks in her chin, pulling a knowing face. 'You couldn't make some of it up.'

'Really?'

She holds up a hand. 'No, don't ask me. I'm bound by the ethics of confidentiality.'

But she's dying to tell him.

Sean torments her with silence for a moment and then he asks: 'So what would a relationship counsellor advise in my situation?'

'A counsellor wouldn't advise anything. They're supposed to listen and help people come to their own decisions. They're never supposed to interfere.'

'So you can't help me?'

'In my professional capacity, no. But as your sister . . .'

Sean tries not to smile.

'As my bloody brilliant sister, what do you think?' he asks. 'I can't see any way out of this mess.'

'There's always a way,' says Lola.

CHAPTER 52

For three days he thinks about what Lola told him. On the fourth day he gets up early and takes a cup of tea to Belle, and he sits on the bed beside her, takes her hand and says: 'Belle, we're going about this the wrong way.'

He says: 'You're like a square peg in a round hole. And so am I. The way we are, the way we're living, it's not good for any of us, least of all Amy. You need to find out what it is *you* want, what you really want, and once you've done that we must find a way to make sure you get it.'

Belle looks up at him, childlike. He feels a surge of both pity and frustration.

He tries to remember what Lola said, how she said to phrase the words so they wouldn't sound critical, aggressive or demanding.

He says: 'You said you've never been happy here, in this house. Well, that's nearly all our married life, Belle. That's a lot of time for somebody to be unhappy.'

'I know.'

He rubs his chin.

'Maybe your affair with Lewis was a way for you

384

to try to escape this unhappiness. And when that didn't work, instead of trying something else, we've gone back to how it was before. That's all we've ever known, you and I, and it doesn't feel right to me any more, and I think maybe you feel you're back in the same old cage.'

Belle leans forward, her eyes wide.

'That's exactly how I feel!' she says, and Sean says a quiet, internal 'thank you' to his sister. 'Sean, you understand! At last you're beginning to understand me! I do feel like I'm trapped. I thought being a wife and a mother and living in a nice house in a nice place was what I was supposed to want, but it's not. It makes me feel like I'm being buried alive.'

Sean nods. 'I know,' he says.

And it's true. He does. For the first time ever, he appreciates how it feels to be Belle and he is sympathetic.

'So what is it you do want to do with your life, Belle?'

'I don't know.'

'Then let's find somebody you can talk to, somebody who can help you work it out.'

'I'd like that.'

'I'll help you,' says Sean. 'I'll be there for you. But when we've worked out what's right for you and what's best for Amy, then I'm going to do what's right for me.'

CHAPTER 53

Fen used to think she was different from other people. Now she knows she is exactly the same as everyone else, and knowing that is a relief, it makes her feel less lonely.

She knows that most people go through life doing the best they can with what they have, and that sometimes good people do bad things when they are desperate and desperate things when they're trying to protect the people they love. Other people are sometimes hurt along the way. All you can do is do your best.

She has made a resolution. From now on, she'll stop thinking so much and get on with her life. She is going to do the best she can for Connor.

She will be a better mother. She'll take him out more, she'll make friends with the other parents at the school and talk to people in the park, invite the neighbours round.

And she'll put more effort into her work. She has already suggested to Vincent that they start a reading group affiliated to the shop. It will mean him having to make shelf space to accommodate some more modern novels, but he was not averse to the idea. He told Fen that she would have to be Person In Charge of the reading group and Fen agreed. She taped a notice in the shop window and already more than a dozen people have signed up. It means twelve book sales for Vincent and a new group of friends for Fen. It's probably the first time she's ever taken the initiative at work and Vincent is pleased. Lately, he's started hinting that he wants to spend more time with his family. He's considering semi-retirement. He'd like Fen to take over the reins, he said. Before, Fen would not have considered herself capable. Now she thinks she might, with his support, be able to run the shop by herself.

For a while she drank out of *The End of the Affair* mug, but Vincent accidentally-on-purpose knocked it off the counter and broke the handle. She put it on the shelf, meaning to bring in some glue, but she hasn't bothered to repair it. These days Fen drinks her coffee from *Brave New World*.

In her bed, warm beneath the forget-me-not duvet, Fen yawns. She rubs her eyes.

The first thing she needs to sort out is her finances. She is broke, at the far end of her overdraft. She misses Sean's rent money. That was what made the difference to her between scraping by and living reasonably comfortably.

There's an easy way to improve the situation.

She will clean out Sean's room. It's been more than a month since his sister came by and she hasn't heard anything from either of them since.

His music system, his CDs, an assortment of clothes and other bits and pieces are still in there. She won't give them away; she'll put them somewhere safe. And she'll turn the mattress and buy some new bedding, then she'll write a new postcard and somebody else will come to live in Lilyvale and a new chapter of her life will begin.

She won't look back.

She's trying not to look back. If she keeps herself busy, if she finds other things to fill her mind, then she can manage without Sean. One day, she hopes, she'll wake up and she'll no longer miss him.

She reaches out and checks the clock on her phone. She has time for a cup of tea downstairs, on her own, before she wakes Connor. She gets out of bed and puts her cream-coloured dressing gown over Sean's green T-shirt and she pads barefoot downstairs, shivering a little. The central heating has warmed the air, but the vinyl that covers the kitchen floor still holds the night's chill.

She fills the kettle and plugs it in, setting it to boil. She takes a mug from the hook and pours in half an inch of cold milk from the bottle in the fridge. While she waits for the kettle to boil, she steps over to the window and gazes out.

Something is different.

The green wooden gate at the end of the garden is open and a single set of dark footprints are clearly defined in the dew on the grass. Fen follows the footprints with her eyes, and they lead from the gate across the lawn to the undercroft.

Fen's heartbeat ratchets up several notches.

She takes a deep breath.

She unlocks the back door and walks down the steps. The concrete is stone-cold beneath her bare feet and the autumn air chills her lungs.

She peers through the window of the undercroft, but it's dark inside and she can't see anything.

She pushes opens the wooden door. It's heavy. It creaks.

It takes her eyes a moment to accustom themselves to the gloom, but slowly the shape of him comes into focus. He's in the corner, between the lawnmower and Connor's pushchair, beside the stack of flowerpots and the recycling boxes, huddled and shivering and hollow-eyed.

He is wearing a big old coat, and his arms are wrapped around himself. His face looks very tired, even in the shadows.

Fen tries to breathe slowly. She tries to stay calm and not give way to the earthquake that's going on inside her. She steadies herself against the door frame.

'Hi,' he says, casually.

'Hi.'

They nod at one another awkwardly.

'Fancy meeting you here,' says Sean.

Fen smiles and tucks her hair behind her ear.

'When did you get here?' she asks.

'In the early hours. I slept in the car for a while. I thought it'd be warmer in here but it wasn't.'

'Why didn't you let yourself into the house? You still have a key, don't you?'

'I thought it would be presuming too much.'

'Oh.'

'You're wearing my T-shirt,' he says.

'Do you mind?'

'Not at all.'

'I was going to wash it and send it back to you.'

'Don't. It looks better on you.'

'Actually, I wasn't going to give it back,' she says. 'I was going to wear it forever.'

He smiles.

'What happened?' she asks. 'Why are you here?'

He scratches his chin.

'It's thanks to Lola. She made me understand that Belle couldn't help being how she was, and she put her in touch with someone who could help.'

'Oh?'

'Yeah, she's in counselling now, working out what she wants.'

Fen looks at her feet.

'What does she want?'

'She's not too sure yet. Some space, for the time being. But that's beside the point. I've also had some time to work out what I want, what's right for me.'

'Oh?'

'And that's you, and Amy, and Connor. And us – if that's all right with you. I've told Belle. She knows and she's OK with it.'

'But . . . How? Belle won't want to lose Amy.'

'She won't lose her. Amy can see Belle whenever she wants, but mainly she'll be living here, with us. Sorry, I'm presuming again. I mean we need to talk about that first, obviously.'

'Are you sure it'll be all right this time? Are you sure Belle won't change her mind?'

'She's had her chances. She's made her choices. It's our life now. If you want it to be our life, I mean – that is, yours and mine.'

Fen's mouth is dry. She swallows.

'And the kids, obviously.'

She looks down at herself, at her pale legs, her thin feet and the tattoo around her ankle.

'I thought you might be . . . pleased,' he says.

Fen turns. She looks out of the undercroft door and squints against the brightness of the morning.

Sean sighs. He says quietly: 'You could always to tell me to fuck off, Fen. Nobody would blame you.'

He stares at her. She feels his gaze on her face, her shoulder, her back.

She has a million questions. She has a million doubts, a million insecurities. But she is certain of one thing. She isn't going to do or say anything she may later regret. She is going to leave the door to her future wide open so that every opportunity has its chance to blossom.

'The kettle's on,' she says. 'Would you like some tea?'

He says: 'I thought you'd never ask.'

Fen reaches out her hand to help him up, and his cold fingers close around hers and she knows that this time he has chosen to come to her. He has not washed up at her door by accident.

This is a better time. Everything is better now and somewhere in her heart Fen knows she need not worry. She sees their future reveal itself, one moment at a time, like new frames on a film, and although she does not know what will happen, she knows that Sean and she will be together for as long as their hearts continue to beat.

\#